IRREPLACEABLE
Replaced
Book 3

NOLON KING
LAUREN STREET

STERLING & STONE

Chapter One

GRAVEL CRUNCHED like bones under the tires, a dark symphony to Nina's ears as Will steered them through the silent countryside, with the road unwinding like a gray ribbon under their tires. For the past hour, she'd been resisting the urge to touch the ravine of mottled tissue, a reddened trail running from her right cheek to her jawline, then down the side of her neck.

Back home, she forgot about her scars except when she was applying her makeup, and when her hair was down, most people didn't even notice them. But she'd thoughtlessly tucked her hair behind her ear in the snack aisle of the truck stop where they'd fueled up, and a little girl had asked her mother loudly, *what's wrong with that lady's face?* Nina had turned, bolted for the restroom, and stayed there until Will texted her to ask if she was okay.

And she was okay, once she was back in the car with him.

They had been driving for a little over two hours since their plane had touched down in Bismarck, a lot longer than she had imagined they would be on the road before arriving at the bed-and-breakfast where Will was taking her. But the world outside his Infinity was blurring into a streak of earliest twilight as they roared down the highway.

They were on this trip to celebrate their engagement after six perfect months together — he'd swept her off her feet the night Annie and Bruce had introduced them, and the romance hadn't slowed ever since. Will liked to joke that fate had brought him to Chicago to meet her — he claimed to hate city life, preferring to live in small towns like the one he'd grown up in, but this was the first time he'd ever taken her outside the city limits.

Nina had no idea why he'd picked North Dakota for their first getaway together, but he'd promised her that this trip would be something special.

She'd imagined he was taking her someplace charming, with well-maintained farmhouses and cute picket fences and shops with old-fashioned hand-painted signs. But so far, they'd mostly driven through ranch land dotted with decaying barns and clusters of depressed looking cows in fields wrapped in barbed-wire fences. They'd passed sad-looking motels, gas stations that sold livestock feed and vapes, and the occasional roadside strip club. Signs for the same four fast-food chains every few highway exits.

But once they'd left highway, that's when she'd started to feel anxious, and even more so after leaving the last small town behind over fifteen minutes ago. Now they were truly out in the middle of nowhere, pulling off to the shoulder of the road to park beneath a half-dead tree, for some reason. Will's hand left the steering wheel, reaching for something in his coat pocket as the tires crunched to a stop on the roadside.

Only a ticking from the cooling engine punctuated the sudden silence.

"We're here." His voice was a blend of excitement and something unreadable.

"This doesn't look like a bed-and-breakfast." Nina gave him a nervous smile, not wanting to think of all those horror movies that started out with a scene like this. Parked in the shadow of a tree, draped in the ambiguity of dusk.

Will turned to her, holding a blindfold, the fabric like a slice of night in his hands. As he leaned closer, his pendant caught the fading light — a glint of silver in the shape of a rose encircled by a compass.

"Trust me?" He sounded serious, yet playful.

"Is the next step getting into the trunk?" Nina teased as her pulse started racing, reaching out to trace the blindfold with her fingertips.

Their laughter mingled, a soft sound in the quiet.

Then Nina agreed, the fabric falling over her eyes like the curtain before a show, the world disappearing at his behest.

The car moved again, the rhythm of the road a soothing cadence beneath the wheels.

Minutes stretched, elastic and taut with anticipation.

The Infinity finally stopped and Will broke their silence with the warmth of his voice. "Stay put."

He circled around to Nina's side of the car. His firm hand guided her out of the Infinity and up a gravel path as the wind whispered secrets in her ear, the kind that spoke of isolation and profound quiet that only total remoteness can bring.

Another few steps and they stopped. Will's fingers worked the knot free, and the blindfold fell away. As Nina's eyes adjusted, a tangle of breath got caught in her throat.

She wasn't just looking at any house — it was *the house*. The one that had lingered in her browser's history, the one she'd shown Will during quiet evenings wrapped in each other's arms when neither of them felt much like Netflix or chilling. The house that had been the setting of a thousand daydreams now loomed before her, as real as the ground underfoot and the man right beside her.

It must have been magnificent in its prime, although it was clearly in need of renovation now. Three stories with steep gables, a wrap-around porch, and delicate wooden scrollwork whose white paint was now peeling and covered in dust. Yellowing lace curtains graced many of the windows.

Nina couldn't help imagining what she would do to restore its beauty if it were hers: a coat of dove gray paint to freshen the time-dulled gray of the walls, and bright white for the scrollwork and trim to make all those little flourishes sharp and crisp. The curtains would have to go, replaced with something sheer to provide privacy while letting the lights in. Or maybe custom blinds in a contrasting color to highlight the arched windows on the upper floor?

So many possibilities … that she was never going to pursue.

But this house wasn't a bed-and-breakfast, it had been for sale — she'd found it on a real estate website. Will must've arranged for a showing. The realtor would prob-ably be arriving any moment.

"I can't believe we're here in person," Nina admitted with a shiver, her voice reverent with anticipation as they stood before the weathered front door, stirred by a kind of fervent curiosity that only the truly macabre could evoke in her.

Will produced a key with a flourish, a smile playing on his lips as the key's metallic glint caught the last rays of sun. She wondered what kind of deposit he'd had to give the owners to persuade them to trust him with the key rather than going through an agent.

The thought of exploring this ancient treasure without a stranger hovering behind them filled her with delight.

"Shall we?" he asked.

"We shall." Nina wanted to squeal.

The door creaked open to an overture of withered history as they stepped across the threshold. Dust motes danced in stray beams of light to throw ghostly shadows across the walls. With its antiquated charm and unsettling stillness, the house was a siren call to Nina's soul.

"There's something about old houses," she mused aloud, trailing her fingers over a banister worn smooth by generations of hands. "They're like a library full of lives, with all of those rooms just waiting to be read."

"I guess growing up in an orphanage makes you like old stuff." Will smiled.

"You like the old stuff too."

"I appreciate anything that can withstand the test of time."

"Is this a house or a horror movie set?" Nina laughed, looking around at all the disrepair. Shadows clung to corners like cobwebs, and the once resplendent wallpaper now peered through a patina of dust with a pattern faded past the point of recognition.

Their flashlights cut through the gloom, throwing eerie specters to dance along the musty walls.

Will gave her a shrug. "If this house was in any worse shape, it would probably be scary, but if it looked even a little better, someone would have scooped it up for a fast remodel. Even all the way out here."

"What makes you think the place isn't scary?" Then she added, "All the way out here."

"Shall we?" Will repeated without answering her question.

Nina nodded, gesturing for him to lead the way. "We shall."

They wandered the house, and Nina narrated the unseen, with her predictions of each room's purpose unfailingly accurate.

"Drawing room," she declared as her hand hovered over a doorknob.

And so it was, complete with dust-shrouded portraits gazing down from high walls.

Will chuckled. "I'm pretty sure the big double doors were a dead giveaway."

But as they continued, her guesses grew uncannily precise. "Linen closet," she asserted before opening the door to a cramped space crammed with moth-eaten fabrics.

Will raised an eyebrow but said nothing, the playfulness in his eyes dimming to something more thoughtful.

The main bedroom was their final stop, a grand space where twilight held court.

Nina approached the window, peering out into the encroaching night as she whispered. "It's so isolated."

The vast nothingness stretched beyond like a physical presence. Flat weedy ground for hundreds of yards, and a sparse tree line in the distance. Possibly planted to mark the boundary between this property and someone else's.

Nina imagined looking out this window every day, having the luxury of so much space around her instead of the six feet between her rented house and her neighbors' houses on either side, back in Chicago.

Will joined her at the window, his proximity a warmth at her side even before he took hold of her hand.

Nina was still grappling with the magnitude of the

moment as she turned to Will, alight with a mixture of astonishment and affection.

"Thank you," she breathed, "this house … it's just as lovely as I imagined."

Will watched her with a hint of trepidation. "Do you mean that?" he probed, the depths of his eyes seeming to search hers for any sign of hesitation. "Because I bought it for you."

"What?" The question escaped her lips, a whisper lost in the vastness of their new bedroom. Was Will wasn't messing with her right now?

But as she stared at him, the gravity of his words continued to slowly sink in.

"I wanted you to understand how serious I am about you. About us."

She should have been deliriously happy. But somehow she also felt trapped. A house. It was so… permanent. She'd barely had a week to get used to saying *fiancé*. Why did agreeing to spend the rest of her life with Will feel like less of a commitment than buying a house with him?

And not just any house. Her dream house. No, her *fantasy* house, which wasn't quite the same thing. A fantasy wasn't meant to come true, it was meant to be an escape.

This house was far too big for two people — even if they had children right away, they wouldn't need this much space. It felt embarrassingly extravagant. And impractical.

Still, she wanted it more than she'd ever wanted anything, despite the fear that fluttered in her stomach when she tried to imagine this house as her home, possibly for the rest of her life.

"It's my wedding present to you," Will said with the tone of a confession. "I know we haven't even talked about setting a date yet, but I couldn't risk losing this place. I'm the someone who scooped it up for a remodel. I just knew it wouldn't be fast."

"I'm not in a hurry." Nina laughed, overwhelmed by the suddenness of change, her life different from one blink to the next.

She was lost for words beyond that.

"Come on, Nina — I need to know what you think!"

"What about your job?" she asked.

"I can work from anywhere, and if I have to be in Chicago, I'll catch a flight out of Minot." he shrugged. "When do you want to move in?"

She didn't want to think about that now — this house still seemed like a fantasy, an escape into the completely unreal. Deciding to quit her job and move out here into the middle of nowhere would make it real, which meant wrestling the painful practicalities. She could already hear Annie's reaction: *are you fucking kidding me?*

She'd be isolated out here, with only Will for company and the nearest store a twenty-minute drive away. And they would be taking on the job of renovating an old house that probably needed even more work than they could tell from looking at it.

But when she thought about what this house could become if they put the love into it that the place deserved, Nina realized she wanted to do it.

Once it was in good shape, they could probably sell for a lot more than Will had paid, if they decided to move back to Chicago. When she thought about it like that, as an adventure they would be embarking on together, her flutters of fear bloomed into excitement.

"Soon," she said, loving the way his eyes lit up at her answer.

She pondered the rooms they had just wandered through, the quiet whispers of the house that somehow spoke to her soul. This was a leap into the unknown for sure, but who was she to refuse a dance with destiny in the grand ballroom of life?

Especially when Will was at the heart of it all. A home, the tantalizing promise of family, and the love that had become her north star.

With a resolve that surprised even her, Nina wrapped her arms around him.

Their lips met in a long kiss to seal their future.

Nina tugged at his hand. "Dance with me."

Will couldn't resist her playful command.

They danced in the empty bedroom, where dust swirled around them like confetti. No music filled the air, nor did it need to. They had the rhythm of two hearts beating in unison, and the creaking of floorboards singing a tune that only old houses can know.

Her new home seemed to hold its breath, with secrets on the lip of revelation.

Chapter Two

Nina stood on the porch, watching the moving van rumble down the driveway, leaving a cloud of dust to settle on the gravel in its wake. The house stood stoic around her, its windows reflecting the tangerine glow of her first setting sun as a resident.

She was surrounded by the remnants of their city life together in boxes and furniture, most of which belonged to Will. As she unpacked them, Nina's possessions seemed meager in comparison, items mostly scavenged from second-hand stores and estate sales. Each purchase had been precious to her at the time, but seeing them alongside his things for the first time made her feel a little embarrassed.

Nina loved old things, and she loved even more when she found one at a bargain price, undervalued by its current owner. It gave her a thrill to rescue these once-loved items from obscurity, giving them the appreciation they deserved but no longer received in this modern world.

Hours later, her stomach growled as she placed a Waterford vase on the kitchen windowsill, turning it so the tiny chip on the side turned invisible. The way it sparkled in the sunlight, you'd never guess she had scooped it out of a bin in a dusty Goodwill.

The house was starting to feel more like hers. No, *theirs.* And now that she'd unpacked their pans and plates, it was time to fill up the fridge.

She decided to check on Will, to see if he was hungry too.

Her hand grazed the newel post as she ascended the staircase, and to her surprise, it wobbled and came off in her hand.

She examined the wooden piece with a frown, noticing a base frayed from years of use — or total neglect. How much rotten wood would they have to replace to make this old lady beautiful again?

Nina turned back around and headed toward Will's office, ducking her head to see him crouched amid a circle of boxes filled with his papers and books, brow furrowed in concentration as he worked to arrange his new domain.

She held the newel post with an amused tilt to her lips. "Looks like we've got some maintenance to do."

Nina placed the detached piece atop a stack of books.

Will looked up from his box. "The property inspector said there's nothing urgent. Everything can wait until after the wedding."

Nina did her best to keep the flicker of hesitation off her face. Will hadn't been pressuring her to choose a date, but he seemed to be assuming it would be soon. Wasn't moving their entire life to another state and starting over again in a house that needed fixing up enough to focus on right now?

"I think I'll head into town to pick up some groceries." She brushed her hands together as if to rid herself of history's dust still clinging to her skin.

Will stood and stretched his back with a groan. "I could use a break from all this unpacking. And the Infinity needs gas."

He started patting his pockets before glancing all over the office.

"Did you move my keys?" A slight edge of fatigue crept into his voice.

"No." Nina replied.

They were on a hunt for his elusive car keys after that, combing through the downstairs rooms with a mounting sense of confusion. Will's fob might as well have vanished into the floorboards.

"Maybe they're upstairs," Will suggested.

"But you didn't go upstairs?"

"You did."

"I'm telling you, Will, I didn't touch your keys."

But Will was already on his way to the bedroom.

Where he found his keys, nestled innocuously on the windowsill.

"You must have brought them up here with you," he said with a nonchalant shrug.

"No. I didn't." She was positive that she hadn't — she'd been unpacking all morning, just like he had.

Will's gaze never wavered, his voice leaving no room for argument. "I haven't been upstairs since I parked the car."

Nina wanted to protest, to insist that she remembered things differently, but the certainty in his stance and the unwavering assurance in his eyes gave her pause.

Was it worth fighting over, marring their first day in their new house, the house he had bought for her?

She dipped her head in a reluctant nod and a slow exhale, then they walked to the car in silence, trying to ignore the tension suddenly hanging between them.

Will slid behind the wheel, and the familiar purr was a welcome sound as the engine cut into uncertainty.

Overcast skies from the previous evening had now surrendered to a sprawling canvas of blue, lighting up the clouds so brightly they seemed illuminated from within.

A sign for the neighboring town flashed by, its edges corroded by weather and time, the paint faded and barely legible: *JACKRABBIT RIDGE.*

"Jackrabbit Ridge." She loved the name — quaint and homey, and there was probably a story behind it. The kind of place whose thrift store was surely full of treasures from her great-grandmother's era. "When do you want to explore that place?"

"Probably nothing there," Will murmured, his eyes on the road and his tone suggesting an end to a discussion that never even had the chance to get started.

So Nina stared out the window at endless fields of wheat waving like a golden sea, their uniformity broken only by the occasional skeletal remains of abandoned homesteads and discarded farm equipment. An old wheat mill, its gray wood splintered past the point of decay. Not much else.

The desolation was profound, the silence of abandonment speaking louder than any bustling city street ever could.

Glenburn, North Dakota, emerged as a solitary streak of civilization, a sparse thread of Main Street flanked by remnants of commerce and echoes of rural heartland on either side.

Grady's Pharmacy stood sentry to their right, its windows hosting a series of fading product posters amid a few brand new ones that appeared garish by comparison. Glowing neon script offered the promise of home remedies. Thompson's Family Grocer promised delicious local produce via its weathered, paint-chipped sign swaying gently in the breeze.

More refined businesses and amenities like doctors and dentists were a two-hour drive south to Bismarck.

Will was driving to the corner, where the End of Trail Gas station seemed to be a relative hub of unassuming town activity. Old fuel pumps stood like rusty guardians at the gates of the vast, open fields beyond, and three of the six were occupied, once the Infinity was idling in front of one.

With the engine still running, Will broke the silence. "Still happy about the move?"

"As long as you're at my side, absolutely."

But as they cruised along the modest stretch of Glenburn, a flicker of recognition started scratching at her mind. That convenience store — why did it seem so ominous? And that tiny yarn and crafts shop on the next block gave her a strong sense of deja vu. But she was sure she had never been here.

Was it just the sameness of small-town rural America? It seemed so familiar, she had a hard time brushing it off like that.

Maybe she'd seen it in a documentary. Or… in one of the true crime podcasts she loved to listen to.

"You don't seem happy. Is something wrong?" Will asked.

"I think there was a murder in this city. Glenburn, North Dakota."

He sighed. "You should really stop listening to all those podcasts. They always get the gears turning in your head."

"I like it when my gears are turning." She shrugged. "There's nothing better than having a great puzzle to solve. I enjoy playing along, seeing if I can figure out the big reveal before Riddles in the Dark gives it to me."

"Did you figure out the murder here in Glenburn?"

"I'll tell you when I remember the murder."

"If there's a mystery to solve in Glenburn, I'm sure you'll crack it. But please, let's not make our new home a stop on the true crime tour."

Will grinned and got out of the car to gas up.

The pump clicked rhythmically as another vehicle rolled to a stop at the adjacent pump. A man emerged, his movements mechanical as he also gassed up.

A woman's eyes met Nina's from inside the car, her stare intense and unwavering.

And it didn't stop.

Nina thought she had gotten used to being stared at, but somehow it was different out here in the country than it had been in Chicago. Maybe because of the relative anonymity the city granted its inhabitants — she'd never see the starers again, and they'd never know who she was. And the people she saw everyday had learned not to look so hard after they'd gotten to know her, to treat her like a person instead of a victim. But out here, wouldn't everyone know that she and Will had bought the old house? Would she have to tell the story over and over again, until the whole town knew? Would they whisper pityingly behind her back until she finally moved somewhere else?

Nina's scar was a memorial of the accident that had stolen her parents and childhood. She had no memories of anything before waking up in a hospital all alone — the doctors had guessed she was about six, but whoever had dropped her off had disappeared after handing her over to an emergency room nurse, covered in blood and unconscious.

At the orphanage, she had been told it was probably a car accident, her cuts the result of shattered window glass.

Even though she couldn't remember that accident, she would never be allowed to forget it had happened.

Not unless Nina avoided people for the rest of her life.

That moment when a new acquaintance's eyes would inadvertently drift to her scar seemed to punctuate every introduction. Their face would flicker with pity, curiosity, or discomfort before they regained their composure.

At social gatherings, Nina would often catch the caboose of a hushed query whenever she approached a cluster of partygoers.

Every varietal of, 'What happened to her face?', most often followed by an embarrassed hush from the person queried.

But Will had met her gaze squarely, his own eyes reflecting an empathy born of similar loss, never once flinching at the scars of Nina's past. He'd lost someone too — Rose, his first love — when he was only a teenager, so he understood what it was like to have your life ripped away from you. To start over from scratch and build a new one in the devastation of of the present. His loss had laid the foundation for a bond unmarred by the superficial judgments so common in this world.

The man finally finished gassing and got back into his car in time for Nina to see the woman say something to him — a beat before he pretended not to look over at her.

Nina sank lower in her seat, her body curling instinctively away from their scrutiny.

The gas pump clicked off, and Will replaced the nozzle.

Climbing back into the car, he found Nina almost hidden from view, cramped down as if trying to squeeze into the footwell.

"What are you doing down there?" Will asked.

"I didn't want to be stared at anymore," Nina

confessed, meeting his gaze with a fragile smile as she straightened herself in the seat.

"They're gone," he assured her, reaching out to squeeze her hand gently. "I'll be right back — I just need to pop inside the station real quick to grab some oil, and then we can get out of here."

He stepped out of the car, leaving Nina alone with her thoughts and the ghost of all those stares that lingered even in their absence.

Chapter Three

WILL PUSHED OPEN the door and a jangling bell cut through the hum of the AC.

The Gas & Go's exterior was a collage of weathered advertisements and neon beer logos. The interior was cramped and claustrophobic, reeking of rubber and stale coffee.

Will's thoughts lingered on Nina, her vulnerability hidden behind the facade of toughness she wore like armor. Rosie had been brave, just like Nina. Except for the scar, Nina could almost be Rosie, with her icy-blue eyes, elfin features, and sleek blonde hair — upon seeing Nina's profile photo for the first time on Insta, he'd been stunned at a resemblance he wouldn't have thought possible.

Being with Nina dulled the loss of Rosie, helped him feel close once more to the first woman he'd ever loved. He could never tell her that, of course. All Nina needed to know was that he loved her too. Did it matter why, as long as he was good to her?

He even loved Nina's scar, because it reminded him that she wasn't Rosie. It helped him forgive her when she didn't do what Rosie would have. It wasn't Nina's fault that she wasn't Rosie.

And it wasn't her fault that the locals were making her uncomfortable. They couldn't see in her what he did: the imperfect echo of his perfect Rosie. It was his job to protect that echo, however faint it might be.

The sooner he found the oil, the sooner Nina would be safe back at home.

Rows of shelves were a time capsule of rural commerce, housing an eclectic mix of car essentials and last-minute shopping regrets. A key cutting machine stood in the corner, surrounded by a carousel of uncut keys. There.

Will passed the key-cutting machine to grab a liter of oil, the container cold and heavy in his grip. Then to the alcohol aisle, where bottles stood in formation like soldiers on parade, labels gleaming under the fluorescent lights.

The middle-aged clerk had a busy mustache hanging over his lip like a caterpillar. He watched Will move through the aisles, sizing him up from behind a counter cluttered with lotto tickets and local maps.

A surge of annoyance tightened Will's jaw. His gaze hovered over the wine section, a parade of overpriced mediocrity. An offense to his standards.

He turned to the clerk with a half-grin. "You wouldn't happen to have a 1960 Beaulieu Vineyard Georges de Latour Private Reserve Cabernet Sauvignon, would you?" The name of the wine rolled off his tongue with ease.

But it didn't catch the clerk off-guard like Will expected.

"Nope." His mustached twitched in amusement. "But I've got a '74 Château Montelena Cabernet in back. Eight hundred bucks. Want me to bring it out from the cellar?"

Surely the bottle's contents had long since turned to vinegar, assuming the clerk wasn't joking.

"I'll pass." He set the oil in front of the clerk. Up close, Will could see the name *James* stitched on his lapel.

"Passing through town?"

"I just bought the place off Highway 12, at the Junction."

"No shit." The man's hands stilled, the scanner beeping into silence. "You bought the old Byrd estate?"

Will thought he detected shock and a hint of something darker.

"That's the one," he confirmed with a nod. "Bought it off the bank after the previous owner defaulted on the taxes."

James leaned forward, eyes narrowing as his voice winnowed down to a whisper. "You shouldn't have done that, it don't matter how good of a deal you think you got."

Will tried to hide his annoyance. "What makes you say that?"

His eyes locked onto Will's with an intensity that made the air in his cramped store feel suddenly charged. "You know about the murder, right?"

"Of course I do." Will gritted his teeth. His biggest fear from the second he'd hatched his plan to buy the house had been that someone would mention its history to Nina.

When she'd told him about a podcast discussing the murder in Glenburn, Will had gone numb. He wanted her to be happy in their new home; his happiness depended on her happiness. They'd both been trapped in the past for so long, he wanted them to move forward together, into the life he had once hoped to give to Rosie.

But now that life would be Nina's, assuming he could make her happy.

James continued, oblivious. "Happened about twenty years ago on that property of yours. Glenburn's never stopped talking about it. Police said they caught the guy, but around here? We ain't buying it. Most of us think the real culprit's still out there, maybe closer than we all think."

He leaned forward, as if proximity could lend truth to his words. "Some folks swear the killer's been living there the whole time."

"I don't want to hear any more." Will turned to leave, sick to his stomach at the thought of someone poisoning Nina's feelings for their new home.

"There's also talk of hauntings," added James.

"*Hauntings?*"

Will took the bait, even if he scoffed while repeating the word. Not because he was curious, but because he had to know what Nina might hear when she went shopping in town. Maybe he should do all the shopping, at least until they'd lived in the house long enough that she would dismiss the rumors.

James shrugged with a glint of delight in his eye to tell this story to the apparent sucker who had bought Glenburn's famous murder house. So certain that he knew the real story. "Lights flickering on and off in the dead of night when nobody's supposed to be there — unexplainable shenanigans like that have been happening on the Byrd property for years. Didn't the real estate agent mention any of this?"

Of course she hadn't. She'd been legally obligated to disclose the murder, but why would she sabotage the potential sale with lurid rumors?

Not that Will hadn't expected there'd be a few, given what had happened at that house. But he would do his best to quell them, for Nina's sake. And for the sake of their relationship.

"You believe that there are ghosts just because there are supposedly lights on the property? Despite countless other less ludicrous possibilities, like faulty wiring in an old, rundown house?" Will couldn't help but roll his eyes as a touch of sarcasm edged into his tone, hoping to kill the man's enthusiasm for spreading ghost stories about their new home. "If there's a killer behind bars, then clearly the police think they caught the right man."

James hummed a non-committal "uh-huh," with a knowing look that further stoked Will's irritation. But better to be dismissive and let the conversation die than to make a bigger deal and make the man even more determined to push his point. Will couldn't keep Nina from interacting with the locals, but he could discourage them from scaring her. Or worse.

Will shook his head and handed over cash for the oil, then left the Gas & Go without another word as the clerk burned a hole in his back with that gaze.

Nina looked up as he approached the vehicle, her eyes searching his as he slid into the driver's seat.

"What took so long?" She sounded slightly concerned, but mostly curious. "Everything okay?"

What would be the best way make it a non-issue right from the start?

"The guy in there was filling me in on our new home's apparently infamous past."

"Really?" Nina perked up, her eyes brightened at the glint of intrigue. "Tell me more."

"The place is supposedly haunted," Will replied in a flat voice, hopeing she would dismiss the claim as quickly as he had.

She looked even more disappointed than he'd hoped.

"That's what they always say about old houses. I was hoping for something more exciting."

"More exciting than a haunted house?"

She shrugged. "Did he say anything else?"

"That's about it."

Nina leaned back in her seat, looking bored. Mission accomplished, for now.

The truth would swallow them in its time, but Will saw no reason to accelerate the inevitable.

Chapter Four

FADING light draped their home like a shroud, its eerie calm disrupted by the crunch of gravel under tires as Will steered his Infinity up the last stretch of driveway. Their new home's windows were like blind eyes turned toward the dying day. In the full light, she'd found the place charming despite its state of disrepair, but now it seemed to have an aura of despair. She could see why the locals said it was haunted.

She wondered if it was the quiet she was reacting to. She'd spent most of her life in the hustle of Chicago's noisy streets, but had quickly learned to tune out the sounds of sirens wailing, trucks rumbling, people yelling, dogs barking, grackles cawing — a distant cacophony that served as the soundtrack of her days. Here … Nina didn't even hear frogs croaking. Not a single cricket chirped. Not even the whine of a mosquito.

Her gaze abruptly shifted upward, to a fleeting silhouette dancing against the bedroom windowpane in the waning light.

"Look, up there, in the bedroom window!" Nina pointed, surprised to see her finger trembling.

But then the specter dissolved into the encroaching dusk, a moment before Will turned his head.

"It's probably just the light playing tricks with the shadows."

"Yeah, probably."

Most alleged ghosts were actually the result of someone's imagination getting away from them. She and Will had spent the whole day inside that house and seen nothing but rooms lacking the love and attention they deserved. Once the renovations were finished, the place wouldn't look creepy anymore, even at twilight.

Maybe she could find an antique street lamp to put out front, where it would cast a cheery glow over the front yard.

The car rolled to a stop, its engine settling into silence as they both got out, then went to the trunk where they could unload the groceries.

Nina paused in front of the trunk while waiting for Will, her eyes drawn back to the upstairs window. *Trick of the light.* Another quirk that she'd just have to get used to.

Just like the creaks and groans that the orphanage used to make each night as it settled. She hadn't slept at all her first night there, but within a few days every little sound had become a comfort — the old building talking to her as she drifted off to sleep.

She would get used to this house too, and soon every shadow would become an old friend, telling her where the sun was in its passage across the sky.

Still, there was a part of her that wondered if they had forgotten to lock up when they left and someone had come in. Someone who could be waiting for them to walk in, unaware that danger lurked inside their new home.

City instincts that she would need to unlearn, after a life lived behind doors reinforced with deadbolts and chain-locks. Crime rates out here in the country were supposed to be much lower, weren't they?

Will came up beside her, and she forced a smile, shrugging off a chill that had nothing to do with the evening air.

He unlocked the trunk, and they each grabbed an armload of groceries, then approached the porch together.

The clicking tumblers as Will unlocked the door made the knots between her shoulder blades relax a little. They hadn't forgotten.

"We should've gotten spare keys cut while we were in town," she said.

"Slipped my mind. Next time, for sure." He unlocked the door, then followed her inside, setting his bag on the kitchen counter before leaving to bring in the rest.

Nina set her own two bags down on the countertop with a soft thud. She couldn't resist scurrying to the back door, to make sure it was still locked. It was.

A quick tour of the lower level revealed that all the windows were intact, no sign of a break-in.

Trick of the light.

She made it back to the kitchen in time to start pulling produce out of one bag just before Will appeared with two more. He gave her a peck on the cheek, then left her tucking the veggies into the refrigerator crisper while reflecting on their first trip into town.

She had kept her hood pulled up the entire time, though it made for a flimsy shield against the curious glances that inevitably wandered toward her scars. The selection at the market had been modest, a scant variety compared to what she was used to. No Whole Foods or Garden Gourmet out here. Not even an Aldi.

But they now owned a lot of fertile land, and by

summer she and Will could be reaping a harvest of their own. A well-tended garden would bring another note of cheer to the property.

Will returned with the remaining groceries, clinking with the promise of a chilled evening wine. She made room in the refrigerator, cool air brushing her face as she slid the bottle onto the shelf.

Tonight's dinner would be fettuccine, Nina finally decided after much internal deliberation. She wanted to make their first meal in this house a memorable one, and considering Will's love affair with pasta, the heavier the better. Fettuccini was perfect.

But then Nina realized that she'd forgotten the most important ingredient.

"What is it?" Will asked.

"I forgot to buy basil."

"It'll be just as good without basil." He sounded convincing enough while leaning against the kitchen counter, watching her profile against the windowpane. But Will wasn't the one cooking, and he didn't know what he was talking about.

Was she annoyed at him? Or at herself, for subconsciously sabotaging the dinner she'd wanted to share for this first night in their new home?

She barely glanced at him, her eyes still out the window. "I bet there's a garden out there."

"With a full bed of basil I'm sure." Will laughed at her, not with her.

Now she *was* annoyed with him.

"There's a garden out there," Nina repeated, this time more emphatic, almost defiant in the face of his skepticism. "And I bet there is basil in it."

She started walking toward the door.

"You can just make something else. I'll be happy with

anything you—"

"I'll be right back."

"Do you want any company?"

Nina exited the kitchen into the cooling embrace of their sprawling backyard, and the vastness of fields beyond that stretched to the horizon.

"I'll be fine on my own," she called over her shoulder to Will.

Nina kept walking without waiting to hear his answer.

The open field behind her new house was a canvas of earthy tones, with rocks and stones half buried in the dirt. She still could scarcely believe that all this land was actually hers.

Nina couldn't shake the sensation of being observed. She cast a glance behind her to see Will's figure retreating from the deck.

She kept walking toward the garden shed that loomed ahead.

Its door groaned in protest when she got there, refusing to open for Nina until she forced it from its frame with a hard shove from her right shoulder. It finally swung open to an interior cloaked in shadows.

The air was thick with the scent of metal and earth. Rows of gardening tools and shelves packed with jars full of seeds lined the walls. Surely there had been a well-tended garden here on the property at one time.

She exited the shed and looked back at the house. Will was no longer on the porch.

She shivered, feeling abandoned even though she'd told him she didn't need his company. With the sun setting, shadows deepened around the house, transforming her dream home from fairy tale fantasy to something grimmer. Or Brothers Grimmer.

She had the urge to return to the brightly-lit kitchen,

where she'd be surrounded by the comfort of familiar things.

But if she went back without finding some basil, Will would give her that *I-told-you-so* smirk that always infuriated her, ruining their first night in the new place.

Of course there would be basil, even if it had gone to seed. Who planted a garden and didn't plant basil?

She circled the building and her breath hitched at the sight of a fenced area, overgrown and neglected. Rows of wooden beds like a cemetery of aspirations, its withered plants like headstones in a graveyard of intent.

She pushed the gate, its hinges crying out with a high-pitched keen as she entered the forgotten sanctuary. Her boots disturbed the dirt as she walked between the rows, her heart racing with the promise of discovery until she halted in front of her biggest surprise of the day, even though it was the sight she had come out here to find: a solitary basil plant, drooping in the shadows.

Nina reached out to caress a lonely leaf, its edges brittle with neglect.

She crushed it gently, bringing the leaf to her nose and inhaling a pungent scent that spoke of summer kitchens.

She carried the basil back to the house, wondering if it really meant anything that she had found such an unlikely plant, still clinging to life in an unlikely place.

Nina shook off an icy chill that didn't come from the breeze as she approached her back porch, pretending like it didn't feel like the property itself was watching her.

She would put a couple of wrought iron lamps out here, too. Something to turn the maw-like porch into a cozy place to watch the sun set while she sipped peppermint tea.

She'd have to remember to plant some peppermint, when they got around to the garden.

Her steps were light on the old wooden floor, echoing off the high ceilings as she made her way to Will's office from the kitchen, still clutching the uprooted basil like a prize.

She nudged the door open with a gentle push, her eyes taking in a room that already looked nothing like the rest of the house. Will's office was a capsule of order, with every stick of furniture neatly arranged and his technology all in its rightful place, computer hard-drive softly humming on the desk and monitor aglow. His books were already arranged on the shelves.

His modern-minimalist furniture looked completely out of place here. But this was his space, and she'd restore the rest of the house to its former glory. She hadn't noticed any antique shops in Glenburn, but the consignment store might yield a few gems. If not, she could fly back to Chicago and go shopping with Annie.

"All set up." Will swiveled in his chair to face her.

"I can see that." She smiled. "Maybe you can help me with the living room next?"

"Of course." He nodded at the basil in her hand. "You're kidding me."

Nina held up the branch she'd plucked from the plant, still slightly dusty from the garden. "Isn't that weird?"

"I'm glad you found some basil, because now you can make the fettuccini, but I don't know how 'weird' it is."

"You didn't seem to think I would find anything out there," Nina argued. "But there was a garden, and this was the only plant even remotely alive."

"I'm glad it was there." He shrugged.

"That doesn't strike you as odd *at all*. This exact herb, in a neglected garden, when we needed it? How I knew it would be there?"

"It was an herb garden. I guess basil is just the hardiest herb?" Another shrug.

Nina wasn't sure why she felt like arguing with him — she was the one who'd insisted there would be basil in the first place. Maybe because he hadn't been surprised like she'd expected.

Or maybe Nina was still unnerved out by how different their new home looked in the gloom of twilight. She still couldn't stop thinking about that shape in the window.

Trick of the light.

Will's attention was already drifting back to the monitor, and she could tell the conversation was starting to annoy him too. It would be a terrible start to their new life to spend their first night here fighting.

So she left the office with a sigh and returned to the kitchen.

Nina washed and minced the leaves, their fragrance rising in the air with a sharp, fresh scent that filled the room. Her sauce simmered on the stove, bubbling as the fettuccine rolled to a boil, the nest of golden noodles almost ready for their creamy bath.

She prepared a salad, simple greens due to a meager selection in the produce section, but still a nice splash of color to accompany their meal. By the time she was finished, the noodles were al dente, ready to strain and toss in the rich, redolent sauce.

Nina found a box marked *CHINA* and sliced the tape with a knife, lifting the flaps to reveal a collection of delicate plates patterned with roses, their edges kissed with gold.

She had never seen them before. But they were beautiful. Maybe Will had bought them, another present to celebrate their engagement?

An ugly question rose up before she could stop it: had

he bought these plates long ago, to give to the woman he'd loved and lost?

No, that wasn't fair to use the tragedy of his past as an excuse for jealousy just because she was annoyed with him right now. Rose was dead and Will had worked hard to heal from her loss. Nina was the new love of his life.

She picked up two of the rose-patterned plates and set the table for their first dinner in this house with a flourish: smoothing out the linen tablecloth, arranging the china with care, placing the crystal glasses so they caught the light and threw prisms against the walls.

The wine bottle gave a soft pop as she pulled the cork.

"Dinner's ready!" Nina trumpeted, standing back to admire her display of domestic perfection as he entered the room.

"Looks great," Will said, taking in the spread and pointing at the bottle of wine chilling in the bucket. "You know, the wine really should have been left out to breathe."

His words deflated her like a pin in a balloon.

"I'm sorry, I didn't think of that. Next time, I'll remember." A flush of embarrassment warmed her cheeks. But she was sure that when he tasted the pasta, he'd forget everything else. Velvety sauce clung to the strands, with a sprinkle of freshly grated Parmesan on top, and the salad sat crisp and dressed on small plates.

They took their seats, glasses clinking in a toast before they each took a sip of the slightly-too-chilled wine.

Will's eyes narrowed slightly as he peered at the plates. "When did you buy this china?"

Nina glanced at the empty box were she had unpacked them and then looked back at Will. "I figured the china was yours. It was with our things."

She pointed to the box.

"I've never seen them before." He nodded at where it

read *CHINA*. "That looks like your handwriting, not mine."

Nina examined the scribbles on the cardboard as well as she could from the table. "That doesn't look anything like my writing, and it's definitely not my china. Maybe the previous owners left it here?"

"The house was empty when I bought it, and when we walked through together. Remember?"

Nina couldn't argue with that. Maybe the moving company had mixed someone else's things in with theirs. But it seemed petty to pursue it. She would rather get back to the excitement of moving into their own place, not squabble about basil and dishware.

The clatter of utensils on their plates punctuated the quiet as they ate.

She broke the silence first. "I'm thinking of job hunting once we're settled."

"Are you sure?" Will paused, his fork mid-air. "I thought we'd work on the house first, get married … then, maybe start a family?"

Nina looked up, surprised by his hopeful tone. "I would love that. I just wasn't sure if you wanted me to work or not."

"I want you to do whatever makes you happy," he affirmed with a smile. "I want whatever you want."

She smiled back, grateful for the moment of connection.

But every time she glanced down at her plate, that flicker of unease returned, and her mind wandered through the rest of their dinner.

First thing tomorrow, she'd find *her* dishes and store these in the back of a cupboard somewhere.

After dinner, she gathered the dishes, her hands working as her thoughts continued to meander in circles.

Darkness outside the kitchen window seemed to press against the glass.

For a moment, Nina could have sworn she saw a shadow flicker across the lawn — a ghostly wisp of movement that vanished as quickly as it appeared.

"Will?" she called, her voice tighter than she intended.

He was at her side, the concern clear in his features. "What's wrong?"

Nina nodded at the window. "I thought I saw something outside."

He grabbed a flashlight from the drawer and together they stepped out onto the back porch, the beam cutting a swathe through the darkness.

They scoured the backyard and found nothing.

Another trick of the light?

"It must have been my imagination," Nina muttered in embarrassment as Will locked the door behind them.

He started back toward his office, but Nina wasn't ready to let their evening end.

She caught his necklace between her fingers, playfully tugging at his chain, glancing down at the rose and compass as she led him upstairs.

Only in the bedroom, with Will entering her from behind, could the fervor of their affection eclipse her anxieties, and the urgency of their union finally speak louder than the shadows.

Chapter Five

A HIGH-PITCHED SCREAM jolted Will awake, piercing the stillness of his night. Truly bloodcurdling. He realized that the ear-scraper was coming from Nina.

Adrenaline surged through his veins as he snapped on the bedside lamp, illuminating the room in a harshly-artificial glow.

Sharp shadows seemed to slink away, retreating into the corners.

Nina was a pale figure of terror, her body pressed against the wall, pointing at the bedroom door, trembling with the aftershock of her fright.

"Someone was there — *watching us!*" Nina's voice was a strained whisper, her eyes wide with the rawness of paralytic fear.

He never should've told her what the gas station clerk had said about the house being haunted. Now she had the idea in her head, and it would be even harder to persuade her to let it go.

He couldn't stop the exasperated thought: *Rose wouldn't have let her imagination get the best of her.*

But that just meant it was up to Will to help Nina do better. Starting with showing her that he was taking her fear seriously, then dispelling it.

Will unplugged the lamp, its cord trailing behind him like a lifeline as he raised his makeshift weapon. Bare feet met the cold floor with urgency, his lamp held aloft to confront the imaginary intruder.

The hallway was shrouded in an even heavier darkness beyond the beam of his makeshift lantern. He ventured out, heart pounding, every step an echo in the silent house. His breath seemed too loud in his ears.

Not because he was afraid — Nina's shriek of terror had flooded his system with adrenaline as it had ripped him from his dreams.

He checked each bedroom methodically, under beds and behind every door, but found nothing.

Except … a window was open in one of the bedrooms, its curtains billowing in the breeze. Nina must have left it open.

He approached the window, his muscles tensed for action as the cool night air washed over his skin. Peering out at the yard below, he saw nothing but weedy ground that needed mowing — or even better, replacing with a real garden. Nina could plant all the basil she wanted.

He secured the window and returned to the bedroom, satisfied even though his heart was still racing from the adrenaline surge.

But Nina was still a statue of fright.

"It's okay," he assured her. "It was only the wind."

"I saw someone, Will."

He rubbed the sleep from his eyes, trying to bring the world into focus, wishing he could just go to sleep instead but knowing he would be lucky to doze off before dawn, despite his exhaustion.

"A nightmare, perhaps?"

She wrapped her arms around herself as she shuddered. "I know what I saw. And it wasn't a dream."

"Okay, Nina." Will sighed as a wave of exhaustion washed over him. "I'll check the house again, just to be—"

A THUD echoed through the house, seeming to vibrate through the floorboards.

He tensed, and even in the dim light, Nina could surely see the shift in his stance.

"I'm sure you heard that," she said.

Will nodded, already on his way back out of the bedroom. Was it possible that she really had seen something?

What if the ghost stories told by the locals contained some grain of truth? He didn't believe in ghosts, but he did believe in burglaries and home invasions.

He descended the stairs, his footsteps cautious as he approached the front door, which was now ajar. He knew it had been closed when he'd headed upstairs — Nina must have gone out to the car for something before joining him, and failed to shut it completely.

A cold gust of wind greeted him as he moved forward to close it.

"Nina?" He slipped into the living room and hid in an alcove full of shadows.

His body thrummed with adrenaline, thanks to her carelessness. It was petty of him, but he wanted her to feel the same way. Besides, if she was annoyed, it would snap her out of her fear. This was a teachable moment.

Nina's voice followed the sound of her feet on the stairs, soft and drizzled with worry. "Will … where are you?"

He waited, anticipation bubbling to the surface until she was close enough and—

Will leapt from his hiding spot.

Nina's scream tore through the stillness. Raw and piercing, as it echoed off the walls.

Seeing Will bent over in uncontrollable laughter, her fear sparked into a tempest of irritation, terror now boiling into vexation at his jest.

Just like he'd known it would.

"That's not funny!" She swatted him on the arm. "You scared me half to death!"

He wrapped his arms around her, chuckling as he pulled her close.

"I'm sorry," he managed between lingering laughs. "But I have heard that fear can be an aphrodisiac."

"You're such an asshole." She hit him again, but laughed as if trying to prove she was okay with it, awkward as she sounded.

"But you're not afraid now," he pointed out. "You're welcome."

"I'm going back to bed." She turned around and headed toward the stairs, obviously mad at him but trying not to show it.

Had he miscalculated?

Will gave her a moment, knowing it would be better that way, listening to the sounds of her tentative footsteps, soft hesitations on the creaking wood beneath.

But he was still buoyant with the remnants of laughter and feeling a twinge of guilt for his prank. Nina was already under the covers with her back to him when he returned to the bedroom.

The mattress dipped under his weight as he sat down beside her. "I'm sorry, okay? It was a stupid joke, and I didn't—"

Nina turned to face him, her eyes still rimmed with fear

and irritation. "You think this is funny? I was terrified, Will. I thought—"

He reached for her hand, holding it gently. "I know, and I thought the joke might jolt you out of it. But I'm an idiot for not taking how you're feeling seriously. I should have been there for you, not hiding in the shadows."

"Can we not do that again? Ever. Please."

"I promise." He shook his head. "No more scares. Not even in a horror movie."

"I still like watching scary movies. I just don't want you jumping out of shadows. The last thing I want to feel is afraid in my house."

That was the last thing he wanted, too.

"I'm sorry," Will said again.

He settled into bed and Nina inched closer to him.

"Can we close the door tonight?" The question made her sound vulnerable.

But she still should have known not to ask.

"You know I need to hear the fire alarm if it goes off." Even though he should not have had to explain himself, Will added, "It's a safety thing."

When he went back to the hardware store to copy his keys, he'd buy smoke detectors for every room. Deadbolts for the front and back doors.

He would also start checking to be sure Nina had locked up before he got into bed.

Nina sighed her acquiescence. "Stay up with me until I fall asleep?"

"Of course."

He petted her hair as they lay in the dark. Listened to her breathing, deep and even, willing himself to stay awake like he promised.

But time slipped by despite his resolve, and sleep crept

upon him with a stealthy wave that slowly pulled him under.

Chapter Six

Morning light filtered through the curtains, spilling over the rumpled sheets where Nina had spent the night chasing the barest traces of sleep. Skirting the edges of true rest, her mind reluctant to plunge into the depths of unconsciousness after all the eerie occurrences that had peppered their previous day.

Not that it apparently mattered much to Will, who lay tranquil beside her, his chest rising and falling with the steady breath of undisturbed slumber. How could he be so impervious to anxiety when it dogged her every moment?

She told herself that was a good thing. Once of them had to stay calm in the face of danger. Will's ability to keep his head was why she could rely on him.

She didn't remember getting out of bed last night — she'd woken up standing on the other side of the room, screaming at the dark shape in the doorway of their bedroom.

There had been incidents at the orphanage for months after she'd arrived: she'd wake up screaming in a corner of the dormitory in the middle of the night, not knowing how she'd gotten there. The social worker assigned to the orphanage had told her that sleepwalking could be triggered by trauma, just like amnesia.

Eventually, she had grown out of the sleepwalking, but the amnesia remained. Nina still couldn't remember a single moment of the accident or her life before. She didn't even know her real name. The orphanage caretaker, Mrs. Lambert, had helped her choose a temporary name once it became clear that her memory wasn't coming back any time soon.

Nina Turner was supposed to be a placeholder, but by the time she'd graduated from high school, it had become her name.

She peeled herself from the bed with a sigh and padded across the cool hardwood floor to the bathroom. The promise of a hot shower dangled before her like a carrot in front of a weary horse.

She stepped into the bathtub and turned on the tap, expecting a welcoming cascade of hot water, but the shower head mocked her without so much as a drip.

She twisted and turned with mounting irritation. No water. Not even a sputter or a cough of air from the pipes.

A string of curses escaped her lips as Nina left the bathroom, movements jerking around as she wrapped herself in a towel.

Back to the bedroom, to see that Will was already out of bed.

She descended the stairs and found him in his office, not surprised in the least to see him sitting amid a cocoon of glowing screens, already on the day's first call, if she was guessing by his headset. He looked tired. She felt guilty for waking him up over what had probably been a nightmare.

Although they'd both heard the the thud a few moments later. But he hadn't found an intruder — in fact,

Will had been so unconcerned that he'd decided to jump out of the shadows to startle her downstairs.

Now she felt less guilty.

He glanced up at her, and she mouthed a single word with exaggerated clarity: *Water.*

His eyes met hers, a brief flicker of confusion crossing his features before he offered her a noncommittal shrug and returned to his call.

She went to the kitchen and tested the sink, hoping for a different outcome. But the faucet just made a gargling sound as a trickle of water rushed out, then nothing.

She wandered into the larder next, the narrowness of the room pressing close around her as she eyed the empty shelves, still waiting for provisions to stock their new life.

Nina reached for a box of cereal and a sudden wave of deja vu shimmered through her body, causing a moment of paralysis before the sensation faded.

But she *had* stood in this same spot and reached for the same shelf before — just last night. The half-filled packet of fettuccine still rested right there next to the cereal where she'd left it.

She grabbed the box and shook it for comfort on her way to the cupboard.

She pulled out a bowl, then was struck by another lighting bolt of curiosity, the kind that was coming all too often around this house.

She looked down at that intricate rose pattern on the bowl in her hand and set it down on the counter, remembering the exchange that had sparked some of last night's tension.

A compulsion led her back to the living room, to the box marked *CHINA,* where she scrutinized that handwriting for a second time, now looking at the loops and lines more like a riddle to be solved.

She crouched down to study the strokes. She was sure that wasn't her handwriting.

Why would Will insist otherwise?

Suspicion was an insidious vine already twining around her thoughts.

Was Will lying to her about the china? The only reason she could come up with for doing so was that he had bought the dishes for Rose.

Or maybe they had belonged to Rose, and he'd been hanging onto them for all this time.

Did he really think Nina would be jealous of a dead woman?

They hadn't talked much about Will's first love, other than that he'd worked through his grief in therapy, and had finally accepted his first love was gone. But he clearly did not want to discuss the details, and Nina had respected that.

She appreciated that he never pressed her to talk about her amnesia around the accident that had scarred her, or what her parents had looked like. They'd agreed to leave their respective pasts behind and look into the future together.

But now Nina wondered if that had been the right decision. What if Will wasn't done grieving Rose?

Another reason to put off setting a date for the wedding. A long engagement would allow them to be sure they were both ready.

Nina returned to the kitchen and drenched her cereal in milk. Then she carried her bowl out to the porch. The back door creaked softly on its hinges as she stepped out.

The morning air was a crisp embrace as she meandered the grounds, the crunch of her cereal a solitary accompaniment to the rustle of dry grass underfoot. She could already sense the first stirrings of fall, and wondered what their first winter would be like. She was used to Chicago winters — frigid wind blowing in off the lake to cut through your clothes and chill your skin, treacherous ice on the sidewalks when the snow melted and refroze.

Nina turned to make her way back to the house. A glint near the ground caught her gaze. Curiosity drew her nearer to the source.

She set her bowl aside, fingers working to clear the encroaching grass from what appeared to be a window pane embedded in the earth.

Definitely not a trick of the light.

The realization dawned slowly — a basement, or the ghost of one, lay hidden beneath her feet. The prospect of discovery got her heart beating faster.

Or was that fear?

Maybe she should wait until Will got off his call before she tried to explore it. Who knew what she might find down there?

Or who. What if she really had seen an intruder last night?

Cereal now forgotten, Nina circled the house, seeking other signs of this subterranean enigma. Another window, similarly concealed by the overgrowth, came into view on the opposite side.

Was there an entire level to their home that they had yet to uncover?

But if so, where was the entrance?

Morning sun cast a golden sheen over the old glass, creating a canvas of light and shadow. Nina stood, contemplating the concealed windows, and caught a movement from the corner of her eye.

Will, framed within the pane as he watched her, an eyebrow arched inquisitively, his silhouette a portrait of curiosity as he stood in a wash of light.

Relief washed through her as she lifted her hand in a wave, then turned back toward the house as he ducked back inside.

Will was long gone when she got back to the kitchen. She set her bowl and spoon in the sink, then started her search through the house, starting in the living room and ending in front of his office door, which was closed.

She felt a little insulted that he'd seen her wave, but hadn't even lingered long enough to say good morning before returning to work.

Maybe he'd had to hurry back for a meeting?

Will wouldn't want to be interrupted, so her hand did nothing more than hover over the doorknob as she barely dared to imagine opening the door without knocking. Even when she did knock, he was usually grumpy that she'd broken into his thoughts.

If the door was closed, then he had a reason.

So Nina withdrew to the living room, a frown spreading across her face as she surveyed the space. She hadn't found storm doors or any other kind of entrance outside, so the way into the basement had to be somewhere inside the house.

But she'd explored every inch of the house. How could she have missed a stairway leading down there? Did it lurk behind a concealed door?

The idea both thrilled and terrified her.

She swept through the lower story, examining every floorboard for evidence of a trap door and every wall panel for a hidden entrance.

Finding nothing in the other rooms — sitting room, den, utility room, dining room, living room — Nina returned to the kitchen, where the only conceivable place for a hidden door was.

She went back to the larder, her gaze tracing the shelves, walls, and ceiling.

With a start she realized that the back of their pantry did not align with the home's exterior. There was an unac-counted-for space, a gap in the architecture that could only mean one thing.

Nina reached for the sturdy shelves opposite the door and planted her feet, gripping the wooden frame as she pulled. But the shelves refused to budge.

But she was persistent, determination fueled by the knowledge that answers were only a few drops of elbow grease away.

With a groan of old wood and a whisper of dust, the shelves finally gave way, swinging open to reveal a hidden door.

And behind it, shrouded in the dim light filtering in from the pantry, was a staircase leading down into the pitch black basement below.

Chapter Seven

A silence settled in the office as Will ended his call.

It only lasted a beat before he heard the distant yet distinct sound of movement, a soft cadence of footfalls. Nina had a way of moving that was almost a whisper, but right now she was bustling all about.

He leaned back in his chair and listened, trying to decipher her intentions. Was she taking measurements? It sounded like she was rapidly making her way through every room downstairs.

Or it could be she was still mad that he'd scared her last night, and she was making noise to let him know?

He stood to stretch and heard her call his name.

He opened the door and heard it again.

"Will!"

He walked toward the sound and found Nina standing in the kitchen.

"Is everything okay?" he asked.

"The water isn't working."

Will had figured that when she'd interrupted his call to

mouth the word, but now she looked more upset than irritated about it.

"That's weird, because it was working fine last night." He crossed to the sink and turned the knob.

Nothing happened.

"Great," Nina said. "Now you've seen it for yourself. What are we going to do about it?"

"I'll call someone." He turned to go.

"That's not why I called you."

Will turned back around, raising his eyebrows in query.

"I was outside eating my cereal, trying to wake up, I guess, when I saw some windows in the ground."

He frowned, hoping the flare of panic he was feeling wouldn't show on his face, but for a second he was thrown back into the darkness of his past, disoriented and nauseous as he lifted his throbbing head from the earthen floor. *Rosie?*

Not now. He bit the inside of his lip to bring himself back to the present before he asked, "Like basement windows?"

"Right." Nina nodded. "But I couldn't find the entrance. Until I finally did."

He frowned harder, and the darkness retreated a little further.

Will had learned long ago that anger could beat the darkness back. But it wasn't fair to take that anger out on Rosie.

Not Rosie, Nina. It wasn't fair to take his anger out on Nina.

Will forced himself to sigh, hoping he sounded patient. "Do you have to be so cryptic? I've only got a few minutes before my next call."

Nina started walking toward the larder. Will followed her

inside to a door at the rear. She hesitated, her hand hovering over the wood, a shadow of doubt crossing her features before she nodded at the wood and left Will to yank it open.

The hinges groaned in protest after apparent years without disturbance, then the door swung ajar and a gust of stale air rushed past them.

The darkness crowded closer, and his mouth went dry. But what was he going to tell her, that he was afraid of basements?

Or worse, tell her why?

His hand found the light switch, and he flicked it on.

The flare of light illuminated a staircase before the bulb died with a startling **POP** and went dark forever, plunging the basement back into darkness.

He peered into the abyss but saw only black. The metallic taste of fear — or maybe blood — in his mouth. He'd bitten his tongue. He was on the verge of a panic attack, but he refused to let her see it. He thought about the bottle of pills stashed in his office desk. A sign of weakness that he'd never let Nina see.

"I don't have time for this," he said. "I'm going back to work."

Nina grabbed a flashlight from an open box on the floor. "You're going to let me go down there by myself?"

He heard the unspoken question: *Would you let Rose go down into the basement by herself?*

Of course not. Will would have done anything for Rosie. And he had.

Which was why his heart was beating so fast right now. He wondered if he was having a heart attack rather than a panic attack.

They descended the stairs together.

Stale air enveloped them, thick with the scent of dampness and decay. Her foot hit the concrete floor a beat behind his, but then she led the way with an unspoken certainty, her instincts apparently guiding them to the home's vital systems. Including the water intake valve for the house, right next to a decrepit-looking washer and dryer.

The water intake valve that was in the *off* position.

But that was impossible, because they'd had water yesterday.

The intruder.

What if Nina hadn't been sleepwalking? What if she really had seen someone, perhaps a burglar hoping that the house's new owners would have something worth stealing that they hadn't yet secured?

That didn't make sense. What kind of burglar snuck in and turned off the water?

Nina made an exasperated sound, then strode over and tried to turn the valve for about half a second before she turned to him expectantly.

Will forced himself to join her despite his desire to run screaming back to the light, to flee the darkness pressing against him. He turned the valve clockwise, grunting with effort until it finally gave. The sound of water came rushing through the pipes.

"There," he said gruffly. Will wanted to bolt back up the stairs to the kitchen, where sunshine streamed through ornate windows draped in tattered lace. But he refused to let her see it. "Let's go try the water now."

"How did it get turned off?" Nina asked, instead of agreeing and leading him back upstairs.

"I guess it turned off somehow while we were sleeping."

"That really sounds logical to you?" She looked at him.

"Old homes are weird." He shrugged, desperate for this conversation to be over.

Will promised himself that he would buy the biggest, hardest to force open deadbolt on the market as soon as his meetings were over.

Then another thought occurred to him.

"Maybe there's another valve somewhere else, and this is just a backup," he said.

"Why would there be two valves?"

"What's your explanation? A ghost turned our water off?"

He regretted snapping the second he saw the hurt twist her features. Will had only seen that expression on Rosie's face once, and he'd vowed to never be the cause of it again.

If he wouldn't do it to Rosie, he shouldn't do it to Nina.

"I know, it doesn't make sense, but ..." He forced another sigh, trailing off in search of a plausible explanation to end the conversation so he could get out of this small, dark space before claustrophobic terror squeezed his heart to a stop. "The bank could have had the water on halfway or something when they foreclosed on this place. And we've been moving all around the house since we got here, so maybe all the vibrations as we've been moving things around nudged it somehow."

Nina looked incredulous. "You can't possibly believe what you're saying right now."

"Do you have a better explanation?"

Because he didn't. Not unless he decided to start believing in ghosts.

Or in burglars who broke in to mess with the plumbing.

Her skepticism was obvious as the daylight outside, her arms crossed as if warding off his half-baked theories. But she didn't offer a better one.

"Fine," Nina conceded with a huff, turning on her heel with a swish of her robe that signaled the end of the conversation as she started back toward the stairs. Finally.

"Every home has its quirks," Will said as he hurried after her, quickly closing the hidden door behind him. "This one's just quirkier than most."

She walked straight to the kitchen sink and turned on the faucet. Gushing water sounded like a victory cry.

"I'm going to take a shower," she said.

Then Nina left the kitchen and Will returned to his office, fumbling the bottle of pills his shrink had given him out of his office drawer and swallowing one dry.

Nina didn't know about the panic attacks that he'd mostly learned to control — he'd kept them from her because she would want him to talk about it. She thought sharing the nightmare of his past was going to help somehow.

But Will knew the darkness was waiting to suck him back down again. The darkness that had taken Rosie away from him.

He couldn't open that door to the basement in his own soul — because he would never get out of it again.

He needed to focus on his future, and his future was Nina.

Will settled back into the curve of his chair, the leather softly groaning under his weight. The house was silent again, except for the distant sound of water pelting the shower floor as Nina washed away her morning frustrations.

Will couldn't shake the unease clinging to him, a persistent whisper echoing her skepticism.

The front door had been open last night, and so had the window.

But why would anyone come in just to turn off their water? It didn't make any sense.

There had to be another explanation. And he had to find it before Nina got even more curious about their new home's secrets.

He wouldn't be going back down into that basement again.

And he had to make sure she didn't either.

Chapter Eight

Nina's mind was still foggy as water cascaded over her, failing to wash away the unease that had settled within her since going out in the garden last night. Steam enveloped her in a warm shroud that offered a temporary respite from the chill of so much unknown, but it wasn't enough.

She stepped out of the shower and caught a strange reflection in the mirror — her visage carved with lines of tension that felt foreign on her face, and made her look and feel like someone else.

She dressed quickly and descended the staircase, feeling almost in a rush as she made her way back into the kitchen, drawn by an unwelcome whisper that refused to still itself.

The basement had hidden beneath the tall, weedy grass for who knew how long, but she'd spotted it less than twenty-four hours of moving in.

The larder door concealed itself like a secret, yet she'd found it as if led there by an invisible thread.

It was as if the house wanted her to unravel its secrets.

All she'd had to do was listen and it had told her where to look.

She shook her head, but the disquieting thoughts only rattled around without leaving. The house seemed to be watching her, its old bones creaking in a language she might be on the cusp of understanding.

She ventured outside, pulling her coat tighter against the morning chill.

She walked far enough out that she could turn and stare back at her house, its form no longer a puzzle of architecture with pieces she could not figure out. It was back to looking like it belonged in a storybook, just like it had online. Intricate scrollwork gracing the edges of steep gables. Sun glinting on the pointed-arch windows. Elegantly-carved railings that wrapped around the back porch, just like they did in the front.

But still she shuddered, remembering how sinister it had seemed last night.

Will's figure loomed from his office window upstairs, his silhouette a curious punctuation mark as she raised her phone to take a picture, ignoring his stare as she captured the house, freezing it in time to study it later.

She turned around to explore more of the property, wading through gnarls of overgrowth in search of hidden gems. A fat clump of trees stood guard around what appeared to be a thicket of rosebushes, thorns peeking out like soldiers on watch.

Then she saw an anomaly amid all the green, a lump obscured by the wild growth.

And like so many other seemingly unexplainable impulses on this property, Nina almost wanted to blurt the words: *wishing well.*

Her boot nudged at the earth, through all the weeds,

until wood greeted her toe with a solid and yet somehow expected response.

She fell to all fours and began to clear the debris until she revealed a curved edge of rotting timber. A wishing well, half-eaten by time, yet unmistakable in its purpose.

Nina recoiled, her heart a drumbeat of pulsing shockwaves, partly awed by what she could only acknowledge as a chilling discovery, this wishing well that had crept into her imagination before it manifested right there in front of her, leaving her with a cold seed of fear in the soil of her gut.

She stepped back, breath visible in the morning air, bowled over by the knowledge that her new home held more than creaking floorboards and eerie-feeling drafts.

The secrets of this place had somehow projected themselves onto her own subconscious in a way she could no longer write off as mere coincidence. First the garden, then the secret door to the basement. Now, the well.

The realization that her life was now irrevocably entwined with this place settled upon Nina like the early morning mist — pervasive and inescapable.

Why did the house feel so familiar?

The question played on an incessant loop as she traced her steps back to the house. Into the kitchen, then right to the living room.

She turned in a circle, studying the place, each corner of the living room seeming to whisper her name in an eerie chorus that knew her uncomfortably well.

The monotony of all that faded baby blue wallpaper struck her differently now. Sterile and alien, it was almost as if she could see right through it to a pattern of roses behind it — vibrant and red, climbing the walls as if they were truly alive.

She walked to the wall and reached for a seam in the

paper, its edge begging her to turn it. She tugged, the thick wallpaper yielding to her with a reluctant hiss.

Then she kept pulling and pulling, the sound of tearing wallpaper punctuating the silence until the truth lay bare before her. Roses, their colors muted with time but their existence undeniable.

The revelation was another crack in her facade of reality.

Again: *How had she known?*

A sense of certainty had guided her hand, as if she was reclaiming something lost.

"What are you doing?" Will's entrance was sudden and jarring.

Nina startled, dropping the corner of the torn wallpaper she had been peeking behind.

"I knew about the roses."

"We have a rose garden too?"

She lifted the wallpaper higher, so he could see the roses underneath. "Do you want to tell me that's not weird?"

He shrugged: *Not weird at all.* "Didn't you see like a quadrillion pictures of this place online?"

"No." She shook her head, the motion resolute. "The only photos I saw were of the house as it is now. Blue walls, no roses."

"Maybe you saw the roses somewhere, a tear you didn't notice."

Nina looked around. "Where?"

"Maybe in another room?"

"I found a wishing well outside—"

"A wishing well?" He looked both exasperated and confused, as if she were babbling incoherently instead of articulating the facts of her morning.

"Plus the door to the basement and everything else.

How do I know about those things, Will? Why does this place feel like a puzzle—"

"Because you want it to be," he replied before she could finish. "You are a keen observer, and thus you've been making some excellent guesses. Maybe you're remembering things you read on the real estate listing."

But a hollow of doubt in Will's voice betrayed him.

"Why would I guess that the wallpaper covered more wallpaper?" Nina didn't wait for an answer, because Will wouldn't have one unless he made it up. "There's something here, something about this house that resonates with me, and I don't know why, or how to explain it."

His patience waned as Nina pulled at the wallpaper again, revealing more and more of a floral pattern that should have been foreign to her.

Except that one of the roses was a splotchy brown, much darker than the others. Some kind of stain?

"What do you want me to say, Nina?" His voice crackled with a frustration he couldn't hide. The tension was getting worse. They had only suffered a few fights in their time as a couple, but they had all started like this.

Nina's hands fell to her sides, the torn wallpaper forgotten. "I don't expect you to say anything. I just … it feels so familiar here, and I can't explain why. From more than what I saw of this place online. It would be nice if you could hear me instead of finding new ways to tell me I'm imagining things."

"I can hear you just fine, Nina. But if you want me to agree that there's something haunted about this place—"

"I never said it was haunted, I said that it felt familiar and—"

"But you already *know* why it's familiar!" He threw his hands up in the air and shook them with exasperation. "You obsessed about this place online for weeks. That's why I bought it for you. What other dots could you need to connect?"

Now he sounded angry.

Nina needed to get out of there before the argument got brutal.

She headed for the door, grabbing the car keys off the hall tree.

"Where are you going?" His voice softened, the edge of impatience giving way to concern.

"I need to go for a drive."

"I'm sorry." Will reached out, his hand gently enclosing over hers and taking the keys. "I didn't mean to upset you. We're both on edge, that's all. The move, this house … it's been a lot."

Her resistance waned under his sincere-sounding apology.

It was true; they were frayed, nerves raw from the stress of new beginnings and unexplained phenomena.

The promise of comfort was a temptation Nina couldn't ignore.

"I'll take the rest of the day off, we can unpack together," he said to sweeten the deal. "And I'll make dinner tonight, so you can relax."

She smiled and followed him back into the living room, looking around at the wreckage of their walls, shadows entwining like the roses beneath the paper.

And all the countless secrets in this place.

Chapter Nine

Dinner was a mostly quiet affair, despite the clinking cutlery. Forks and knives clattering against rose-covered porcelain punctuated a heavy silence that hung between them like a curtain.

Will was starting to resent that Nina insisted on continuing to use the china she'd found — and accused him of hiding among their things. It felt like an accusation: *You loved Rosie more than you love me.*

Nina was precious to him in her own way. Because with her, he could have the life that he would never share with Rosie.

But for that to happen, she was going to have to stop picking at his past. Will couldn't love her if he kept falling back into the darkness. So he was going to have to set better boundaries.

"I'm going to call a professional to inspect the basement." He set his fork down on his empty plate. "Please promise you won't go down there until we're sure it's safe."

"Are you afraid I'm going to be attacked by the water valve?" she joked.

Will could feel the throb of an angry headache building behind his eyes. He'd taken a second pill before cooking, in hopes that it would bring him back to zen.

Not even close.

He must have looked exhausted, because her voice softened. "Why don't you go to bed?"

He offered her a weary smile, accepting the tenderness of her kiss on his cheek. That was more like it. "Thanks. I think I will."

A cool draft caught his attention on the way upstairs.

The front door was ajar again. How could she be so careless, especially after screaming her lungs raw about an intruder?

He pushed it closed, the latch clicking into place with an air of finality.

"Nina!" His voice echoed in the foyer. "Make sure the front door is locked when you close it."

"Of course," she said.

Will turned around to find her looking at him. "You need to make sure it's latched."

"I know how to work the door." And the angry ember started crackling again.

He should have said it more gently, but it was too late for that. And Will didn't have the energy to apologize. Besides, she hadn't said sorry for leaving the door open.

He needed to make it to the hardware store tomorrow. He wasn't just going to add a deadbolt, he would also replace the existing locks. Just in case the key that the realtor had handed over to them wasn't the only one floating around.

"Can you get me some aspirin?" Will pinched his brow. "It feels like I'm coming down with a bad one."

"I'll bring it upstairs with me."

Nina went to the kitchen to get him a glass of water

and some aspirin as he made his way to the stairs, down the hall, then into the bathroom.

Will's familiar nightly performance unfolded in an unfamiliar place. He braced his hands against the cool sink, leaning in close to the mirror. Toothbrush bristles rasped against his teeth, a methodical scrub as he attempted to cleanse away the sour taste of their spat.

The faucet gushed cold water over his hands and face, a bracing chill that sluiced down his skin and cooled the heat of frustration. All he wanted was for her to forget about the past and focus on the life they had now. He'd bought her the house. He'd told her she didn't need to work. He'd devoted himself to giving her a perfect life.

Rosie would've been ecstatic — she was also looking for what came next — but Nina couldn't let anything go.When he emerged from the bathroom, Nina met him with two aspirin and a glass of water.

"We'll get another bottle for upstairs next time we're in town," she said while Will took the pills and glass.

"Thank you." He downed them with a swallow of water. "And I'm sorry about today."

"Me too. It was stupid."

"We won't be stupid tomorrow." She laughed.

They hugged.

Nina pulled away. "Get to bed. I'll clean the kitchen. And thanks again for dinner. Your pollo asada was better than my fettuccini."

"It wasn't a contest."

"Get to bed," Nina repeated, then turned around and trotted down the stairs.

He entered their bedroom and went straight to the window, driven by a sudden need to make sure the window was latched.

The he surrendered to bed, the mattress yielding to the

contours of his weary body. The pillow cradled his head, a soft cloud in the darkness, and sleep rushed in like a tide over sand.

But Will awoke in darkness to a throbbing pain pulsing behind his eyes.

The hallway lights seared through his eyelids, an invasive brightness that should not have been there, no matter what time it was.

His breath hitched as he shot upright, the sheets tangling around his legs.

"Nina?" His voice was barely a whisper, strained by the edges of an inexplicable fear.

But Nina was right there next to him, a gentle rise and fall of breath beside him in the darkness, her presence a temporary anchor.

Cold sweat beaded on his forehead as he swung his legs over the edge of the bed.

The light in the hall swung gently, a pendulum of soft light making distorted shadows dance across the walls in a ballet of darkness and light.

"Nina!"

She stirred beside him, her own alarm mirroring his as she sat up, her eyes wide and searching.

Floorboards creaked as he stood, loud as a thunderclap in the silence.

"Stay here," he instructed.

She reached out, her fingers brushing against his arm. "What is it?"

Will didn't answer, his gaze fixed on the oscillating light fixture. Another impossibility. But there it was.

"You forgot to turn out the light." The conviction in his voice was thin.

"I haven't been out of bed," she whispered with a tremor in her voice. "I was asleep."

Will reached for the lamp on his nightstand, the same makeshift weapon from last night, and moved toward the door, his movements brusque with adrenaline.

Nina's hand clamped onto his wrist. "Call the police."

"Are you kidding? How long do you think it would take for them to get out here? We're not in the city. We're on our—"

"I know we're not in the city, but—"

A THUD echoed downstairs and propelled him into motion.

He shook her off and made his way to the stairs.

The front door loomed open when he reached the bottom, gaping open like a dark mouth. The night air whispered in as he peered outside with his hand on the doorknob.

The driveway was empty, their car alone under the gazing moon. No one in sight.

Nina could have forgotten the hall light, but the swinging fixture? And the open door?

The uneasy feeling in his gut refusing to subside as he closed the door and—

Will heard a noise in the kitchen. A soft skittering that raised the hairs on the back of his neck.

He entered the room, barely lit by the moonlight.

Something brushed against his ankle, and he shouted out loud, heart pounding in his chest as a surge of adrenaline coursed through his veins.

His eyes darted around, searching for the source of the unexpected touch.

He saw the glowing eyes of a cat and felt a second blink of uncut terror, followed by a full-bodied flush of relief.

But Will yelped again when a hand landed on his shoulder.

He spun around, his heart leaping into his throat, only to meet Nina's anxious gaze.

"I thought I told you to stay upstairs," he said, his relief tinged with irritation.

"I heard a noise. I had to make sure you were alright."

"There was a cat. I don't know how it got inside."

They both knew the cat wasn't responsible for the swinging lamp that shouldn't have been on. Nor had it opened the front door that Will had been certain to lock.

"I watched you latch the front door," Nina reminded him unnecessarily.

Will redirected to the only other possible answer that wasn't terrifying. "Isn't it possible that you were sleepwalking?"

"No, I was not sleepwalking, Will!"

"You told me you used to, back at the orphanage. After the accident."

"We were *both* in bed. And you were with me when we both heard that thud. Again."

"The cat could've knocked something over, after you let him in. Or maybe you did—"

"I was *not* sleepwalking!" Nina scooped up the cat and marched into the living room, presumably to check the front door for herself before tossing it outside.

"If you were, how would you know—"

Nina let out a blood-curdling scream that pierced the silence, echoing through the house and sending shivers down his spine.

Will ran into the living room to see her jabbing a finger at something he had apparently missed on his circuit a few minutes ago.

Someone had nailed a dead bird to their living room wall.

A threat from a past he'd left behind.
Only now, it was threatening Nina too.
What if he couldn't protect her?

<h1 style="text-align:center">Chapter Ten</h1>

Nina's fingers tightened around the mug as she listened to the hushed whispers of the house while waiting for the police to arrive.

She perched on the edge of the kitchen chair. Cold from the floor crept up into her legs as warmth from the chamomile tea seeped into her fingers.

Will had prepared the kettle for her with a quiet urgency after calling the police, suddenly solicitous as she remained frozen in dread and disbelief. Hard to believe that a few months ago she had been stalking her supposed dream house online, but now it felt like a creeping nightmare that had them dangling above its bloody maw.

There was no doubt now — someone had been inside their house.

Or maybe Will was playing some horrific practical joke on her, a million times more awful than jumping out of a shadow and yelling *boo!*

Either possibility was terrifying.

But she doubted he would have called the police if the

dead bird had been his idea of a sick joke. No, Will would be laughing and trying to convince her not to be mad.

Unless he realized he'd crossed the line and now had to go through the motions of a police visit in order to mollify her?

But why? It made a lot more sense that some local had taken offense to them buying the Byrd house.

Maybe the gas station clerk who had tried to scare Will with his ghost stories?

Or was she grasping at straws?

She could hear Will's restless pacing in the living room, his heavy steps thudding against old wooden floors. His shadow occasionally flickered across the threshold while they waited for the cops.

He had been right about how long it would take them to get there. With nearly a half an hour between call and response, there was no way Nina could ever count on local law enforcement to save their necks in an emergency.

Living out in the country was supposed to make her feel safer, but now she realized that was an illusion too.

Footsteps finally crunched on the gravel outside, and her heart hammered against her ribs.

"They're here," Will called out to her as his pacing came to an abrupt halt.

Nina rose, her fatigue and fear battling an urgency to just do something already.

She darted into the living room, coming up behind Will as he opened the door. The arriving officer was a lone silhouette against the pale wash of her headlights, her solitary gait still reassuring against the backdrop of this surreal-feeling night as she approached their porch, introducing herself when she got there with an assessing gaze.

"I'm Officer Angela Rivera." She nodded at Will and Nina.

Tall, willowy, with a no-nonsense demeanor. The woman radiated competence. Her stern face was not unkind, and her cropped hair appeared more practical than stylish.

"What's happening here?" Rivera asked.

"There was someone in the house. They …" Nina paused, the words sticking in her throat like thorns on a stem. "Whoever it was, they nailed a dead bird to our wall."

Rivera' eyes darkened, a flash of concern and perhaps something else crossing her features before the expression receded back into neutrality. "Show me."

Will led the way, back straight, like a soldier leading his commander officer into the fray. Rivera entered the house, her boots thudding solidly on the wooden floor as he took her to the bird.

Nina lingered at the edge of the living room, unable to bear the macabre display that had turned their home into a crime scene.

"Do you have a plastic bag for this?" Rivera called out.

Nina scurried to the kitchen, returning moments later and handing the bag over to Will, who delivered it to the officer just as she finished donning her gloves.

Rivera emerged into the kitchen, holding the tiny dead bird, now a sad piece of evidence in that plastic bag.

She laid the bag on the table, then pulled out her notepad and pen. "Walk me through what happened."

Will recounted a short tale of shadows and fleeting figures that made Nina's blood run cold yet again. Rivera listened, asking the occasional question while nodding along, her pen constantly scratching across the paper.

"Can you take a look around the house before you go?" Nina asked.

"Of course. That's why I'm here." Rivera gave her a nod. "I'll make a sweep of the house. You two wait here."

Nina went to the kitchen, where she cradled herself, the sleeves of her sweater offering scant comfort as Will joined her but said nothing, sharing the space with silence yawning between them.

The tightness around his eyes and mouth made her think he was actually scared. Maybe as scared as she was.

Something inside her relaxed. Whatever this was, at least they were in it together.

She traced the grain on their table with a fingernail while he stared into the darkness outside.

"Did you find anything?" Will asked Rivera on his way into the living room after hearing her descending the stairs.

Nina jumped up and followed him, with the question that haunted her more poised on her lips. "Or anyone?"

"Nothing and no one." Rivera shook her head. "This place is empty as a tomb, except for you two."

That didn't make Nina feel better.

"Poor choice of words." Rivera gave her a smile. "Sorry about that."

"Do you think we should leave?" Nina asked.

"Like I said, there's no one here right now except for you guys. I'll look around outside, give the entire property a once-over before I hit the road, but I'm guessing you're fine. If there was anyone here, then I'm sure they got scared off—"

"What do you mean 'if there was someone here'?" Nina asked. "What about the bird?"

"I suggest changing your locks and getting some security cameras as some smart first steps." Rivera hesitated, then finally said the part that perhaps explained why she seemed bothered. "Do the two of you know about the history of this place?"

Then, when neither one of them answered her fast enough. "About the Byrd family?"

"The Byrd family?" Nina repeated, turning to Will and searching his face for an answer, but finding only an unreadable expression.

"There was a murder in this place," Rivera told them.

Nina turned to Will again.

But that time, he had the grace to look ashamed.

And Nina said, "I know why I remember this place now."

Chapter Eleven

NINA WATCHED the taillights of Rivera's cruiser dissolve into the night.

Isolation wrapped around her like a shroud. She was alone with Will again, but that once-cherished solitude now felt like an accomplice to this home's malevolent history.

Will had known all about that history, but he'd chosen not to tell her.

With a deep breath to steady her nerves, Nina walked to the kitchen.

She filled a bucket with hot, soapy water, the potent scent of detergent still failing to mask the undercurrent of something metallic in the air.

She gripped the handle tighter than necessary on her way to the living room, then started scrubbing the blood-stained wall with all her might. Throwing her shoulder into the cleaning, vigorous and determined, each stroke of the sponge another futile attempt to cleanse this place of its past and most immediate present.

"How could you not tell me?" Nina's voice was low as

she heard Will approaching her from behind, the words sharp as her scrubbing intensified.

"I didn't want to scare you," said Will with a weary sigh.

"Scare me?" Nina scoffed, tossing her sponge into the murky water with a splash that sent droplets scattering onto his pant leg. "Knowing my interests, please explain what it is about that would have scared me."

"I don't know." He shrugged, his sarcasm in full bloom. "Maybe the part about someone being murdered here."

"Lies scare me, Will. I'm never afraid of the truth."

"You're afraid of the truth sometimes."

"Do you really want to argue with me about this right now?" Nina glared at him.

He blanched, looking even more afraid than he had before, while they were waiting for Rivera to arrive.

Good to know that she was scarier than a dead bird. Whatever that said about her. And their relationship.

Nina turned to the wall again. Her scrubbing had done little to erase the stain.

Fitting, since the truth of this house couldn't be so easily wiped away.

The Byrd home. The realization settled in Nina's mind, with an eerie familiarity that turned her stomach. She remembered the case, and all the morbid curiosity that had her combing through every detail and theory. An unsolved puzzle that had haunted the fringes of her memory often enough that it felt startling as it percolated to the surface of her real life right now.

Nina couldn't believe that she hadn't connected it to the house while drooling over the listing. No doubt the realtor had mentioned the murders when Will was buying the house and he'd decided she didn't need to know. If he'd mentioned it, she would've put it together immediately.

Not that knowing would've stopped the intruder from breaking in. But that didn't assuage her anger one bit.

"What do you remember about this house, Nina?"

"There was a podcast series about it."

"Of course there was." Did he sound relieved?

"I read everything about the case after hearing the series ended. I even joined a Reddit community so I could post my theories. And please don't start — I'm not in the mood for you to make fun of me right now."

"I have no plans to make fun of you. Now or later. What do you think happened?" His curiosity was not merely academic. Personal, probing, and perhaps even desperate.

Nina paused, the bucket forgotten at her feet. "The uncle had an alibi, but I think it was him anyway, or at least that's what I thought at the time."

"Why do you think the uncle did it? And you don't think that anymore?"

"Because he wanted the Byrd fortune." She shrugged. "I'm not obsessed now, so with a little distance, I guess I don't really know what I think."

Will glanced at the wall. "Why don't you stop scrubbing? I'll open a bottle of wine and you can tell me everything you know about this place."

Her hands stilled, the sponge slipping from her grasp and sinking into the crimson-tinged water. She exhaled with a gust of breath as she stood, the bucket suddenly too heavy in her hands as she followed Will into the kitchen.

Nina dumped the bucket into the sink with a grimace, watching the diluted blood swirl down the drain, an unsatisfying end to an act of cleansing that felt far from over.

Because even if she could erase all traces of the bird's blood, the murder had left other marks on this house.

She thought about the smear of blood on the rose-covered wallpaper she'd uncovered earlier.

She slid into a chair, its legs scraping softly against the kitchen tiles.

Will uncorked the wine with a muted pop, the sound oddly-comforting in the quiet kitchen. He chose a pinot noir, pouring the deep red liquid into a pair of glasses, its aroma mingling with the lingering traces of detergent and something more primal in the air.

As he set one glass in front of her, their fingers brushed — a fleeting touch that tingled with shared disquiet.

She wrapped her hands around the stem and started to talk.

"I was drawn to the Byrd case for the same reason as everyone else." Then Nina explained before he could ask. "Three victims. Both parents stabbed in their sleep, and a child, who apparently woke up and fought back before the killer slit their throat. The weird thing was that the police report also said there was vomit in the parents' bed, but no toxicology report was ever released."

"Meaning?"

"Meaning they could've been sick. Or—"

"They could've been poisoned?" He blinked hard, like he couldn't process the idea. "Why would you poison someone if you were planning to stab them?"

"That's why everyone in the forum thought it was a coverup, but no one's figured out how it all fits together. And —" She hesitated to tell him what else was under that wallpaper besides roses — it was probably still there. But she needed him to take this as seriously as she did. "Whoever did it painted a Satanic symbol on the wall in the child's blood."

Will got even paler, if that was possible, and he seemed to be hanging on every word. Maybe he hadn't asked the realtor for details. "Anything else?"

"The child was only referred to as 'Panda.' Their identity was never released to the public."

"What information was released?"

"Nothing." She shrugged. "No age or gender. We only have a name that isn't even a name."

"Is there a name that's not released to the public? Or are you saying that even the cops don't have the victim's name?"

"Of course the cops have a name. But money and influence can buy a lot of silence, and the Byrds had plenty of both."

Will thought for a minute. "They supposedly arrested the murderer. What makes you think it was the uncle?"

"He inherited what was left of the family fortune. Although it sounds like there wasn't as much left as he'd hoped."

"What about the guy that every one thinks is the killer?"

"The police pinned it on a drifter. That doesn't mean he did it." Nina took a sip of wine. "Every part of his story makes it sound like he was a convenient scapegoat. The entire town was desperate for someone to answer for the murder, so that Glenburn could go back to sleep."

Will made a disgusted face. That was exactly how Nina felt about it too — it was infuriating that something so horrifying could be swept under the blanket. But despite the podcast and the community that had formed around the story, no one had managed to prove the drifter's innocence. Which made a coverup all that more likely, in Nina's mind.

But then Will said, "You almost look happy that there was a murder here."

Did he think she was some kind of ghoul, fetishizing murder?

Maybe she couldn't blame him him, given how many true crime podcasts she listened to, But it wasn't about the deaths to her, it was about discovering the truth and the hope of finding justice.

"*Happy*? No. That's not the word I would use." She shook her head. "It's more like a sizable piece of the puzzle clicked into place. That nagging familiarity I've been feeling — it's not insanity. It's recognition."

"I'm sorry for not telling you sooner."

"You didn't tell me at all," Nina corrected him with a smile. "But I can see why living in a murder house might bother most women. Just don't do it again."

He smiled back, looking more relieved than before. "I'm glad you're not most women."

They toasted and sipped. Then Nina asked the question she didn't want to ask, twisting the stem of her wine glass in her fingers as she spoke.

"But how is the bird related to all of this? Aside from the family name, I don't remember anything about a bird being related to the case."

The fear was back for a second, flashing across his features before he cleared his throat with a gravelly sound. If she didn't know better, she'd think he was fighting off a panic attack. But he'd never mentioned having them before.

To be fair, she had just dumped a season's worth of gruesome details in a few minutes of conversation. He was probably seeing the house he'd committed to paying off over the next thirty years in a slightly different light now.

"I don't see a connection either. Rivera might be onto something. It could've been a squatter, not happy about us moving in here." He stood from the table. "I'll find a lock-smith in town tomorrow."

"New locks are a great idea." He hesitated. "How do you feel about staying here now that you know?"

"I don't mind, really." A small, wry smile played on Nina's lips as she shrugged.

She felt an unnatural pride in owning a house with such a dark history. And now that she understood why she'd been feeling so unnerved, she felt less afraid. She had been blaming her anxiety on being a city mouse adapting to its new country home, but it was the house, not her.

"You're an odd bird." Will chuckled, shaking his head before wincing. "Not the best choice of words, I guess."

They shared another laugh. The bird seemed less frightening now that Will was on her side, and wouldn't be telling her that she was seeing things.

"Let's get some sleep," he said tenderly.

They glided through the still house together, engaged in a quiet choreography of caution as they triple-checked the locks on every door and wedged chairs under the knobs to create makeshift alarms that would announce any late-night intruders.

The bedroom door whispered shut behind them.

Side by side, they settled beneath the covers. The sheets were a cool caress against Nina's skin, still prickling from the residue of fear. Will's breaths were steady and rhythmic beside her, a grounding metronome to her frayed nerves.

She looked up, tracing shadows in a waltz of dark and light on the ceiling as she begged her mind to quiet.

The sharp edges of Nina's fear dulled as her day of ugly discoveries slowly dissolved into the dark.

The house settled around them, bones of old lumber creaking in a nocturne for two.

Until Nina was finally sleeping.

Chapter Twelve

MORNING LIGHT FILTERED through the curtains to lay a gentle hand on Will's closed eyelids. He stirred as remnants of sleep clung to his psyche like cobwebs.

He sat up with a groan, cradling his skull as a headache started to throb at his temples. Last night could've been a disaster, but somehow it had brought Nina closer to him.

That didn't mean he was out of the woods, though. He would have to find that bitch who'd left the bird and—

The sound of Nina banging around in the kitchen below interrupted his furious thoughts. He had to pull himself together before facing her, to stop his rage from bleeding through. She would feel it, but unlike Rosie, who knew when to let him alone, Nina would keep picking and picking until he exploded.

Not her fault she wasn't Rosie. But Will had to make sure she didn't find out about his stalker before he could take care of it.

He tiptoed to his office to dry-swallow another dose of meds from his desk drawer, then back to the bathroom for a hot water massage on his scalp as the scent of eucalyptus-and-mint body wash slowly woke him up.

Dressed and somewhat more alert, he descended the stairs, wondering if today might bring them another serving of the macabre like yesterday.

Not if I can help it. He would deal with that bitch quickly and quietly, before Nina — or Rivera — caught on.

He saw the picture of pink cosmos under a blue sky now hanging in the living room before his foot hit the bottom stair — a visual bandage covering the spot where the bird had been nailed to the wall.

But at least she hadn't pulled off the rest of the wallpaper, hunting for the bloody Satanic symbol she now knew lurked there. With luck, Nina would forget. And when it was time to redo everything, he'd hire professionals to replace the wallpaper while he took Nina on a vacation.

"You couldn't get the blood off?" Will asked as she emerged from the kitchen.

"The blood came off, but even a blank space will be a constant reminder of what happened." She smiled. "I'll find something better later, but right now I figure these flowers are better than leaving a void where dread can fester."

"Poetic." He sniffed the air. "Do I smell breakfast? And coffee?"

"You do." Nina nodded at the kitchen, then gestured for Will to lead the way.

The table was a spread of simple abundance: crusty bread, the insides fluffy and warm; eggs scrambled to a soft, golden curdle; strips of bacon arrayed like savory brush strokes; and coffee with steam rising in aromatic whispers.

This was the kind of life he'd imagined for them in this

house. The kind of life he would already have if Rosie had lived. But now he was having that same life with Nina.

And that was good enough.

"I'll find a locksmith in town today and arrange for him to come out," said Will as he sat.

"Or her. We don't know that the locksmith will be a guy."

"It's pretty likely."

"What time are we leaving?" Nina asked with eggs in her mouth.

That couldn't happen, not if he was going to put an end to this bird bullshit. He took a sip of coffee, enjoying the bitter heat on his tongue. "I'm going alone."

"You're leaving me here?" The fork clattered onto her plate. "After last night?"

"You'll be fine." He reached across the table and covered her hand with his.

"I'm not staying here alone." She shook her head. "Not with an intruder lurking about."

Will retracted his hand and used it to massage the throbbing in his forehead. "Lock the doors. Keep your phone with you. It'll be fine."

"How can you be so sure nothing will happen in broad daylight? And why can't I just come with you?"

"Intruders look for easy targets. They won't come back now that the cops have been sniffing around."

"That's not reassuring, Will. And you only answered one of my questions."

He had, because any reason he gave her for going alone would just raise more questions.

When he remained silent, Nina abandoned her breakfast after a few bites to let him know exactly how she felt about it.

Rosie would never have given him the silent treatment.

Eager to get on with it, Will shoved eggs into his mouth until his rose-covered plate was empty, his appetite mostly gone. She was still using those damn plates. Was she taunting him with his loss?

No. Even though Nina wasn't Rosie, she wasn't cruel. She probably just hadn't found the box with their dishes yet.

Or maybe she still thought he was lying about having bought them, and that he wanted to use them.

He would have to make sure she wasn't jealous of Rosie. Jealousy was how the whole bird thing had started.

He cleaned up so she wouldn't get any angrier at him, then went to the hall tree where his keys should have been.

"Nina?" He yelled. "The car keys?"

"I don't have them!" Nina yelled back.

"Where did you put them?"

"I haven't touched your keys!"

A chill traced the length of his spine. Unlike last time, now Will had to wonder whether the intruder could have taken them.

The thought sent him on a frantic search through the downstairs rooms.

Frustration blossomed into anger, its roots winding around his reason and squeezing tight. Will was ready to punch the wall when he received an instantaneous return to his sanity when he plunge his hands into the depths of his coat pocket and his fingers brushed against the key fob.

After accusing her of taking them, he should've apologized and told her where he'd found them.

Instead, he stepped outside and closed the front door with a grunt, then walked to the car. Slid behind the wheel and felt cool leather against his heated skin. He turned the engine, pausing through a long moment of hesitation where he contemplated Nina's desire to not be left alone.

But no, he couldn't let her see the tremor in his hands or the way his eyes kept darting to every shadow. He couldn't give her a chance to figure out that there was even more going on than she already suspected. In front of Nina, he needed to remain composed.

Will shifted into gear, the gravel crunching under tires as he pulled away, leaving behind the house, Nina, and a silence that seemed to observe his departure.

He stopped at the gas station first, even though the tank was still mostly full.

He approached the counter where James was thumbing through a car magazine.

"You know anyone who can change locks around here?" Will asked.

"That's one of my side hustles," James replied while looking up from his magazine. "Trouble at the homestead?"

Was he guessing, or did he know? And if he knew, was it just small-town gossip, or could he know something more?

What if he'd helped that bitch sneak into the house?

"No trouble," Will answered casually. "Just pays to be safe."

"Oh yeah?" James gave him a grin.

Will decided it was probably just gossip. In a place as small as Glenburn, everyone probably knew about Officer Rivera coming out to the property last night.

He tried to keep the impatience out of his voice. "Can you change the locks or not?"

"'Course I can."

"What time can you come by this afternoon?"

"I'm off at 2:00." James looked at his watch. "So, five and a half hours from now? I could drive straight there after I punch out."

"Sounds good." Will nodded. "We want the top of the line, the best locks you've got available. And a spare copy of the key for my fiancé."

He turned to go, but then *fuck it.*

"Do you know where I can buy a gun around here?"

James raised an eyebrow, but didn't seem otherwise surprised as he nodded at the door. "Ten miles down the road. There's a place called The Last Stand. Can't miss it — looks exactly like you'd imagine."

Will sighed and went back to his car.

The drive was silent, save for the occasional gust of wind, sounding especially loud as it buffeted the Infinity, like the weather was trying to push his car back toward the safety of Glenburn. Maybe he should've waited to bring Nina out here.

He could've kept the house locked up, waited until she'd agreed to set a date. The sooner he locked her down, the sooner they could be happy together. But he'd thought the house would clinch the deal, persuade her to agree to take Rosie's place at his side.

Not that he would've said it that way to her. But Will had worked hard to earn the life he and Rosie planned out together — a house they could fix up and make their own, then a big family full of love, and a lifetime to grow old together.

He deserved that life, and it had been stolen from him. He was owed, and Nina was the one who could pay him back with her own happiness.

Will wanted to make her as happy as he would have made Rosie.

He was fully committed. He needed her to be too.

The Last Stand appeared on the horizon. A barn converted into a fortress of firearms, standing solitary in a field of overgrown grass, its sign adorned with caricatures of outlaws and cowboys.

Strange that James had predicted the sight was exactly like Will would imagine, and stranger that he was dead on the money.

A giant loomed in the doorway as Will approached the barn.

"James said you'd be coming," drawled the man, his figure a monolith against the wooden beams. "Name's Big Ben. Just let me know how I can help you."

"It's Will."

Shaking hands with Big Ben was like shaking hands with a bear trap. The man could probably crush rocks to dust.

"I'm just looking for a little home protection," said Will.

Big Ben nodded. "Everyone is."

He led Will through the dim interior, where the walls were weighted down by a staggering arsenal that could fully equip at least one small militia.

Big Ben presented him with a compact handgun, its sleek black surface gleaming under the sparse light. "This one's favored by folks looking to keep something handy for unwelcome guests."

Next, he hoisted a shotgun off the rack, the wooden stock worn smooth from use, "If you're looking for a more persuasive argument, this little beauty has a reputation that precedes it."

The rifle came next, and Big Ben patted the scope affectionately as he delivered his well-oiled pitch. "For those with an eye for precision, she's a purty one, and she don't just bark, this bitch bites hard."

The Last Stand's prices for each presented weapon were somewhere between absurd and ridiculous. But Will didn't want to seem cheap. Or to accidentally accuse Big Ben of ripping him off.

"I'm looking for something simpler."

Big Ben handed Will a matte black revolver with a weighty cylinder. "Old-school, reliable, doesn't jam, and packs a punch like a mule."

He set it down with a thud that resounded through the wood. "I could find these for a lot less, back in the city."

"Then you should get back to the city."

Will thought about the dead bird, and whether or not the person who had left it might try something worse. Jealousy drove people to do terrible things. And that bitch had been as jealous as they'd come.

She'd been nothing like Rosie, even though her eyes were the same icy-blue and her hair the same golden shade. But he'd been young and naive back then. He hadn't realized that not all women were like Rosie until it had been much too late.

Will opened his wallet and left with the gun, hating his purchase but knowing that Rosie would've approved.

Chapter Thirteen

Nina's gaze lingered on the desolate highway beyond their house, contemplating what now felt like an oppressive solitude.

With Will gone, the morning stillness seemed to amplify, filling the space with an echo of her heartbeat. She turned from the window, a chill still clinging to her skin as she descended the stairs, her hand trailing the banister, feeling the grain beneath her fingertips.

Nina made sure the front and back doors were locked, even though she had already checked a few times that morning.

Her phone buzzed on the counter, and though the sound was startling, she was glad to hear a lifeline coming in from the outside world.

Annie flashed on the screen, bringing an involuntary smile to Nina's lips despite the tension knotted in her shoulders.

Hey, how's the new place? Will letting you out of the house yet?

Haha, stop it. He's not like that. Nina texted back. *But this house has … history.*

What does that mean? Also, ►►►*Nina!*

Stop it with the red flags. You know I hate that.

And you know I worry about you.

Everything's fine, I promise. Nina assured her.

What was that about the house having history?

Something weird happened last night.

???!!! (SPILL ALL THE TEA!)

We're actually living in the Byrd House, just outside Glenburn.

WHAT THE FUCK? 💀 *The murder house?!*

Their exchange unfolded in a burst of blue and gray bubbles, texts flying back and forth as Nina delved into the last night's revelations.

Have you been in the basement yet? Annie asked.

Once. Haven't had the nerve to go back down. But I will.

Pictures or it didn't happen! 📷

You'll have them. Promise.

Stay safe, love you! 🤗

Love you more. 💚

Nina sent Annie a picture of the home's exterior from the first day.

And Annie replied: 🔪 😬

Nina had some homework to do, but first she went to the kitchen, right for the knife drawer — if Will was going to leave her alone, she wasn't going to be defenseless. She opened the drawer up and wrapped her hand around the chef's knife, then went to Will's office.

She set the knife on his desk with a clatter and powered on his computer, so that she could use his laser printer.

The screen flickered to life.

She opened Chrome and entered her search.

The page loaded for Riddles in the Dark. Nina clicked

to the appropriate series: *Triple Satanic: The Unsolved Byrd Saga Byrd Family Murder*. She scanned the copy until her eyes landed on the article, *Blood on the Byrds: The Unsolved Mystery of Glenburn's Grisly Satanic Sacrifice*.

Nina had read the article before, but this time she read it while her heart pounded against her ribs like a prisoner rattling the bars of a long-forgotten dungeon.

In the sleepy heart of Glenburn, a town where the tallest tales usually involved crop yields, the Byrd family tragedy erupted in scandal. Their home, an architectural relic now shrouded in whispers and sidelong glances, was the grim stage for a disappearance that rattled the bones of this rural community.

Their parents murdered, "Panda," age and gender unknown, was found slaughtered by an unknown killer, leaving behind a crimson-soaked room and more questions than the town has residents.

The true terror wasn't just in the volume of blood that drenched the Byrd domicile or the chilling satanic symbol scrawled on the wall — no, the horror here lay in the silence that followed.

A kid stumbled upon the scene and that sight clawed the innocence right out of him. Same for all of Glenburn.

The rumor mill churned day and night in town, fueled by tight-lipped authorities who refused to unveil Panda's identity.

The surviving Byrds, fiercely private to the point of litigious threats, clutched their secrets like a miser with his very last coin.

The plot twisted further when a drifter was caught in the web of this small-town mystery. His clothing, stained with Panda's blood, seemed to scream 'guilty.'

The trial was swift but the conviction was as satisfying as a mouthful of dust for most folks in Glenburn. Too many questions hung like a persistent fog that the sun of supposed justice couldn't quite burn away.

Panda's uncle dissolved into the mists of rumor. A year after the gavel fell, he disappeared with what remained of the family fortune, perhaps across the Atlantic, to a land far from the prying eyes and wagging tongues in their hometown, far away from the family grave that Glenburn had become.

This Byrd murder is more than a cold case; it's a frostbitten saga.

A BIT OVER THE TOP, but that was standard fare for Riddles in the Dark.

Nina hit *Print* and the machine whirred to life. She wanted Will to know more about their home's past, so that she wouldn't be the only one carrying the knowledge. Even if they never figured out who killed Panda, it would be so much easier to move past it if they could just talk about it.

If she could just help him understand how the whole thing made her feel—

A staccato knock shattered the stillness.

Her head snapped toward the sound, a prickle of alarm running down her spine.

She approached the living room window, peering outside, but the angle offered no view of the front porch. So she grabbed the knife and headed downstairs, passing through the living roomon her way to the front door.

She looked through the peephole to see a strange man standing on her porch. He looked to be about Will's age, or maybe a couple years older. Mid-thirties. He didn't look dangerous, but you never knew.

It would be madness to open the door, considering what had happened here all those years ago, and what had happened last night. How long it had taken Officer Rivera to arrive. And how long it might be before Will returned.

He should never have left her alone.

But she had a knife in her hand.

And Nina refused to live her life in fear.

So her knuckles whitened around the hilt as she gripped it.

Then Nina opened the door.

Chapter Fourteen

THE MAN on Nina's doorstep wore an air of casual confidence, his posture relaxed but his gaze sharp, taking in the surroundings like he had a lease on them. His rugged appeal seemed to match the desolate landscape.

"Hi there." The man tipped his head, greeting Nina with a friendly smile that reached his perceptive eyes. "Name's Steve Berger. I live just over yonder."

He gestured vaguely behind him, but that told her nothing. Will had told her that he closest property was at least a mile away.

She stepped outside, feeling more comfortable with her back to the door while holding a knife.

Steve's gaze fell to the blade and a flicker of amusement passed over his features.

"It's smart to be safe all the way out here. I might have answered my door with a gun." He grinned. "I mean, if I was you instead of me. But I can promise you, I'm as safe as they come." Steve leaned forward and whispered. *"Unless you're a bad guy."*

"I was just making my lunch for later." She met his

gaze with a guarded one of her own, acutely aware of the heat in her cheeks. "What can I do for you, Mr. Berger?"

"Just Steve is fine." He chuckled and tipped his head again. "I saw this place had some new life in it and wanted to say hi. I moved back to Glenburn last year after inheriting the old family plot, but it gets pretty quiet out here. Thought you might appreciate a neighborly welcome."

Nina nodded, her nerves tightening like piano wire pulled taut.

"My name is Nina. My husband Will is in town right now. He'll be back any minute."

"I'm sure he will be." Another grin. "Is there anything I can do to put you more at ease? Other than promising that I don't bite?"

"You could tell me why you're here. I'm assuming there's more to your visit than a 'neighborly hello.'"

"I do have an ulterior motive," Steve admitted with a nod. "You've got me there. But it's still neighborly."

Nina stared at him, waiting.

"I was passing by on the highway while driving home last night and saw the police cruiser. Everything alright?"

"We had an intruder," Nina admitted, a shiver running down her spine despite the sun. "We didn't catch them. That's why Will is in town right now — he's seeing about getting our locks all changed."

"That's a good idea. I would wanna swap out every lock in the place if I were you." Another nod. "If y'all need any help, just give me a holler. I'm happy to lend a hand."

"I'm sure we've got it." She found a smile. "But thank you."

"Did the police say it might be squatters?"

"They did." Nina nodded.

"Makes sense." Steve scratched his chin. "Sometimes

late at night, I see lights flickering on and off over here. I figured the Byrds never really left. But then I heard someone bought this place. And now here we are."

"Did you know the Byrds?"

"My dad was their gardener. Did some handyman stuff for them too. Half a dozen people worked for the family. James Corr at the gas station, his aunt picked up and delivered laundry. Angie Rivera's mom cleaned for them."

Rivera hadn't mentioned that during her visit last night — but why would she? It had been her job to make sure their intruder was gone. And there was no reason for Nina to ask if Rivera had ever been inside the house before.

In a small town like this, maybe she should just assume that anyone could know the layout of the house well enough to break in and mess with them.

She hoped Will had found a locksmith, and that he'd be available to come by today.

She shivered, then flushed as Steve's lips quirked up. She hated that he knew she was scared, even if it was true.

"What did you think of the Byrds?" She asked.

Steve shook his head. "They were your run-of-the-mill rich folks. But this town's got a million rumors since the murders. I've heard everything from the Byrds were running a cult out here to they made their money with a cartel that had them killed to they were just a bunch of snobs who didn't want anyone in their business."

Nina gave him a half-hearted laugh, followed by what felt like a confession. "I was actually printing out some old articles about the murder when you knocked."

His smile was teasing. "And here I thought it was veggies you were chopping."

A tiny laugh escaped her, a discharge of tension.

"You were still living here when it happened?"

"I was just a kid, but sometimes I helped my dad on the job."

"So you've been inside?"

"We weren't allowed in the house, but I helped take care of every inch of the property around it." Steve grinned. "Back in the day, that garden used to grow summer squash bigger than your head. If you want help bringing it back to life, I can show you how."

She did, but she wanted to know what he knew about the murder more.

"Did you buy that Galen Green was the murderer?"

"Not for a second." Steve snorted. "That guy might have enjoyed wandering the earth and getting stoned, but he was just a drifter. Anyone who ever had a conversation with the old coot would know he was in the wrong place at the wrong time. What would he have against the Byrds?"

That's what Nina had thought too, back when she'd first started listening to the podcast.

"What do you think about the uncle?" She asked, mostly to hear how Steve might respond.

"I reckon he's guiltier than Galen, but that don't mean he did it."

"I've never seen any names used in this case. Do you know who found the body?"

"'Course I do." But Steve obviously didn't want to say.

"Who was it?" Nina had to ask after an awkwardly long silence made that perfectly obvious. "Who found the body, Steve?"

She'd hoped using his first name might help, but the discomfort in his expression stayed fixed. He sighed and somehow she knew what Steve was going to say before he said it. A lot like she had known what would be inside each of her new rooms.

He swallowed again. "I'm the one who found the body."

"So you have been inside the house."

"Just the one time. And I wasn't paying a whole lot of attention to the decor."

The revelation struck Nina hard, despite most of her somehow knowing it was coming. But before she could process it further, or spin a reply, the sound of crunching gravel drew her attention to Will's Infinity rolling into view, his face visible through the windshield, etched with either concern or irritation.

The car came to a halt.

The driver's side door swung open and Will's purposeful strides quickly closed the distance between them.

"Everything okay here?" His gaze played tag with Nina and Steve.

"Everything is fine. Steve was just introducing himself. He's our neighbor."

"Ah." A curt nod. "I'm Will. Nice to make your acquaintance."

His tone was civil, but the air felt charged with an unspoken challenge.

"Good to meet you, Will." Steve extended his hand. "I just wanted to make sure that everything was alright around here after what happened last night."

"And what happened last night?" Will challenged, his handshake brief and perfunctory.

"Steve saw Officer Rivera's car here." Nina should not have had to explain.

"I appreciate your concern." Will gave him a nod. "But we've got everything under control."

"Of course." Steve took a step back. "You need anything, just ask. Happy to help."

Will responded with a noncommittal hum, then turned toward the house.

"We should head in." He was already walking.

"Sorry about … you know," Nina murmured to Steve as she lingered. "Do you have a cat by any chance? We found one in our kitchen."

"Nope. Just my old dog, Duke, and the occasional deer wandering through."

"Right. Well, thanks again." Nina gave Steve a little wave and followed Will back into the house, the door closing behind them with a definitive click.

Chapter Fifteen

WILL KEPT his movements slow and deliberate as he carefully tucked his newly-purchased gun into a nondescript shoebox. His hand lingered longer than necessary on the lid before he finally slid the box to the back of the closet, shrouded by hanging clothes and ample shadows.

Descending the stairs, he found Nina waiting, clutching a handful of papers, her expression somewhere between frustration and worry.

"You didn't have to be so curt with him." The edge in her voice sounded sharper inside. "He's our neighbor."

"Even if that's true, he's still a stranger, Nina." His voice was steady, but even he could hear his own irritation.

All he could think was that Rosie wouldn't have flirted with the neighbor the second Will turned his back on her. Nina resembled Rosie so much that sometimes it was hard to remember she was a different person. A person he loved.

But then she had to remind him how much he missed the person she resembled.

He decided to go on the attack. "How do you know he was really our neighbor?"

The silence was weighted down by Nina's realization of her own naivety.

It was worth driving the point home, especially given who was trying to threaten them. Threaten him, actually, but Nina would be collateral damage, and it would be his fault. "Did he show you any kind of identification? Did you even think to ask?"

"You're right," she finally conceded, her shoulders slumping slightly. "I just … I don't want us to live in fear here. And I had a knife with me."

"So I saw." He hated to think how scared she must have been to reach for it. He couldn't help imagining Rosie answering the door with a knife in hand, and felt his failure to protect Nina even more keenly. "The locks are all taken care of. A guy is coming by this afternoon, around 2:30. We'll both feel a lot safer once that's taken care of." He nodded at her papers. "What's that?"

"It's a story about the Byrd murder."

"Enough, Nina—" Will stopped himself before he said too much. "We talked about it last night, we don't need to talk about it again. I want to focus on the future we're trying to build here."

Nina gritted her teeth but swallowed the fight, disappointment clear in the slump of her posture.

"Give 'em here." Will held out his hand.

After a long moment, Nina begrudgingly surrendered the papers.

She watched him walk over to the fireplace, starting a fire before consigning those pages to the flames where they belonged.

He stared until the ink and paper were curling into ash, then turned to Nina. "Let's keep our focus on settling in."

"Fine." Though it sure didn't look that way. He would have to keep an eye on her, to make sure she wasn't digging into the past unnecessarily. "I'm going to unpack."

"Good idea." Will nodded, watching her retreat. "I'll be in my office."

He was sitting in front of his computer a minute later, but the pages he'd burned to avoid reading now stared back at him. Riddles in the Dark was an asinine name for a podcast, and that headline about the Byrd case was a grim, unwanted reminder of the reality he had dragged them both into when buying the house.

Because he was the one who'd found the listing and left it open in a tab on her laptop to see how she would react. She'd been just as fascinated with it as he'd hoped, without showing any sign of recognition. But that stupid podcast—

It didn't change his plan. She'd already agreed to marry him. He could still make it work.

He just had to take care of his other problem first. Before something worse than a dead bird showed up in their house.

Like *her*.

He couldn't believe he'd ever thought that bitch was anything like Rosie.

Will clicked away from the page, then pushed away from the desk. It was time to find his stalker and scare her off for good.

But his phone rang before he could open his laptop, jarring the stillness of his office. *Bruce* lit the screen. Will's boss, and Annie's husband — Bruce and Annie had been the ones to introduce Will to Nina. Putting up with Bruce's bullshit every day in the office was the price Will had to pay in order to meet the woman he wanted to spend the rest of his life with.

Will braced himself for the volleys of crude humor that were sure to be coming his way as he answered the call.

"You know it's not a good time," said Will, instead of *Hello*.

"Because you're working, or because you're still in the honeymoon phase in your haunted mansion?"

"We're not on our honeymoon, and the house isn't haunted. Hearing you ask me that question, I'm wondering why I ever tell you anything."

"Does that mean none of the above?"

"I'm working."

"Doesn't sound like it. Are you wearing an apron right now? I bet Nina has you an all fours. The question is whether she has you cleaning or playing some sex game, like pretending you're a coffee table while naked, with a feather duster sticking out of your—"

"I'm sure there's a reason why you're calling."

"Nope. This is it. I really am just checking in to make sure that you're still being pussy-whipped hard by Nina out there in the middle of Fuck Your Mother, America."

The thing Will hated most about big cities was the snobbery of their inhabitants toward small towns. Growing up in a place like this didn't mean he was stupid, but everyone in Chicago treated him like he must be Einstein if he'd made it all the way to their shitty urban hellscape. "It's Glenburn, North Dakota."

"I know where it is, and what I said."

"Nina's been through a lot. This is a place where she can be happy." Where they could be happy. Not that a moron like Bruce could understand that.

"Happy wife, happy life, right?" When Will didn't respond, Bruce finally got to the point. "TopDrawer wants us to come in for an on-site meeting."

"Why?"

"We're supposed to be evaluating some new software. Together, as a team, to see if we want to sign the contract.

Apparently this shit is more expensive than an all-inclusive month at one of those bullshit resorts that charges you for air. Can you fly out Thursday and Friday?"

"I'll be there."

Now he didn't have to make up an excuse to fly back to Chicago to deal with his other problem. He could kill two birds with one stone, and the company would pay for it.

"You sure you don't have to check with the missus? So she can put her royal stamp on your hall pass or—"

"I'll be there."

"—cross-stitch your permission slip—"

Will killed the call.

Nina gave Bruce's disgusting behavior a pass for Annie's sake, but Rosie wouldn't have tolerated someone like Bruce.

He would work on Nina. As she adapted to her new life, the friendship with Annie would fade away, and it would be good riddance.

He opened his laptop and narrowed his focus to the glowing computer screen.

Once working, hours slipped by unnoticed, until he heard the sound of a vehicle approaching outside and went to the window.

He saw a dust-smothered pickup, its approach stirring a cloud of dirt, seemingly on purpose, as it navigated the long drive up to the house.

The pickup stopped behind the Infinity, then James stepped out and started walking toward the house, holding a bag that Will imagined was full of tools and locks.

And yet Will still had the disquieting thought that no amount of steel and bolts could ever shield them from the shadows cast by history's serpentine reach.

Chapter Sixteen

Nina stood in the kitchen, garlic and basil mingling in the air as she stirred her marinara. Her phone buzzed with an incoming FaceTime.

She turned off the burner and pulled out her phone to see the screen lighting up with Annie's eager face.

"Where's my grand tour of the infamous murder room?" Annie was only half-joking.

With a laugh, Nina left the kitchen and aimed her phone at the mantle where shadows were playing tricks in the light.

"That's where the killer painted all that creepy shit?" Annie asked.

"The one and only. I found a stain that I think might have been blood." She lifted up the corner of a hanging panel of wallpaper to reveal the rusty stain amid faded flowers. "But I'm not ready to pull up the rest of the wallpaper."

Nina wasn't sure she ever would be.

But she was ready to investigate. She pulled out a map printed from the home's layout online.

"Are you taking me to the basement next?"

"You know me so well." Nina descended the creaking stairs after turning the flashlight function of her phone on.

But the tiny light barely illuminated the darkness down here. She let it play over the nearest wall, comparing what she saw to the map.

"Creepy as shit." Annie giggled. "Just like I hoped."

Nina traced her finger along the paper's edges, where the ink depicted something different than what she was seeing with her eyes. That was why she'd printed the map: the very walls appeared to rest at a different angle, and the map showed a corridor where now there was a solid wall.

"What is that?" Annie asked. "What are you showing me?"

"I don't exactly know," Nina admitted with frustrated intrigue. "It's like the house is—"

Nina whirled around at the sound of footsteps behind her.

Will's silhouette filled the stairway, his shadowed expression unreadable. She suddenly felt like she was doing something wrong, even though that was ridiculous. It was their house, and she'd already had to come down here to turn the water back on.

She'd had to guilt Will into coming with her, though. And he'd been on edge the entire time they were down here, even though there was nothing but bare drywall and a cement floor. And the finicky water valve.

Claustrophobic, maybe?

He'd never mentioned it before. He was the calm one who never lost his head.

Except he'd been coming closer and closer to losing it since they'd moved into this house.

"What are you doing?" Will asked gruffly.

"Just showing Annie around," Nina said as she

dropped the blueprint behind her, hating that she felt guilty for being on the phone with her best friend, despite knowing she had every right to be.

She felt lucky that their respective best friends were husband and wife, even though Annie was an absolute doll and Bruce was … a lot. But Will always had a snappy rejoinder for whatever obnoxious thing Bruce had just said, so it was always fun whenever the foursome got together.

"Hi, Annie." Will's greeting was perfunctory, his gaze never leaving Nina's. "Dinner smells great."

Nina put the phone back in front of her face. "I'll call you in a bit."

"You're not seriously—"

Nina hung up the phone, already composing an apology text in her mind.

Will was still staring at her in a way that made Nina feel like she might have done something wrong.

"I didn't know you were still talking to her."

"Why wouldn't I talk to my best friend?" Nina pulled out the map again, unfolding it on a nearby workbench. "Look at this. Doesn't the architecture seem off to you?"

Will's eyes narrowed at the paper as if it were an unwelcome intruder in their lives. "Drop it, Nina. Someone probably made a mistake uploading the map online, or the house got renovated after the blueprints were drafted. You are obsessing over every little possible—"

"You're right." Nina didn't want to hear it. She gave him a tired smile. "Do you smell that?"

"Smell what?"

Nina didn't answer, pushing past him to rush back upstairs and into the kitchen, heart thumping against her ribs as she hurried to rescue the sauce, stirring briskly while still working to ignore the basement's incongruities rattling around in her head.

"Why did you turn the burner back on?" Nina yelled to Will.

He didn't answer.

She finished preparing the pasta, steam rising like specters from the boiling pot. She set the table with care, placing two rose-patterned bowls across from each other.

"Why did you turn the heat back on my sauce?" Nina made the mistake of asking again.

"I didn't touch your sauce."

"I turned it off when Annie called. Before I went downstairs."

"The burner was on when I went into the kitchen. That's *why* I went down there to find you."

"I would never go down in the basement without turning the burner off, Will."

"I thought it was weird, too. Again, that's why I was worried."

Will wasn't hearing her right now, so Nina focused on the flavors, seeking solace in the familiar tang of tomatoes and the earthy hint of basil from her garden. But eventually, she could no longer stand the quiet and felt compelled to break it with the question haunting her mind.

"Are you mad at me?" Her voice was small, almost lost amid the clinking of cutlery.

"Maybe buying this house was a mistake." His words dropped like stones into the well of their disquiet without answering her.

"Why would you say that?" Nina blinked, taken aback.

"You're fixated on it, in the wrong ways. It isn't healthy."

Nina bristled with a mix of defiance and hurt. "I enjoy solving puzzles."

"It's more than that, and we both know it. This is becoming an obsession."

She took a breath and reset herself. "Did you get me a key?"

He reached into his pocket and slid the new house key across the table. "Here."

Her fingers brushed against his as she took it.

"I'm going to Chicago on Wednesday." Will pushed his plate away, even though he'd barely eaten half.

"I'll come with you," she offered.

It would be nice to spend some time with him in the city she still thought of as home, where they'd first met. Reconnect with the way they'd been when they'd first started dating.

"I'll be busy with meetings. It won't be fun for you."

"So you're leaving me here alone? After what happened? After you *just* said that I was obsessed with this place?"

"The new locks should keep you safe. And I'll be back on Saturday."

Nina swallowed a rising bubble of protest. "I can drive you to the airport."

"No need." Will dismissed her with a wave of his hand, then spoke with a tone of finality. "I'll be taking the car."

So, he would also be leaving her stranded.

A pall of silence descended upon the dinner table, broken only by the sharp ringing of cutlery against porcelain. Nina's fingers curled tighter around her fork. Ever since the intruder had left that dead bird, Will had been different, and she didn't know how to bring him back.

An insidious whisper inside her refused to be stilled, and Nina could no longer stay silent. "I really don't like the idea of being here alone without a car."

"Why would you need to go anywhere?" He sure made his question sound practical. "We have groceries, and there's enough unpacking to keep you occupied. Unless I'm missing something?"

"What if there's an emergency?"

"You can always call the neighbor," Will suggested.

"I can't tell if you're being an asshole right now."

"Why would you think that I'm being an asshole?"

"Because you were being an asshole right in front of Steve." She crossed her arms. "I don't want to be stranded here without a car."

"You're not being 'stranded.'"

"What do you call it then, Will?"

"Stranded implies duress."

"Maybe that's what I feel."

"Well, you don't need to. I'll only be gone a few days, Nina. And honestly, if you can't handle being alone here for that long, then maybe we shouldn't have moved here in the first place."

A strained silence lingered between them, until Nina broke it again.

"When you get back, we need to talk about getting a second vehicle. I'll be looking for work after we're married and—"

"I thought you didn't want to work?" Will's expression shifted, confusion and irritation at war on his features. "That you were going to focus on the house?"

"I said I'd think about it." She met his gaze, her own resolve hardening. "I never agreed to stay home indefinitely."

He pushed his chair back with a scrape. "I'll be right back."

Nina simmered in her seat until he returned.

Will sat and slid a box across the table toward her.

"What is this?" Trepidation knotted her stomach.

"Open it." He nodded at the box.

She lifted the lid and found a gun nestled inside — a cold and foreign presence among their dinnerware that filled her with a jarring ripple of chills.

"When did you get this?"

"This morning." There was so little emotion in his reply, considering they were talking about a fucking *firearm*.

"I have no idea how to use a gun."

"I'll teach you."

Was that supposed to make her feel safe? It didn't.

But Nina didn't know what else to say that wouldn't risk starting a fight, so she finally fell silent for good this time.

Will retreated to his office after dinner, leaving Nina to clear the table and wash the dishes. Warm water was a minor comfort, a routine helping her to shelve the unease.

"Goodnight," Will called out, his voice distant.

"I'll be up shortly," Nina replied, her words echoing in the empty kitchen.

Once done with the dishes she texted Annie: *What are you doing later in the week?*

Annie texted back: *Are you asking me if I want to come see the murder house?*

Chapter Seventeen

It was finally Thursday morning.

Gray light diffused through the living room window as Nina perched on the sill with her gaze fixed on the road where a lone car was slowly approaching, its pace clearly out of step on the quiet rural road.

She watched, her heart hitching as the car paused, then executed a deliberate U-turn.

Nina smiled widely and jumped off of the couch, rushing to the front door and bursting outside, running down the gravel driveway with her arms flailing. She probably looked like a human distress signal.

The vehicle hesitated, then yielded, crunching onto the driveway, the dust a veil that lifted to reveal Annie's familiar form. She parked with an abruptness that echoed the thud of Nina's heart, then emerged from the car like a force of nature.

Their embrace was a tangle of limbs, laughter bubbling between them as Annie stepped back, her eyes sweeping over the vastness around them.

"Holy hell, Nina, you really did move to the middle of butt-fuck nowhere."

Nina grinned, a flush of warmth seeping through her. "Come on, park in the barn. God, I can't believe I get to say that!"

Annie's trunk popped open to an arsenal of provisions — wine bottles clinked, bags crinkled, stuffed with an assortment of junk food.

"Emergency rations," Annie declared with a wink. "Can't let you starve in this gothic fortress."

Annie's laughter was a salve to Nina's frayed nerves. She really needed this.

They hauled the suitcase and bags out of the car and made their way to the house, a parade of two.

Annie deposited her suitcase with a casual flick, her gaze roaming the space with a curious awe.

"So this is the infamous murder house, huh?" She turned to Nina, her eyes glinting with mischief. "I need the grand tour — like, right now."

"Don't you need to use the restroom or anything?"

"I peed my pants on the way here." Annie laughed. "Fine. Potty break first, then murder tour later."

Nina put on a kettle while Annie used the bathroom.

Their tour began on the lower floor, with Nina leading Annie through each of the home's spacious rooms. Her eyes darted around to absorb every detail.

"Who knew gothic could be so ... cozy?" Annie quipped. "Also, does everything you say always echo?"

"We just need more furniture."

"Right. That's all you need. What's upstairs?"

"I'll show you." Nina led the way.

The top floor was more of the same. Rooms bathed in slants of light with shadows lurking in all the corners. Nina watched Annie's expression shift from amusement to something more pensive.

"You weren't kidding about the vibe up here." Annie ran her fingers over an ornate bedpost.

"Come on. I know what you want to see next. We're going back downstairs."

Through the kitchen and into the larder, then over to the secret door.

"Cool." Annie grinned.

Nina used her shoulder to heave the basement door through the frame when it stuck. It popped open and a pitch black expanse loomed before them.

"Oh. So this is what it feels like when shit gets real." Annie's voice wavered between trepidation and delight. "I can already feel all the murdery vibes from up here. Maybe we don't need to go *all the way* down."

"I've already seen it." Nina shrugged.

"After you." Annie nodded at the darkness, accepting her dare.

Nina reached over and flicked on the light switch. A flare of light and then back to black as the bulb shorted out. Again.

"Great," Nina muttered, her heart now pounding. "We need a flashlight."

"Of course we do," Annie said, a nervous giggle escaping her. "It's not a proper murder house tour unless we're wandering around in the dark."

Nina retrieved a flashlight.

Its beam cut through the darkness to the unforgiving lines of stairs.

They descended into into shadows deepened by the narrow flashlight beam.

"I swear, if something jumps out at us, I'm suing you

for emotional trauma." Annie joked, her voice a little too high.

"I'll counter-sue you for accessory to reckless exploration."

"I'm not sure your joke works."

They reached the bottom and Nina's flashlight illuminated an expanse of basement. The air was cooler, and still. Like the gloomy room was holding its breath.

She swayed the light slowly around, shining it on every inch of the unsettling space. It was the same as before: bare drywall with a valve coming out of a hole in one wall, rough cement floor, the ancient washer and dryer in the corner, and the hanging lamp that kept shorting out.

It felt so, so wrong, but she couldn't put her finger on why, except: "Tell me that this basement doesn't feel smaller than the rest of the house."

Annie shook her head. "I definitely can't tell you that." Her gaze swept across the room. "But that could just be how this creepy ass place is built."

"According to the blueprint, this basement should be bigger." Her flashlight lingered on the far wall, where the shadows seemed to dance and retreat.

"Definitely something off about it. I also thought the murder room would be more … I don't know the word."

"Fucked up is two words."

"Let's go back upstairs. This place is giving me the chills."

"I've been living with the chills." Nina started for the stairs.

Back in the bright light of the kitchen with the secret door firmly closed, tension eased from her shoulders.

She busied herself with unpacking the grocery bags, while Annie disappeared to the bathroom for the second time.

"Again?" Nina asked.

"The creep factor has my bladder on high alert. "

The clinking of bottles and rustling of bags was a comfort as Nina stowed the groceries. She uncorked one of the wine bottles and poured two glasses as Annie reappeared with a slightly-bewildered expression.

"It's so quiet here. I can't stand the sound of it."

"Welcome to the middle of nowhere." Nina handed her a glass of wine.

They clinked with a toast.

"To being reunited," Annie said.

"And to surviving your murder tour." Nina smiled.

It felt great to have a friend here with her. She picked up the bottle and nodded at the window. "Let's take this outside, get some fresh air."

Annie raised her glass in agreement and gave Nina a nod.

They stepped out onto the back porch. A cool breeze made for a pleasant tickle compared to the stuffy air inside.

"It's a hell of a space," Annie said.

The property was a vast canvas of wild beauty. Overgrown grasses swayed in a sea of green as Nina led the way, her steps unhurried and wine bottle cradled in her arm.

"The garden's this way." She gestured toward a patch of land where nature had run riot. Then back behind the shed, to where stray tendrils of ivy were clinging to the edges of empty beds, and where her single basil plant still stood defiant. Almost thriving.

"I just knew this was here, even before I saw it."

"Cool?" Annie replied, after Nina was looking at her expectantly for a little too long.

"I mean, I *knew it*, Annie. Like, I saw it in my mind.

Same for a lot of the rooms. Most of them. Don't you think that's weird?"

"It might be." She shrugged. "But you were obsessed with Riddles in the Dark, so maybe not. They talked about this place—"

"Not about basil!"

"Gardens have basil."

"You sound like Will."

"Fuck you, too." Annie laughed and took a sip.

Nina mused, her fingers lightly caressing the basil leaves. "There's so much about this place that feels familiar to me. Familiar, but also wrong."

Annie nodded, her eyes taking in the neglected charm. "It's strange, but it's like you were meant to be here."

They left the garden and kept walking as they talked about the possibilities for landscaping the property. The ground underfoot was a patchwork of soft earth and unyielding stones. Trees lined the boundary, their branches yawning into the sky.

A rusted barbed wire fence came into view at the property line, tracing the perimeter, its jagged edges leaving no mistake about borders.

The drone of an ATV punctuated the quiet.

After following the sound they spied Steve, a figure of purpose against the backdrop of wilderness as he repaired a section of fence.

"Steve!" Nina raised her hand in greeting.

He looked up, a smile breaking through the lines of concentration on his face.

"This is Annie, my friend from back home," Nina added.

"Nice to meet you, Annie." He grinned at her. "Has Nina been scaring you with ghost stories?"

"I'm here for the stories. What's a visit to a murder house without a little scare?"

He wiped his brow with a chuckle.

"So, Steve, as the local expert, what's the scariest thing you've seen around here?" Annie asked with a playful glint in her eyes.

"Scariest thing?" Steve propped his tools against the fence, his posture relaxed. "Probably my reflection in the pond after a long night out."

Annie laughed. "What about ghosts? You know I'm here for the stories."

"You ever hear about the midnight coyote?"

"I have not." Annie narrowed her eyes at him. "Something tells me that's because you just made it up."

"Wouldn't you agree that it's awfully early in our relationship for me to be making things up?" Steve asked.

Annie kept the banter going. "I would say that makes it the perfect time. What if Annie isn't even really my name?"

His eyes twinkled with amusement. "Well, 'Annie', I guess you've got me there. But I would strongly suggest you keep at least one eye out for the ghost coyote."

"I thought it was the midnight coyote?" Nina said.

"That's its nickname," Annie rushed to Steve's defense. Steve laughed.

"We'll let you get back to your work," Nina said.

He tipped his head and turned back toward his tools.

"Nice to meet you, Steve." Even the way Annie said his name made it sound like she was flirting.

They were barely out of earshot when Nina leaned over and whispered, "You're married."

"I'm not looking to fuck the guy."

"You just want him to want to fuck you?"

"Something like that." Annie laughed.

"*He's the one who found Panda's body*," Nina whispered, even though there was no longer any need to.

"*No shit!*" Annie whispered back.

Then she got that look on her face.

"Don't do it!" Nina warned.

But Annie was already on her way.

Chapter Eighteen

Annie ran back toward the fence.

Nina tried calling after her, but it was too late.

"Hey, Steve!" Annie yelled.

He looked up and she finished her siren call.

"You should come over for a drink tonight after dinner. We've got plenty of wine, and I bet you have stories to tell." Annie reminded him again. "That's why I'm here."

Nina winced. "I'm sure that Steve—"

"A drink, huh? Sounds tempting."

"She just wants to grill you about the murder. You don't have to—"

"I'm okay with that," Steve interrupted, his eyes still on Annie.

"We're eating at six." Annie gave him a parting smile. "See you any time after that."

Nina shot Annie a dirty look as soon as she could, no more than dozen steps from the fence on their way back to the house. "What the hell was that?"

Annie shrugged, unapologetic. "Don't you want to

know more about what your neighbor saw, seeing as he's a firsthand witness to this case you're obsessed with?"

"I'm not obsessed."

"Ha! And I'm not a true crime junkie who just invited a witness over for murder gossip." Annie laughed. "You can't tell me that he didn't seem happy to be invited. He's probably thrilled that someone is interested in his stories."

Annie wasted no time once back inside, heading straight for her bag and pulling out her laptop, fingers tapping across the keyboard before Nina could ask what she was doing.

Annie told her anyway. "Let's stir up some shit on the Byrd Murder Reddit forum."

"What does that mean?" Nina asked, peering over her shoulder. "What are you planning to do?"

"I'm not *planning* anything. I'm posting an Ask Me Anything about living in the house. People will go nuts for this shit."

It only took half an hour before they saw a strong response on the forum, with the first wave flooded by skepticism.

"They don't believe we're actually here," Nina observed after reading the responses.

"Let's give them proof." Annie smirked, already clicking her phone camera, snapping a half-dozen photos, then uploading them.

Skepticism turned into a deluge of questions, the forum alive with curiosity.

"Now look at them go," Nina said.

"You ready to see what comes out of Pandora's Box?"

The screen flickered with a barrage of queries, some of them truly bizarre.

Nina leaned back in her chair and scanned the relentless stream flooding their impromptu AMA.

How long is the driveway exactly?

Is it really as secluded as they say?

How many bedrooms?

What kind of locks are on the doors now?

Are the windows double-paned?

Must get pretty cold out there.

Nina and Annie took turns with the questions.

Annie: *The driveway is long enough for a good scream. Butt Fuck, Egypt is on the way to this place. Five bedrooms, but one of them feels more like a closet.*

Then Nina: *The best money can buy. I'm not a window person. Like a witch's nipple.*

"How cold is a witch's nipple?" Annie turned to her. "I've always wondered."

Then Annie corrected one of Nina's answers: *The windows are double-paned to keep the ghosts out.*

Theories about the murder were varied and wild. One user insisted it was a cover-up by local law enforcement, another was convinced that the crime of passion was committed by a crazed relative, and yet another argued for a more supernatural explanation, citing the infamous Satanic symbols as proof.

But Byrd91 stole the show with skepticism bordering on aggression. *There's no way you're actually living in the Byrd house. Stop lying for internet points!*

Annie typed: *Internet points? Honey, we're living in a murder house. We have bigger thrills than Reddit karma. We'll save you a seat at the next seance if you're interested.*

Annie closed her laptop with snap. "So what are we making for dinner? Other than sweet love to Steve's stories?"

"How about a stir-fry? We've got chicken, veggies, and I can make a quick sauce."

Annie nodded and rolled up her sleeves. "I'll chop the vegetables."

As Annie deftly sliced bell peppers and onions, Nina took the chicken out of the fridge and began cutting meat into strips.

Annie broke the silence. "I worry about you being all alone out here. And with Will leaving you like this. Can we please agree that's an asshole move?"

Nina sighed, placing the chicken in a bowl. "He bought a gun, for protection."

"Is that supposed to make me feel any better?" Annie paused, her knife hovering over a bell pepper. "About him, or your safety?"

There was a knock on the door before she could answer.

"So out here I'm guessing that could only be Steve or a murderer," Annie joked.

"Unless they're one and the same," Nina joked back. But she couldn't help thinking about the dead bird and wondering if whoever left it would knock the next time they came back, once they realized the locks had been changed.

Nina opened the door to see Steve's tall frame filling the entryway, his presence a strange yet fitting addition to the ambiance.

"Hope I'm not too early," he said as he followed Nina in to the kitchen.

"Perfect timing." The lightness of Annie's voice masked an undercurrent of curiosity and apprehension. "Wine?"

"Sure, thanks." Steve nodded, stepping inside. "Wine sounds nice."

His gaze wandered, taking everything in as Annie

handed him a glass of merlot. He raised it in appreciation before taking a sip.

Then he turned to Nina. "Any more problems with your intruder?"

"*Intruder?*" Annie repeated, sounding deeply concerned. "What intruder?"

"Sounds like something I shouldn't have said." Steve tipped his head. "Sorry about that."

"Not your fault." Nina turned to Annie. "We had an intruder. Maybe someone who was squatting here before we moved in and—"

"What the fuck, Nina?"

"I'm sure she just didn't want you to worry," Steve said.

"No shit!" Annie snapped. "But again: What the fuck, Nina?"

"It wasn't a big deal." She shrugged. "Seriously. The house was empty for a long time. Are you really surprised to find that someone wanted to take advantage of free rent and plenty of privacy?"

"I have no problem understanding the motivations of a squatter, Nina." Annie looked seriously mad. "But I'm having a really hard time understanding why Will would be a big enough fucker to leave you here alone, and without a car, after that."

"He had the locks changed." But when she said it out loud, it sounded like an excuse. Nina fiddled with the hem of her shirt, wanting to retreat into herself as the silence between them grew oppressive.

Until Annie turned to Steve. "So, you found Panda's body: what happened?"

He shifted uncomfortably, the wine glass cradled in his hands. "Yeah, I did." He took a deep breath. "I saw the door open, which was odd. But that wasn't the only reason I went in."

Annie leaned in, her interest piqued. "What else?"

"I saw a ghost." The words tumbled out, and for a moment, the room was still, as if they were absorbing the shock of his statement.

"No way," Nina declared.

"You're fucking with me!" Annie exclaimed.

"Yes way, and I am most certainly not fucking with you. I haven't told anyone about this in years, mostly because I'm sick of folks either looking at me like I've gone loco or thinking it without saying it."

"Fair warning, Steve. We'll probably think you're crazy," Annie said.

"Or maybe not." He shrugged. "She was dressed in a white nightgown, covered in blood. She just stood there, saying 'help me' over and over."

Annie's mouth fell open, her previous skepticism evaporating.

Nina felt it too, something in the set of Steve's jaw, the solemnity of his voice. She didn't believe in ghosts, but his conviction made it clear that he believed he'd seen one.

"I walked in and saw all the blood in the living room." His eyes flickered toward the mantle as a haunted look claimed his expression. "Then I saw the body."

The room suddenly felt colder. He could probably tell her which panel of wallpaper to pull up in the living room, if she wanted to see the Satanic symbol left behind by the killer.

Did she?

Nina shuddered.

"I was spooked," Steve continued. "Just rode my bike back home as fast as I could. To this day I've never pedaled faster."

"How do you know it was a ghost?" Annie asked. "Maybe it was a person begging for help?"

"I've never been sure of much in my life, but I was sure as hell of that," Steve said with finality. "Then and now."

"Boy or girl?" Nina asked.

"What?" Steve seemed surprised by her question.

"Was it a boy's body, or a girl's?" Annie jumped in. "The papers went out of their way to hide Panda's identity, including their gender."

"Girl," Steve said. "A beautiful girl."

The three of them sat in a weighted silence, each lost in their thoughts until the timer for the rice dinged. Nina fluffed it with a fork, then made a quick stir-fry with the chicken and veggies they'd chopped earlier.

Meanwhile, Annie flirted with Steve some more.

Nina had a hard time reining in her disapproval. But if she was married to Bruce, whose idea of subtle was to speculate on what sex toys random strangers might be hiding in their nightstands at home, maybe she would be tempted to flirt with the occasional stranger too.

Dinner was animated, with conversations meandering from the mundane to the macabre and back. The bottle was empty long before their conversation stopped flowing. But eventually it was time to call it a night.

The table was cleared and Steve stood, ready to depart.

He turned to Nina at the front door, a sincere look in his eyes. "Here's my number. If you need anything while Will is away, like a lift to town or help around the house, inside or out, call me and I'll be here as soon as I can be."

His voice held a protective edge. It was easy for Nina to believe that Steve's concern was sincere, and now she felt embarrassed that she'd treated him so suspiciously the first time he'd knocked on her door.

"Thank you." She gave him a nod. "I really appreciate that."

"Goodnight, you two." Steve tipped his head before turning around. "Take care."

The door closed behind him and Annie turned to Nina.

"So Panda was a girl. We're the only people who know that. Besides Steve, that is. And the cops."

"Jesus." Nina shook her head with a laugh. "You can't even wait a second?"

"What is it you want me to wait for? This is a break in the case. Plus, no one's ever mentioned the ghost before. What if your house really is haunted?"

"He didn't see a ghost." Nina shook her head. "But what if he actually did see a girl? And the lighting was weird or something. Do we know if Panda had a sibling? Nothing I've read mentions a brother or a sister. All the articles make it sound like Panda was an only child."

"Same." Annie slowly nodded. "Are we going to post what we learned on the forum?"

"I'd rather wait," Nina said.

"Good point. We don't want anyone else to solve the case before we do." Annie winked at her.

But the rest of the dwindling night had textures of unease and curiosity. They prepared for sleep, the house feeling larger and more ominous than before. Their decision to share the bed was unspoken but mutual.

Nina lay beneath the covers in the suffocating darkness, but Annie's steady breathing was a comforting sound in the otherwise silent room.

Just as Nina was about to drift off, her phone buzzed and jolted her awake.

She looked at the screen and saw *UNKOWN NUMBER*.

She blinked at the message. It was a photo — Will, in a bar, looking unaware that he was being photographed.

A surge of confusion and hurt washed over her.

Who is this? Nina texted.

No reply.

Bruce? she tried again.

But still no reply.

Nina set the phone down with a sigh as the light faded into the darkness. She lay back on her pillow, mind whirling with questions and unease.

She hated who she became when she was jealous, but what was Will doing out in a bar this late at night? Bonding with his coworkers? Shooting the shit with Bruce?

Was that why he hadn't wanted her to come with him — because he was seeing someone he worked with?

If that were the case, surely Bruce would know, and he would tell Annie.

And Annie would absolutely tell her. So it was probably something innocent.

But who had taken that picture and why had they sent it to her?

Annie was already asleep, but her presence was still only a slight comfort amid the sprawling uncertainty of a claustrophobic night.

Nina closed her eyes, hoping that sleep would take her soon, desperate to escape the nagging thoughts now haunting the edges of her consciousness.

A floorboard creaked somewhere downstairs, and it was as if the house itself was settling in for a nightmare.

Chapter Nineteen

MORNING SUNLIGHT STREAMED through the kitchen windows as Nina and Annie sat at the table with a simple breakfast spread between them. Now that Nina was stirring her coffee and it was otherwise silent between them, she couldn't think of a reason to avoid bringing up the message that had been burning her mind to ash since last night.

"I got a weird text last night. Right after you fell asleep."

"Why didn't you wake me?"

Nina retrieved her phone and showed Annie the photo. "It's Will at a bar. Sent from an unknown number."

Annie leaned in to examine the picture. "Any idea why someone would send this to you? Or who it could be?"

"No." Nina shook her head. "And I don't want to ask Will about it either."

She spoke with a definitive edge, closing the topic.

Annie loudly chewed, swallowed, and said, "Do you wanna talk more about Steve's ghost story and what that might mean?"

"Do you think he really believes that story, or—"

"Was he fucking with us?" Annie finished the thought. "I haven't stopped wondering since he told us the story. But if someone was peeling off my fingernails and making me decide one way or another, yeah, I think that dude believes he saw a ghost."

"Why would anyone be peeling your fingernails off?"

"Do you remember the Thompson brothers from Seattle?"

"Oh yeah, of course. I loved that case. Why?"

"Because the brothers had a secret room where they kept the bodies. That's why the police never found them during the initial searches."

Secret room. Maybe that was why the basement was so much smaller than the blueprint said it was supposed to be?

"Right." Nina stood, her chair scraping against the floor. "Come on."

Annie followed her down to the basement, the air growing cooler as they descended. Nina pointed her flashlight at a section of the wall.

"What if there's a secret room behind there?"

While Nina held the flashlight, Annie examined the wall, tapping the surface. In certain places, it sounded hollow, but they saw no obvious door or entrance.

"Do we have any tools?" Annie's eyes sparkled even in the dark. "We could try to see if there's something behind this wall."

"Let's go look in the barn."

"This is very cinematic."

Annie followed Nina to the stairs.

Up into the kitchen and outside onto the porch.

Across the property to the barn.

It loomed large and full of shadows as they

approached, aged wood creaking gently in the morning breeze, the air inside heavy with the aroma of ancient hay and rust.

Once inside, they rummaged through the cluttered space, their search illuminated by shafts of light filtering in through dusty windows.

Annie's hand finally landed on the cold, solid grip of a sledgehammer.

"Found it!" she exclaimed, lifting it with a grunt.

"You look good with that," Nina told her.

"What do you think Bruce would say if I brought this to bed?"

Nina laughed as they headed out of the barn and back toward the house.

Then they were standing in the basement in front of a wall, where Annie handed her the sledgehammer. It was much heavier than Nina had expected.

"Why me?" Nina asked.

"Because it's your house. If one of us is going to accidentally bust a water pipe, it should be you."

"I don't know why my heart is pounding so hard."

"Probably because you're afraid that your husband will be mad at you."

"I am not." But she knew Will *would* be mad if he came home and discovered that she'd taken a sledgehammer to the basement drywall.

And the way he'd been acting, she was a little afraid to find out what he might do.

But if she said that to Annie, the next part of the conversation wouldn't be about secret rooms — it would be about red flags and hasty engagements to men who left their fiancés at home with guns they didn't know how to shoot.

"We're going to renovate anyway," Nina said, more to convince herself than Annie.

She raised the sledgehammer and struck the wall with all her might.

The impact was loud, reverberating through the basement.

It got louder with each subsequent hit, resounding like thunder through the room and tearing through Nina's body with every strike.

Dust filled the air, coating their hair and clothes, making them cough and squint.

When her wrists began to ache, Annie took a turn.

Then Nina again.

But still the stubborn wall remained solid despite their assault.

With every new blow, a mix of fear and excitement surged through Nina, each swing of that sledgehammer giving her yet another release from the pent-up tension.

The burn in her muscles almost felt good.

But as the dust settled, their excitement waned. They'd shattered the drywall, and chunks of it crumbled away to reveal a brick-and-mortar wall underneath.

Doubt crept in, the exhilaration of their endeavor surrendering to a sinking realization.

"We've made a big mistake," Nina muttered, her arms aching from effort. "Will's going to kill me."

She tried to laugh it off, but her heart wasn't in it.

"One last swing for each of us," Annie suggested, gesturing down at the sledgehammer in Nina's hand. "You first."

Nina nodded and put all of her heft into it, gripping the handle like a lifeline and swinging with a final burst of energy.

The sound was different when she struck the wall this

time. A hollow echo that rolled through the basement as the drywall collapsed under the force of the sledgehammer to reveal a dark void beyond.

Nina and Annie stared in disbelief.

But it was only before a second before they were both going at the thing.

The drywall gave way beneath their relentless assault, the once-sturdy barrier now yielding to the weight of determination and curiosity. Nina's arms throbbed more with every swing, but she felt a further surge of adrenaline with every piece that broke away.

Annie tore off the hanging chunks between Nina's swings, face set in a mask of fierce resolve.

A hidden door revealed itself as they tore through the last of the barrier, tucked neatly behind the stairs. Its presence was a shock, despite it being exactly what they had been hoping to find.

The reality of their discovery sent a shiver down her spine.

Nina reached out, her hand trembling slightly as she opened the door.

Then they entered a space that felt frozen in time.

The small room was cramped with a single bed, a rickety table, and a lamp that — once turned on — filled the space with a faint and eerie glow.

Bible pictures hung from every wall, and not the kind with comforting verses Nina remembered from Sunday school. These were harsh and brutally-judgmental:

Whoever spares the rod hates his son, but he who loves him is diligent to discipline him; Children, obey your parents in the Lord, for this is right; Whoever curses his father or his mother shall be put to death.

Nina found herself flashing on the orphanage dormitory, even though it had been nothing like this — the girls' room had been on the top floor, with plenty of windows to let in the light, and cute pictures of cats and dogs hung on the wall. This basement room was the opposite of that.

It was almost like she was having a reverse deja vu attack.

Or maybe she was overwhelmed with empathy for whoever had been confined down here. Knowing she'd been lucky to escape this fate, while someone else had not.

"It's like an evil Mr. Rogers set in here," Annie said.

But the joke fell flat as her voice wavered.

Nina didn't laugh, or even smile at the quip as they traded a glance.

Annie picked up a magazine from the table. An issue of Octane from just a few months ago. "This is *not* twenty years old." Her voice was edged with fear and disbelief. "Someone was living here recently."

The possibility that their intruder had been staying in this hidden room, right beneath their feet, had been an unnerving possibility. Now it was a violating probability.

But how had they gotten in?

They must've had a key to the front door and come in through the larder, shutting the secret door behind them.

"How long do you think this has this been here?" Annie seemed too afraid to voice more than a whisper.

"Long enough," Nina replied, her gaze sweeping the room again.

Every detail seemed to scream of a past filled with misery and despair.

She caught sight of the bedside table, then approached it tentatively and pulled open the drawers. She found a stack of journals inside, their covers worn and pages jaundiced with age. She and Annie traded a look then began to read.

The first journal described a world of pain and isolation. The writer referred to themselves and others only by animal names: Panda, Koala, Grizzly, Polar, Kodiak, and Sloth. The words painted a picture of lives lived in shadows.

Home life was a prison, devoid of friends, social interactions, or normal schooling, the writer's world limited to the confines of this hidden room. It soon became clear that the writer was Panda.

The story unfolded in heartbreaking detail. A life of misery and longing, a soul yearning for freedom, and a glimpse of the world beyond these walls. Panda despised her life: the strict confinement, and the oppressive control exerted by her parents.

The turning point in Panda's journal was her daring escape. She described sneaking out of the house, stealing a bike, and venturing to Jackrabbit Ridge, the nearest town past Glenburn.

That was when Sloth entered the narrative. And the tone of the writing shifted.

Panda's words were suddenly imbued with a sense of longing. An aching love for Sloth. For the first time, she spoke of happiness, albeit fleeting and only stolen in moments away from her oppressive home environment.

Nina and Annie sat in silence, the weight of Panda's story settling between them. A voice crying out from the darkness and history inside this hidden room.

"This is amazing," Annie said. "I want to read every one of these."

"We could open a bottle and get started."

"Except I can't." Annie shook her head. "I have a flight in two hours. I should already be out of here."

"Fuck."

"Agreed." She nodded. "I could change my flight. Stay a little longer?"

"No. You should go." Nina hated the prospect of being alone in the house, but was practical enough to know what needed to happen. "Will's coming back in the morning. I'll be fine."

"And you don't want him to know that I stayed with you." Annie winked. "Got it."

Annie didn't argue as they left the hidden room, which made Nina want to defend Will, but it was true, she didn't want him to know that Annie had stayed with her, even though that was ridiculous too. She was a grown woman who had every right to invite a friend over for a visit when her fiancé was out of town, especially whe he was spending time in bars when he was supposed to be on a business trip.

She didn't need Annie to point out the red flags. But what was the point in talking about them when Nina didn't know what she wanted to do about them?

They ascended the basement stairs into the kitchen, Annie leading and Nina following as she cradled the small stack of journals like a newborn.

Annie packed her bag reluctantly before she turned to Nina with an earnest expression. "Promise me you'll keep in touch. I want updates on everything. Especially those diaries."

Nina nodded through a knot in her stomach. "I promise."

"And you'll be okay here alone?" It didn't look like Annie would believe a word she said.

"Remember, I have a gun." Nina tried to sound more confident than she felt.

"Tell Steve I said goodbye." Annie pulled her into a hug. "I'm only half-kidding."

She left after a final wave.

Then Nina stood there, watching until Annie's car turned onto the highway.

The weight of emptiness settled around her in the house as she locked the door behind her.

Then she made her way back down to the basement to clean up amid a whirlwind of unanswered questions.

Chapter Twenty

Nina's hands moved almost mechanically as she swept away the remnants of their frenzied discovery, gathering debris into garbage bags.

The journals were an unbelievable find — she might be the first person in the world to read Panda's diaries other than the girl herself. Who knew what she might discover as she pored over Panda's innermost thoughts leading up to the murder.

She might be the one to identify the killer and get justice for both Panda and for Galen Green, the man who was still in jail for her murder.

She half-wished that Will was going to be away longer, because she was sure he would have some reason why he didn't want her to read the journals. She would have to be sure to hide them someplace safe until she'd solved the case. The basement, probably.

Based on his reaction before, she was pretty sure he wouldn't come down here again if he didn't have to.

But that was okay. She kind of liked the idea of having a secret hideaway that he didn't know about.

A creak from somewhere overhead made her freeze in the middle of tying another bag. Then she heard footsteps, and her heart started beating hard against her ribs.

She had promised Annie she was safe thanks to her gun, but the weapon wouldn't do her any good upstairs in the bedroom.

She hadn't even thought to bring it down into the basement with her after Annie had gone. That decision might now be the death of her.

Except that was obviously ridiculous. Nina was being paranoid and—

More footsteps. Definitely not her imagination.

Right upstairs, in the kitchen.

She was trapped, if whoever was on the ground floor descended the stairs.

A wave of panic washed over her. She looked at the sledgehammer. Unwieldy, but at least a possible weapon.

Nina gripped the handle and hefted its weight as she tiptoed up the basement stairs, pausing at the top and listening intently.

The footsteps were further away now, their pace unhurried through the house.

Maybe Annie was back? Her car could have broken down, or she could have forgotten her computer.

Though thinking on it now, Nina had a distinct memory of Annie slipping the laptop into her bag.

"Annie?" Nina dared to call out as she entered the kitchen.

Her only response was the resuming of footsteps.

She tightened her grip on the sledgehammer as the sound of footsteps grew closer.

"Annie?" Louder this time, and filled with an excruciating note of hope.

Nina raised the sledgehammer with a pounding heart,

ready to defend herself against whoever was in her house, bracing herself against the approaching footsteps.

She entered the living room just as Will stepped into view, looking surprised and confused as he held a bouquet of blue hydrangea and orange roses.

The flowers were gorgeous, and Nina was speechless. Still gripping the sledgehammer, she felt a swirl of emotions: relief, confusion, and a simmering anger.

Then she realized that she'd left the journals out on the kitchen counter. She hoped he hadn't seen them.

"You're lucky I didn't knock you out." Her grip on the weapon relaxed, but for some reason she didn't put the sledgehammer down.

Will looked perplexed as his gaze shifted from Nina to the sledgehammer and back again.

"Annie?" He raised his eyebrows. "Why did you call out her name?"

Some tension left her body as she finally lowered the sledgehammer with an exhale, still not letting it go. "Annie came to stay with me. She just left about a half hour ago."

His expression shifted from confusion to annoyance. "Why didn't you tell me she was coming?"

"You were working."

"I should have known."

"It was spontaneous." She bristled at his tone. "Annie had some free time, and I needed the company. You were busy working, so what does it matter?"

"It matters because you should have told me." His voice was firm, and his stance rigid.

Frustration bubbled inside her, a rising tide that threatened to spill over. "I was planning on telling you. But from what I understood, you wouldn't be back until—
"

"I wanted to surprise you."

"Mission accomplished." Nina nodded at the flowers. "Are those for me?"

"Who else would they be for?" And then, almost as if he couldn't help it: "I didn't know there was even a chance that anyone else would be here."

What was his problem? Was he afraid that someone else would see him bringing flowers to his wife? Or was it specifically Annie who he didn't want to come home to?

Maybe because Annie would assume that the flowers were an apology for leaving Nina alone to fend off the intruder's next visit, and Will knew it.

Bruce might have even said something to Will about it.

Although, if he had, why wouldn't he mention Annie's visit?

Nina sighed and took the flowers from Will, bringing them into the kitchen. She pulled a vase out from the cabinet and filled it with water, carefully arranging the hydrangeas and roses with her back to Will, unable to shed the unease now slithering like a snake through her body.

Unease about Will's unexpected return, their almost-argument, and her lingering thoughts of the hidden room and its secrets.

And fear that he'd notice the journals before she had a chance to hide them again.

She turned around to find him staring at her.

"Why do you have drywall in your hair? And what's with the sledgehammer?" His voice mingled between concern and bewilderment. "Do I even want to know?"

Nina couldn't help glancing back at the secret door in the larder, still slightly ajar, and realized that she didn't want him to know.

But she didn't know why, any more than she understood why her first instinct had been to hide the journals. She just knew that she didn't trust his reaction.

Even though there was no reason for him to be angry at her for wanting to explore the house that he'd bought for her — knowing it held exactly the kind of secrets she loved to discover.

She couldn't tell him about the secret basement room.

Or the journals she'd found inside.

She couldn't tell him about inviting Steve over to dinner.

Apparently, she couldn't even let him know that Annie had stopped by for a visit without risking his anger.

Why didn't she trust the man she'd agreed to marry?

Red flag. That's what Annie would've said.

And it was getting harder for Nina to disagree.

"The sledgehammer is for protection. And you probably don't want to know the rest." She put the vase in the kitchen window, where it looked cheery in the golden sunlight streaming through the window. Then she scooped up the journals casually as she turned and strode out of the kitchen, calling over her shoulder without looking back, "I'm taking a shower."

She hurried upstairs, listening for signs that he was following, but he must've been hungry, because she heard the sound of one of those damn rose-covered plates clinking as he set it on the counter.

She slipped the journals into her nightstand drawer, pushing them to the back behind her sleep mask and e-reader. Next chance she got, she'd take them back down to the secret room and read them there.

Then she headed for the bathroom, to clean off the evidence of her remodeling project.

It was too late for Will to call anyone tonight about inspecting the basement. With luck, he would forget all about it by tomorrow.

But in case he didn't, she'd photograph the hidden room to preserve everything as Panda had left it.

Nina was now determined to crack this case, no matter what.

Chapter Twenty-One

THE WEIGHT of the day was still clinging to Will as he prepared for bed beside Nina.

His trip to Chicago had been demanding, more draining than productive. Testing the new software had proven to be even more tedious than expected, and he'd had to put up with Bruce's nonstop oversharing, which got more revolting as the trip went on. He didn't know how Annie could stand being married to the man.

Another reason to think that Annie wasn't a good influence on Nina. He'd been unable to hide his annoyance upon learning that Nina had asked her best friend to visit the second he had left the house and she hadn't mentioned it to him.

Rosie would never have gone behind his back like that.

But then, if Nina had been Rosie, he would have taken her to Chicago with him.

Nina spit into the sink as she finished brushing her teeth.

Then she said, "Did you go out at all while you were in Chicago?"

Why would she ask that? Was she descending into jealousy? There was no way she could know about the other thing he'd gone to Chicago to do.

"Nope." He caught her eye in the mirror and shook his head. "All work. Testing until we were too tired to do anything else."

But even as the words left his mouth he could see that Nina seemed skeptical, more than usual.

No one, not even Bruce, had known about his other errand.

Except Sarah, who'd seemed surprised to see him on her doorstep and had strenuously denied stalking him.

She had denied leaving the dead bird in their living room, too.

Of course he hadn't believed her, because Sarah was the only one who would ever send him a message like that. After that whole mess with the cockatiel—

No. He wasn't going to think about that. He'd been younger then, and still devastated from losing Rosie. Sarah had looked a lot like Rosie too, although her nose was less sharp and her blonde hair wavy rather than curly.

But her character had been nothing like Rosie's. He hadn't seen the warning signs of her jealousy until it was too late. Then she'd blamed everything on him. And the police believed her.

He'd thought Nina was above that kind of jealousy. But he'd learned his lesson — no talking about Rosie, no matter how many times she asked. Nina had to believe that he was over his first love, and that she was the only woman for him.

Will could sense her discomfort as they settled into bed, emanating from her body like a silent alarm. He lay back, exhausted, yearning for the comfort of sleep, but Nina's nightstand lamp was still on, and she seemed glued to her tablet.

"I've had a long day, Nina. Made even longer so I could get home to you sooner, since you were so unhappy about being 'stranded.' Can we please turn off the light?"

She hesitated, then with a quiet sigh, she powered the tablet down and reached over to turn off the lamp.

The room fell into darkness, save for the faint moonlight filtering in through the curtains.

Will turned toward her, reaching out, hoping to bridge the gap forming between them. But Nina remained still, her body tense and unyielding.

He considered his options for what might soften the mood, but tension was a blanket that suffocated every word before he could give it voice.

Will reached out again, but her body was unresponsive to his touch.

"Are you mad about something?"

"No." Her voice was flat, devoid of the warmth he yearned for.

"Then why don't you want to …?" The rejection would hurt more if he said it out loud.

"I thought you wanted to sleep."

Will lay back, feeling a chasm opening between them as he turned over, facing away from her and letting the nighttime silence envelop him.

After several long minutes, the soft rhythmic sounds of Nina's breathing beside him began lulling him into a state of drowsiness, enough for reality to blur in the light of his oncoming dreams.

He had no idea how long he had been sleeping when Nina jolted him awake with a shake and her urgent whispering.

"*I hear something.*"

But he'd had the locks changed before leaving, and the two of them had the only keys. So the only thing she could be hearing was the creaking of this old house.

"Is it you?" he grumbled.

"No. I—"

A sudden crash shattered the quiet and jarred Will all the way out of sleep.

He leaped out of bed, urgency propelling him in a flight across the room.

Maybe the intruder had discovered that their key no longer worked and had decided to break in the old-fashioned way.

He retrieved the gun in dim moonlight, its not-yet-familiar weight a cold reassurance in his hands. He checked the chamber.

"Stay here." His voice was firm, but she was already shaking her head.

"There's no way I'm letting you go down there alone."

So they crept downstairs together, every creak of the old house amplifying their collective anxiety. Eerie shadows transformed the familiar into the unknown. The perfectly safe into the sinister.

The house was silent as they reached the landing, but he felt an uninvited presence lurking in the darkness.

"Fair warning!" Will called out into the darkness. "I'm armed and excited to pull the trigger on any asshole I find inside my house in the middle of the night!"

His heart beat in a machine-gun rhythm despite the bravado of his tone.

Floorboards creaked underfoot with every step, echoing through the silent house. Whoever was down there would hear him coming. He tightened his grip on the gun.

Still no response, but now he heard a rustling in the living room.

And a scuffle of movement that seemed too erratic for a person.

"I will fill you with bullets!"

The silence persisted, stubborn and eerie, as Nina crept toward the living room beside him.

They entered together, Will's finger resting just outside the trigger guard.

He reached for the light switch and flicked it on.

The room flooded with light, banishing shadows and revealing the source of the noise like the lifting of a veil, transforming his fear into a bewildered gust of laughter.

Their uninvited guest was actually a pair of intruders: that same frantic cat from the other night, now chasing a bird that had somehow flown into their living room.

"Jesus Christ," Nina said after a long exhale. "How the hell did that cat get inside again?"

"Maybe you left a window open?" Will suggested as he lowered the gun.

"Of course I didn't leave a window open." Her reply was sharp as her gaze swept the room. "Paranoia and negligence are opposites."

"Fine. Maybe it was Annie. It's not like we checked every room before bed."

But they should have. He would from now on.

The bird eyed them warily, now perched atop a curtain rod.

Will set aside the gun, grabbed a nearby wicker basket, and carefully approached the bird, moving slowly to avoid startling it further.

With a well-timed swoop, he covered the bird with the basket. Gently sliding a magazine underneath to secure it, he carried his feathered captive outside.

The cool night air greeted him as he lifted the basket

and watched the bird beating a hasty retreat into the night sky.

Then Will turned back around to find Nina still standing in the living room with her arms wrapped around the cat and an expression of reluctant affection on her face.

"You need to put that thing outside," said Will, with as much finality as he could muster.

"The poor thing is trembling." She met his eyes with a silent plea. "Maybe we should keep it?"

"That cat probably belongs to someone else, Nina. We can't just keep someone's cat."

"Who could it possibly belong to? Steve is our nearest neighbor, and he already told me that the cat isn't his."

"Well, it's not ours either." Will stood by the door, holding it open, waiting for Nina to put the cat outside.

Reluctantly, she did, setting it on their front porch, where the cat hesitated for one long, pregnant beat before darting into the night.

They secured the house together, methodically checking every door and window and finding them all closed and latched. Will was irritated and confused, his thoughts circling back to how the cat and bird could have possibly gotten into the house with every window and door secured.

Will was far more troubled than he wanted Nina to know.

"How can you be sure that Annie didn't open a window? Maybe the bird and the cat got in while I was gone, and they've been inside this whole time."

"Stop blaming Annie. She didn't open a window. You should be much more concerned that the intruder could be back."

"So you're suggesting that someone picked the new locks just to toss a couple animals inside our house? Why?"

"I don't know. Maybe it's like Rivera said, the intruder wants to scare us."

"Maybe you were sleepwalking and you let them in. That makes more sense than any intruder."

"I was up here with you!"

"You could've come back to bed after letting them in."

"I did not sleepwalk, Will."

"How would you know, if you were asleep when it happened?"

Nina looked so angry, for a second Will was worried she was going to slap him. "I would know."

He rubbed his eyes, exhaustion from the travel and more seeping into his bones. "I'm too tired for this."

"I'm calling the police. I think we should have Rivera or someone else come check on us."

"Fine. You do that. Tell me what happens in the morning." He started toward the stairs. "I'm going to bed."

He slipped back under the covers, where the softness of his pillow and the warmth of his bed soon pulled him back into a heavy slumber.

His last thought was that Nina didn't appreciate everything he was doing for her. The life that he was trying to give her.

The life that Rosie had wanted.

Chapter Twenty-Two

Now that Will was ensconced in his office on a call, Nina locked the bedroom door and removed Panda's journals from her nightstand, sorting through them to find the earliest one.

She flipped to a random entry:

You already know that life at home is … terrible. I guess I can say that here.

Koala and I are both homeschooled, although the first part of that word is a lot more true than the second. It's like we're sheltered from the whole entire world here. Hidden away might be a better way to say it.

We're not allowed outside, because we "might catch colds." No friends, because they might be the "offspring of demons" or something equally ridiculous. And public school? According to Grizzly and Polar, they only teach blasphemy in those tainted classrooms.

Poor Koala gets the brunt of their vile nonsense. They tell me that my birthmark is the stain of Satan of my face. I've stared at it in the mirror a thousand times, trying to see the evil they speak of. All I see is a splash of red, like an accidental flick of paint from a brush onto the canvas.

Nighttime is my sanctuary. I lie awake as the house sleeps, my eyes fixed on the stars outside my window. They twinkle like distant dreams, worlds away from the suffocating walls of this house.

Those stars are my silent companions, my secret keepers, the bearers of my hopes for a better life.

I FOUND a recipe for chicken Cacciatore in one of Polar's old cookbooks today, nestled between the pages like a secret awaiting discovery. Of course she would never cook something like that. Polar never makes anything with flavor. Koala calls Polar's food "bland central."

There is never any adventure in her cooking. Or her life. That's why I can only dream of the day I make that recipe myself.

Koala wants to cook too, and I really want to teach her the little I know. Sometimes we pretend we're in the kitchen together. That Polar and Grizzly are gone. Or maybe even dead. Me and Koala are chopping and stirring and laughing while making whatever we want to make.

Maybe one day I'll have Polar's china. The dishes and bowls are covered with the most beautiful roses. Pretty enough for me to dream about. One of the few things about this place that I don't hate.

THE REALIZATION HIT her like a sledgehammer to the stomach. The china. It had belonged to the Byrds.

But the house had been empty when they'd let the movers in. How had the family's china gotten mixed in with their things?

The intruder. She and Will had left to buy groceries, and Nina had only noticed the box later that night, when she'd been looking for their dishes. Someone could've snuck in to leave the box of rose-covered china while they were out.

But why? And how did they get it in the first place? Was it possible their intruder as a member of the Byrd family?

The uncle. As far as Nina knew, he was still alive. As far as she could remember from the podcast, he'd never even been a suspect, the police were so certain that the drifter had killed Panda.

But if the uncle had snuck these dishes into the house, what message was he trying to send? Were they meant to be a threat? How did rose-covered dishes square with the dead bird on the wall?

None of it made sense.

As she read the passage again, Nina had another thought, this one hitting her even harder than the first.

Who was Koala? She wasn't the uncle. And Polar and Grizzly were clearly adults, surely Panda's parents.

Nothing she'd heard on the podcast or in the news had mentioned another child. Was it possible the Byrds had two children, but they'd kept one a secret?

Again, why?

Panda had called Koala *her.* So, a sister.

Nina kept reading.

THERE'S A PROBLEM. A big one.

Grizzly caught me with a Cosmopolitan magazine. Just a harmless thing, really, but to Grizzly and Polar it's contraband, and all contraband is bad. I found it on the road during one of my rare excursions outside. The pages were filled with images and stories about lives that read like the opposite of mine.

My punishment came swift and harsh like always.

Grizzly converted the basement into a bedroom for me — a cell, more like. I was confined there, away from Koala, and away from the meager comforts of my bedroom.

Those two weeks were an eternity. Each day dragged into a desolate landscape of solitude. The basement is a place of shadows and whispers, where ghosts seem to linger in the corners, watching me with unseen eyes.

But even amid the gloom, I could at least cling to the stars. They are always my beacon in the night, a reminder that there's a world outside this terrible place.

Maybe I'll be part of it someday.

MY DAYS ARE BLENDING into each other. The only thing different is this slow creeping of time that reminds me I'm still here, still trapped in this house that feels more like a prison.

Life beyond these walls seems like a distant dream, but it's a dream I cling to with all of me.

Our days are structured in a way that makes it feel like we're in the Army. Me and Koala are both only allowed out of the basement for meals and 'school.'

We eat our meals in silence, they watch our every move. Every bite.

But the worst part of each day comes in the evening. Bible lessons with Grizzly.

The name is a cruel joke, a mask for the horror that it really is. It's not about salvation or scripture. It's about control, about breaking us down until me and Koala are empty shells, compliant and subdued.

It's always the part of day I dread the most, the time when the shadows in my heart grow the darkest.

I've started using the old coal tunnel to sneak out of the house at night. It's my only escape, a brief respite from the suffocation of my existence.

. . .

Nina stifled a gasp of fear, even though there was no way Will could hear her all the way in his office.

A coal tunnel. In the basement. Big enough for a girl to sneak through.

That must be how the intruder was getting in. She was torn between her desire to jump out of bed and rush to the basement and her desire to discover what other secrets Panda's journal might reveal.

Nina promised herself she would find the tunnel later today, and turned the page.

Two nights ago I did something that I've never done before. It was reckless and daring. That made it the most exciting night of my life.

I stole a bike. I rode it for as long as I dared before coming back home.

The rush of wind in my hair, and the freedom of all that highway under my tires was intoxicating. I knew it couldn't last, but at least for an hour I was free, unchained from the burdens of my life in a basement.

Maybe I could run away forever? Stay on that bike long enough for someone to save me.

But as the adrenaline faded, reality set back in.

Of course I couldn't really run away. Not with Koala still trapped in the basement. Younger, smaller, more vulnerable. I wouldn't be able to take care of her if I took her with me.

And where would I go?

How far could I get before they found me?

The logistics of escape are a maze with no obvious exit.

So I went back home and hid the bike where it wouldn't be found.

I returned to my cell in the basement, to the life I long to leave behind forever.

But for right now, I can only wait. A few more years until we can escape this hell together. I'll keep dreaming until then. Of the stars, of open roads, of a life where I'm no longer just Panda, trapped in a basement.

And for now I'll keep praying that I don't get caught.

Grizzly and Polar always seem to know everything.

EVERY DAY I WAIT, hold my breath, wondering if Grizzly or Polar will discover my secret.

But the coal tunnel, my path to freedom, remains apparently undetected. It's my secret now, my small piece of power in this suffocating existence.

They have no idea that I've tasted the outside world, that I've felt the wind on my face and the thrill of freedom in my heart. With each passing day, their ignorance gives me a sense of strength, a feeling of control that I've never known before.

In this house, even the smallest victories feel monumental.

I'm planning to leave the house again. I can't help it. The pull of the outside world is too strong, the desire for freedom too intense. Last time, I biked all the way to Jackrabbit Ridge. I saw a group of kids, laughing and talking, alive in a way that I've never experienced with anyone other than Koala, and never without worrying that Grizzly or Polar might hear us.

I wondered what it would be like to have friends while watching them. To be part of their world. They seemed so carefree. So normal.

The longing was enough to drown me.

That time, my escape didn't go unnoticed. Grizzly found dirt on the basement floor. My stupid fault for tracking it in. I panicked and blamed it on the cat, our only other living companion in this dreary place.

Polar took him out behind the shed and drowned him. Just like that.

The guilt eats at me. I can still hear the yowling in my mind, see the cat's trusting eyes looking up at me. I feel sick, sick with guilt and grief and a rage that burns deep inside me.

I have to be more careful. My secret escapes can't put anyone else at risk, not even a cat. I have to be smarter. I can't let Grizzly and Polar find out, or take this away from me.

But the lingering fear never leaves me.

The incessant terror that they'll find out, and make me suffer the consequences is unbearable. It's a cage tightening around my heart.

I have to be strong. Especially for Koala.

I will keep my secret. And I will keep dreaming of the stars gleaming over open road.

Then one day, I will leave this bad place behind. For good.

Chapter Twenty-Three

Nina snapped the journal shut as she heard Will's footsteps in the hallway.

She shoved the little book back into her nightstand drawer, then jumped up to unlock the bedroom door, pulling it open just as Will reached for the knob.

"You're awake," he said awkwardly.

"I was just about to do laundry."

And check out the basement to look for the secret tunnel in the secret room.

Will gave her a look she couldn't read, then nodded. She grabbed the laundry basket and set it on the bed, then opened up the suitcase he'd left in the corner, still packed with his dirty clothes from his Chicago trip, and started loading them into the basket.

"Coffee in the press downstairs," he said before leaving her to her chores.

A moment later, she heard him settle into his office chair as he muttered something about customer support.

She snatched up the laundry basket and headed downstairs. As she passed his office, she saw that the door was slightly ajar. She could hear the soft tapping of keys coming from inside.

Great. He wouldn't be coming downstairs for a little while. She had plenty of time to investigate.

The secret room loomed in her peripheral vision as she entered the basement, but she forced herself to ignore it as she turned the dial on the washing machine and heard it humming to life.

She dumped the clothes in with some soap, then made her way back upstairs, intending to pour herself some of that coffee Will had mentioned, to help her wake up while she searched.

But the door leading into the larder was closed. She didn't remember closing it.

She gave it a shove, but the door wouldn't budge. She hadn't noticed a lock before — had she missed it?

Nina knocked gently at first, then louder when she heard no response.

"Will?" Her voice was tinged with worry.

Still, no answer.

Now she was feeling claustrophobic, her heart pounding as her lungs worked harder to suck in air. Was this what a panic attack felt like?

She felt some sympathy for Will's reaction when she'd insisted he come down here to look at the water valve. Had he ever been locked in a dark place like this?

She'd never pushed him to talk about what happened to Rosie, or for anything that he didn't feel like volunteering about his childhood. And he'd barely volunteered anything.

Nina wondered if he'd had parents like Panda's, who'd locked him in a basement or an attic, or maybe a closet.

She didn't have to imagine how easy it would be to fall

apart while locked in a small, dark space with no idea when someone might open the door.

She was close to falling apart right now, even knowing that sooner or later Will would come looking for her.

She would be terrified if the only person who could let her out was the person who'd shut her up in here.

"WILL!" She banged harder on the door. "WILL, CAN YOU HEAR ME?"

Nina could picture him sitting behind his desk, eyebrows narrowed at the screen, door closed and AirPods in, to make it even clearer that he did not wish to be interrupted.

She sat on the top stair, her gaze fixed on the shadowy basement depths.

A flicker of movement caught her eye, and there it was — the cat, meandering through the dim light.

"The tunnel," she muttered under her breath. Of course. Panda had found her escape through the tunnel. If it was still there, Nina should be able to get out the same way. Assuming no one had blocked it off since Panda's death.

Their intruder's ability to sneak in even after the locks had been changed suggested that the tunnel was still accessible.

Gathering herself, she descended the stairs toward the cat.

It paused in front of her. Turned its head and meowed as if beckoning her to follow.

Nina obliged, trailing behind the feline through the basement, over to a far corner, where it passed behind a bare-edged full-length mirror leaned up against the wall.

She moved the mirror to one side, revealing the entrance to a small tunnel, barely visible in the shadows.

The cat trotted into the darkness.

Nina hesitated, a mix of fear and intrigue battling within her.

Then she got down on her belly and crawled cautiously into the tunnel.

Rough cement turned to dirt beneath her. The confined space was claustrophobic, the air stale and thick with the scent of earth. Occasionally, she felt the hardness of metal embedded in the ground, the remainder of the track that once brought coal in for the boiler, back in the days before central heating got installed.

She felt her chest tighten along with the narrowing tunnel. Panic fluttered inside her like a trapped bird. But Nina pushed forward, even as the walls seemed to close in around her.

For a moment, she was stuck, the weight of the house pressing down on her, forcing the breath out of her lungs in punctuated gasps as the sudden fear that she would be trapped forever in this forgotten passage suddenly gripped her body like a vice.

With a burst of adrenaline, she managed to wriggle free.

The tunnel was too narrow to turn back around, the path behind her now as daunting as the unknown ahead.

She crawled onward as the rough walls scraped her hands and knees. Darkness was absolute, a void to infinity. Her only guide was the faint sound of the cat ahead of her, practically prancing as its soft paws padded against the dirt.

Time softened in the tunnel's embrace. Her thoughts blurred as she focused solely on moving forward, each inch gained a small victory against the suffocating darkness.

The space finally began to widen, giving way to a larger area.

She saw a wooden door ahead, part of it broken and askew on its hinges.

With trembling hands, she pushed it open.

Same as Panda must have done all those years ago, escaping her home prison without Grizzly or Polar (obviously her parents) knowing.

Nina emerged from the hidden passage near the road, heart pounding in her chest like a war drum. The world seemed blindingly bright after all that burrowing darkness.

She stood there disoriented, trying to process what had just happened.

The cat, her unexpected guide through that maze under the house, now sat calmly at her feet, looking up at Nina as if nothing out of the ordinary had happened.

She bent down and scooped it up into her arms, its warmth and soft fur grounding her as she began walking back to the house.

Will appeared at the front door, his expression concerned and confused as he spoke. Edgy, if not outright angry. "What the hell happened to you?"

He rushed down the steps to face her, eyeing the cat on his way.

Why was he so angry? She hadn't done anything wrong.

Nina opened her mouth to explain how she'd been trapped in the basement until the cat lead her to the tunnel. But then she realized that she would have to tell him about breaking through to the secret room and what she'd found inside — and some part of her rebelled at that. It was his home too, he had the right to know. It was possible that the tunnel was how the intruder was getting in.

But she was afraid that if Will found out about the secret room, he might forbid her to go down there, maybe even seal it off to keep her from exploring it. And she had to unlock its clues.

Nina couldn't tell him about the secret room or the tunnel or the journals, because she didn't trust him not to get angry and decide for her. He was so adamant about letting go of the past and moving forward — despite the fact that he definitely hadn't moved on from Rose.

She could hear Annie's voice in her head: *Red flag! Red flag!*

Annie was right. If he'd acted like this a month or two ago, Nina would have broken up with him. Or asked him for some space. The fact that they were living together now complicated things, but it wasn't the engagement, or the fact he'd bought her a house. If she flew back to Chicago and showed up on Annie's doorstep tonight, her best friend would usher her to the guest room and tell her she could stay indefinitely.

But she felt a strange responsibility to Panda. If she left now, she might never find the clue that would point her toward the real killer. Nina was staying until she did — or was sure she never would.

So she said, "I was digging around in the garden, and I must've stepped on the cat, because she yowled and ran off. I felt bad, so I followed her out here, to make sure she was okay."

Will's expression said he thought she'd lost her mind. "Were you digging or just rolling around in the dirt? You're filthy."

"I tripped." A lame excuse but she failed to think of anything better.

"When you stepped on the cat?"

Nina nodded. Then before Will could say anything else, she blurted, "We're keeping the cat. And we're naming it Whisper."

Will looked at her, then at the cat, and in a defeated voice he said, "Whisper it is."

He started back into the house.

Nina followed, still cradling the cat in her arms. She waited until she was sure he'd returned to his office, then put Whisper down and mumbled, "good kitty" before hurrying to the larder, the door still ajar as she'd left it.

She pushed on the hidden door to the basement, and it swung open easily.

But it had definitely been stuck before. She opened and shut it several times to see if it might jam.

It did not.

Nina couldn't help wonder if Will had noticed she'd gone down with the laundry and had decided to play another joke on her by holding the door shut when she'd tried to come back up. Just like he'd jumped out of the shadows to try to scare her before.

But if that was so, why hadn't Will been laughing when he came out to join her? Why would he be so angry if his prank had worked?

She would make a point to leave the hidden door ajar in the future. Find a rock to use as a doorstop to wedge it open, if need be, so she wouldn't get trapped down there again.

Nina went upstairs and shed her dirty clothes, but decided to open her laptop and navigate to the Riddles in the Dark forum before hopping in the shower.

Then over to the Byrd Murders page where Annie had posted pics and invited questions.

The forum loaded and Nina noticed a new direct message from Byrd91.

She clicked on the message.

Byrd91: *You're not really in the Byrd house.*

Nina: *I am.*

Byrd91: *Prove it. Tell me something about the basement.*

Nina paused, thinking. Then, she typed out one of the Bible quotes she remembered from Panda's journal: *Whoever spares the rod hates his son, but he who loves him is diligent to discipline him.*

Byrd91: *Children, obey your parents in the Lord, for this is right.*

Her heart skipped a beat.

How did they know another of the quotes on the wall? That was much too specific for Nina to believe it was a guess.

Nina: *Who am I speaking with?*

Byrd91: *That's not important.*

Nina: *I found some journals in the house. They seem to be written by Panda.*

Byrd91: *What do they say?*

Her fingers hovered over the keyboard. Nina knew she should be cautious but felt a strange connection with this anonymous source, or at least a belief that they could scratch her itch of curiosity like no one else could.

Nina: *They're written in code. It's like Panda was hiding something.*

Byrd91: *Of course they were hiding something. What kind of code?*

Nina: *No names are directly mentioned in the journals. I'm trying to figure out more about the Byrds. Grizzly and Polar were the parents, right?*

Byrd91: *Yes.*

Nina: *And who was Koala?*

Byrd91: *Panda's younger sibling.*

Another piece of the puzzle clicked into place.

Nina: *Are you Koala?*

The screen remained static. She stared at the blinking cursor. Her—

"Nina?"

She slammed the lid of her laptop closed and slipped it under the bed.

Whisper meowed softly, as if sensing the change in the room's atmosphere.

Nina stood, scooping up the laundry basket and heading for the stairs.

Will was waiting for her in the hallway with an expression of tentative hope. "I was thinking that maybe we could go out for dinner tonight? I found a place in Glenburn."

Nina forced a smile, wishing she was really feeling it. "Sounds nice."

"Can't wait." He smiled back.

His seemed real.

She went to take her shower.

But no matter how hard Nina scrubbed, she didn't feel clean.

Chapter Twenty-Four

THE RHYTHMIC CHOPPING of Nina's knife against the cutting board was a small comfort she desperately needed. Will had promised dinner out, so she would keep lunch simple.

Cooking was an anchor. The meal was half done and she felt almost all the way grounded by the time Will came into the kitchen. Same as always, his presence filled the entire space immediately.

He wrapped his arms around Nina from behind in a hug that was both surprising and familiar. More comforting than the cooking, if she allowed it to be.

"I love you," he murmured, his breath warm against her ear.

The sincerity she heard in his voice gave Nina pause. Her heart fluttered with mixed emotions. She knew how he could be, on both sides of the emotional spectrum.

And that made her heart like a bird trapped in its cage.

"I'm heading into town to pick up some office supplies," he said. "Need anything?"

Besides for you to explain to me why you're so angry these days?

"Some chives, maybe. And Napa cabbage, if they have it. I was thinking about making a stir-fry tomorrow."

"You got it." He kissed the side of her neck, then left her alone with her thoughts.

She still couldn't explain why she'd lied to avoid telling him about the tunnel. Explaining how the intruder had gotten into their house would make him feel better — knowing the tunnel was blocked should help him relax, knowing they were now safe and that there would be no more late night intrusions.

Feeling unsafe was probably the source of his anger, so telling him about the tunnel should put a stop to their fighting. Right?

But some part of her warned that telling him would make things worse, and she had no idea why.

Nina watched him leave, his Infinity disappearing down the driveway as her heart beat with apprehension and relief.

She finally had the house to herself.

At the very top of her list of things to do was check for a DM from Byrd91 on the forums. But Nina had barely been alone for five minutes before there was a knock at her front door.

She expected Steve, because unless Will was back, who else could it possibly be?

But she was surprised to find Officer Rivera standing on her porch with an expression stuck somewhere between concern and curiosity as Nina opened the door.

"Is Will home?" Rivera asked, her eyes searching past Nina into the house.

"No," Nina replied, her voice steady despite the surprise. "He just stepped out."

"May I come in?" Rivera's request was polite yet firm,

still holding Nina's gaze with an intensity that hinted at something more urgent than casual conversation.

Nina hesitated a beat, then stepped aside so the officer could enter.

Rivera wasn't even fully inside before Nina blurted her most pressing question. "Do you know anything more about the bird?"

Rivera nodded, her voice even. "Vet said that a car hit it."

"So, the bird wasn't killed intentionally?"

"Yes." Rivera nodded. "According to the vet."

A small wave of relief washed over Nina.

"You look relieved."

"Of course I'm relieved. That's better than a bird being murdered to leave us some sort of twisted message."

Rivera nodded, but there seemed to be something she was keeping to herself.

"How are you finding it out here?" Rivera scanned the room.

For what, Nina didn't know.

"Fine," she responded, perhaps a bit too quickly.

Her heart rate ticked up as Rivera leaned against the kitchen counter, posture relaxed and gaze alarmingly sharp.

"I read Will's file," said Rivera.

"Will has a file?" Wouldn't he have to have committed a crime for the police to have a file on him? "What are you talking about?

"I'm talking about Will sending a dead bird to an ex-girlfriend. She felt threatened enough to report him to the police."

Her mouth felt suddenly dry. She blinked twice in rapid succession, then stared at Rivera.

"I'm taking it you didn't know about that slice of your fiancé's past?"

"No." Nina shook her head, finally able to swallow. "No, I did not."

Rivera studied her for a moment. "Any reason Will might want to scare you?"

"I can't think of any reason." She shook her head. "He even bought a gun so I would feel safer."

"You don't feel like he might be isolating you?" Rivera raised her eyebrows. "Have you been dependent solely on him?"

The officer's suggestion struck a nerve.

Nina tried to laugh it off, but it came out forced. "Of course not."

"Please don't be offended, it's part of my job to ask," Rivera said slowly. "Has he ever been violent with you, or expressed violent intentions? Threatened you in any way?"

"No," Nina said, although from Rivera's expression, she wondered if her answer had come fast enough to sound like a false denial. "He's never hit me, or threatened to."

"Have you ever been afraid that he might?"

That should've been an easy *no* too, but the same part of Nina that didn't trust Will with knowledge of the tunnel didn't trust him not to get that angry, either.

She was ashamed to admit her fear, because either she was overreacting, which wasn't fair to Will, or she was staying with someone she should leave, which made her feel like an idiot, and anything he did to her if she stayed, it would be her fault, wouldn't it?

Red flag! Annie's voice screamed in her head. It was getting harder and harder to argue with that voice.

But Nina was the only person in the world who could

get justice for Panda. If she left now, she might never find the clue that singled out the killer.

Will would be back from his errands any minute, and Nina had no desire to explain to him why Rivera had stopped by. Things were complicated enough as it was.

"I'm not afraid of my fiancé, but I appreciate your concern." Nina glanced toward the door: *Time to go.*

"Well, if you ever need anything." Rivera handed Nina her card. "Call."

Nina took the card with a nod.

She stood in the doorway watching the officer leave with a chill creeping up her spine, the featherweight card feeling like a brick in her hand as a whisper of thought she couldn't quite grasp got louder and louder and LOUDER.

It only occurred to her then that maybe she should tell Rivera about the tunnel. At least let her know that part of the case could be closed.

But it would seem like she was afraid of Will if she asked Rivera not to mention it. And Will be furious if he found out that she had been hiding it from him. Nina was sure of it, even though she couldn't explain why.

She would find a more permanent solution for blocking it instead, and once the intrusions stopped, Will would finally relax and they would get back to the place they'd been before leaving Chicago.

Or so Nina hoped.

As the door clicked shut, she was struck by a haunting thought: *Was this house, her supposed engagement present, really a cage whose key was held by a man she no longer trusted?*

Chapter Twenty-Five

WILL ADJUSTED the rearview mirror as he navigated his Infinity through the winding roads to Glenburn, Nina in the passenger seat, staring at who knew what. The sunset, perhaps. It was pretty spectacular, painting the evening sky in shades of eggplant and orange.

Silence reigned inside the car, except for the softly humming engine. He'd had to take another dose of meds this afternoon after looking out his window and seeing Nina on all fours in the grass outside, looking like she'd been rolling in the mud.

He had rushed out, thinking the worst, only to discover that there was no attack and she had simply been playing with the goddamned cat.

But it could've been worse. She could've been poking around in the basement.

Rosie never would have scared him like that. The more time they spent here, the harder it was for him to see Nina filling her shoes.

Maybe it *had* been a mistake to buy the house. Maybe he should have kept Nina in the city where she was happy.

But that felt like compromising on the vision he and Rosie had shared. If he could just help Nina see what they could have together, their lives could be perfect.

"It's cute," Nina opined with a nod as the restaurant he'd chosen came into view.

"*Cute?*" Will repeated.

Grass was the nicest place in Glenburn, the closest Nina could ever find to the kinds of places they'd left behind in Chicago. But this place was better, because you didn't have to tolerate all the noise and stench and traffic to enjoy it.

Rosie would've loved it. She hadn't been spoiled by the decadence of city life.

"Rustic." Nina tried another word.

"It's definitely that."

The wooden facade was weathered to a soft gray, with creeping ivy climbing its edges like nature's embroidery. A pair of fat oak barrels flanked the front entrance, over-flowing with a vibrant array of wildflowers. A hand-painted sign hung above the door, its curling letters beckoning diners inside the restaurant.

"Have you ever eaten here?" Nina asked.

"When would I have eaten here?"

"I don't know." She shrugged. "When you came to look at the house. Before you bought it."

"No." He shook his head. "I wanted to wait until we could try it together."

Grass was a cozy haven inside, with warm light raining down on the wooden tables and polished bar. Walls were decorated with vintage farming tools and local artwork. The restaurant felt inviting yet intimate.

Nina's posture subtly shifted as they approached the hostess stand, a hint of her usual self-consciousness creeping in. Will noticed the way she seemed to shrink ever so slightly, her gaze darting to the hostess then quickly away.

"No one is looking at you," he reassured her with a whisper.

"I'd feel more comfortable somewhere darker, less visible."

"Would you mind seating us at a table in the back?" Will asked when they approached the hostess, pointing toward the farthest corner. "Over there would be perfect."

"Of course." She nodded, plucking two menus from a stack before leading them to a table.

Will scanned the wine list as a server approached their table.

Her smile was wide and welcoming. Early twenties, with bright eyes and a cascade of auburn hair. "Good evening. I'm Bailey, and I'll be taking care of you tonight. Can I start you off with something to drink?"

Will glanced at the wine list again. "Yes, we'll have a bottle of the Chateau Ste. Michelle Cabernet Sauvignon, please. And some water for both of us."

"Excellent choice," Bailey nodded, jotting it down. "I'll be right back with your wine and water."

He opened his menu, unsure of how to initiate the conversation he wished to have with Nina.

She did the same, browsing the menu with her gaze, and fingers tracing the line of entrees. She didn't seem excited about anything. Probably comparing each dish to the overpriced versions she was used to eating in the city.

She would come to appreciate this place. Will would keep bringing her here until she finally did.

"What are you thinking?" he asked.

"Maybe the salmon. Or the steak. I don't know. How about you?"

"Salmon swims, steak walks. Either way, they both end up on a plate." He shrugged. "We could do both."

"Steak never walks. Cows walk before they're steak. Salmon always swims."

"Good point." He hoped she couldn't tell how annoyed he was right now. But food would help. "Why don't we both order a steak, and we can split an order of salmon."

"Yummy." Nina smiled and closed her menu. "So, how was Chicago?"

"It was all work, as usual."

"And you never got to leave the office?"

"I already told you that I didn't." He tried not to snap. "Why do you keep asking?"

"Just making conversation." She shrugged, her gaze flitting away for a blink before meeting his again. "If I'd been in Chicago, I would've taken advantage of the town."

Will wondered again if Bruce had seen him with Sarah and had passed the info on to Nina through Annie. But he was sure that Bruce knew nothing about his ex — including that Will had gone to Chicago to warn her away from Nina.

More likely, Nina's jealousy was petulance triggered by his absence. She had wanted to come with him. He'd refused to allow it, so she naturally imagined him with another woman. When all he wanted was to marry her and start enjoying the life that had been stolen from him when Rosie died.

The life he deserved.

Nina would deserve it too, if she would just let herself.

Bailey returned to the table, opening the wine and pouring a taste for Will.

He nodded his approval, and she filled their glasses.

"Are you ready to order, or do you need a few more minutes?" Bailey asked.

They placed their orders, then Bailey whisked away with a promise to return soon.

The restaurant hummed around them. A soft buzz of conversation and the clinking of cutlery that made for a pleasant soundtrack to their own private world.

Will took a sip, appreciating the wine's depth and complexity.

But Nina seemed lost in thought, her gaze occasionally wandering to the other diners before returning to him. Her jealousy was so unbecoming, but Will didn't know how to dispel it without telling her the truth and upsetting her more. It was hard not to resent that she didn't appreciate what he'd just done for her, even though she couldn't possibly understand that she was finally safe.

But then Nina surprised him.

"This was a nice idea, going out tonight." She reached across the table to touch his hand. "Thank you."

"I thought we needed to get out of the house." Her hand felt warm on his. "How is Annie doing?"

"She's good." A pregnant sigh. "I wish you two would get along better."

"We get along fine."

"You're both important to me."

"But I'm more important, right?" Will teased lightly, a half-smile playing on his lips.

"Of course," Nina said.

He wanted to believe her.

Then Bailey was back with their food, setting beautifully-plated steak and salmon on the table. Will inhaled the aroma of grilled meat and savory seasonings.

Bailey left and the silence returned to their table as he and Nina ate in another lingering silence, punctuated by forks and knives on their plates amid all the conversation rolling toward them from neighboring tables.

Will savored his steak, cooked to surprising perfection, while Nina mostly ignored hers, seemingly keen on eating more than her share of the salmon.

"What if we moved up our wedding date?" He finally broached the topic that had been highest on his mind, not counting her obsession.

If Nina was immersed in wedding preparations, she wouldn't have time for jealousy or obsessing over their new home's history or finding a new job. Once she was officially his, it would be easier to push for kids.

And now that he had taken care of their intruder, they could finally settle in and make the house their own.

"Neither of us have families to invite," he added. "We could go to the courthouse next weekend in Bismarck."

"I really want Annie there." Nina's voice soft but firm, fork paused in front of her mouth.

"Of course." He tried not to show the flicker of annoyance on his face. "We wouldn't want to forget about Annie."

Bailey came back with a dessert menu, but Will waved her away. He just wanted to get home and go to bed.

"Let's go for a drive before heading home," Nina suggested on their way to the car.

"A drive to *where*?"

"How about Jackrabbit Ridge?"

That was how she wanted to end their evening out? Seriously?

Jackrabbit Ridge was the kind of total shit hole that tourists ate up, with hundred-year-old buildings that had peeling paint and hand-lettered signs that weren't vintage so much as too expensive to update when business depended on a summer's worth of tourists to shore up the losses of the other three seasons.

Nina would probably find it adorable.

But he didn't. He knew exactly what it was like to grow up in a decaying small town whose economy was dying by inches.

"I change my question from *Where?* to the much more appropriate *Why?*"

"Why not, Will? What else do we have to do?"

"We could go home and celebrate." He hoped his suggestive tone would tease out the coy smile he loved so much on her.

Instead, it earned him a deflated sigh. "I'm a little sore from all the work in the garden today."

Liar, he thought, pasting on a smile as he opened the car door for her. "Then let's go home and get some sleep. We've got a lot of planning to do tomorrow."

Maybe she would be more receptive at home.

But once there, they got ready for bed fast, and their goodnight didn't go like Will had been wanting or expecting. She reached for her e-reader and his patience snapped.

"If you're going to read that, I'll sleep in the office."

"No, I won't read it." Her reply came quick, almost desperate.

But Will was already halfway to the door. "Read. It's fine."

He entered his office to see the stupid cat — Whisper — lounging on the couch.

He scooped it up without a word and put it outside.

Then Will settled grumpily onto the couch.

Nina appeared in his doorway moments later, looking apologetic.

Good. She should apologize, after rejecting an evening's worth of attempts to make her feel wanted and cared for.

"I'm sorry, Will. Please, come back to bed." She came over and stood next to him.

Her approach was gentle, and her touch inviting. His anger and frustration melted away under the warmth of her seduction.

That was more like it.

Chapter Twenty-Six

I RETURNED to Jackrabbit Ridge again.

That same group of kids was there, and their laughter was a melody I longed to be part of.

Then I met Sloth. He was different from anyone I've ever met before. He seems to know everyone in Jackrabbit Ridge, but not me. That's why he kept looking at me with such curious eyes. Like I was a puzzle he felt desperate to solve.

Sloth is kind, with an attentiveness that feels both comforting and unnerving. I find myself drawn to him, his easy demeanor and genuine interest in me.

It was strange and exhilarating, finally talking to someone who knew nothing about the prison of my everyday life. Sloth can't believe that I don't have a phone or an email address.

"How do you stay connected with the world?" he asked.

I just gave him a sad smile. What else could I say?

We agreed to meet again, away from prying eyes at a secluded spot by the river.

My heart almost stopped when I sneaked back home to see Koala on my bed, her eyes wide with fear and excitement.

Panic surged through me, wondering if she had told Grizzly or

Polar about my escapes. But Koala crossed her heart as fast as she could, swearing that she hadn't breathed a word and never ever would. I believed her.

Koala would never betray me. She would never do anything to hurt me.

And besides, Grizzly hadn't come down with his belt. If he knew where I'd been, I would be bruised and bleeding before I went to sleep that night for sure.

Koala was eager to hear about my adventures outside of the house. We curled up on the bed together, and I told her everything, not even needing to elaborate on my story because the truth was unbelievable enough. I painted a picture of freedom and wonder that I could barely believe myself.

Koala's eyes sparkled with amazement as she asked a million questions about the outside world.

Is it true that people who don't go to church turn into stone?

Do stars fall from the sky because they are angels coming to visit us?

Do people who listen to music other than hymns get cursed?

Does lightning strike people who think bad thoughts?

Worry gnawed at me the next time I went to meet Sloth.

What if he didn't show up? What if his interest in me was only a fleeting curiosity that had already left him?

But as I approached the riverside, I saw Sloth waiting alone.

He greeted me with a smile and a small bag of candy — Pop Rocks. I had never tasted anything like candy before. The sensation of them exploding in my mouth was like nothing I'd ever experienced. Or even imagined. The candy was magical, because every burst was like more freedom exploding in my mouth.

We walked along the river, talking and laughing. Sloth held my hand, and for a moment, I imagined I could live a different kind of life, one where holding hands and eating candy was normal. Not a sin that would earn me yet another lecture and the belt.

Koala was waiting for me at home again. I gave her some of the Pop Rocks I had saved. Her delight was infectious, her joy at the simple pleasure made the risk even more worth it.

Now Koala is even more enthusiastic about my outings with Sloth.

We agreed to meet again on Friday night.

But Kodiak is coming to the house.

And Kodiak's visits always mean pretending that everything is "normal."

Kodiak called the authorities last time. Then a man and a woman showed up here at the house, wanting to take Koala and me away.

Grizzly and Polar made sure that didn't happen. They made me and Koala lie. We both had to say that we liked living in our prison, except we had to pretend it we got to live upstairs, in the nice part of the house, no matter how many times or in how many different ways that man and woman asked us.

But Kodiak is kind, and always bring gifts and smiles for me and Koala, no matter how much Grizzly and Polar disapprove.

The best part about Kodiak's visits is being allowed upstairs to cook. Shepherd's pie for sure, and always some other stuff.

With Kodiak here, Grizzly will stay away from our room for Bible readings.

So for a few days me and Koala can escape from the worst terror of our nights.

Chapter Twenty-Seven

Nina's eyes fluttered open to gentle morning light filtering in through the curtains. The other side of the bed wasn't just empty, the sheets were cool to the touch.

So Will had been up for a while.

She stretched, the prior night lingering like a half-forgotten dream. After Will had finished, Nina had waited until she was sure he was sleeping before sneaking the journals out of her nightstand and taking them down to the hidden basement room to read without fear of discovery.

First, she had dragged the trash bags full of drywall to the tunnel's entrance and plugged it, to be sure the intruder couldn't surprise her if they returned.

Then she'd spent half the night devouring Panda's musings, searching for clues.

Nina couldn't be sure, but she'd bet that Kodiak was the uncle who had disappeared after inheriting what little was left of the family fortune. And then there was Sloth, Panda's new friend, although Nina suspected he would become more to her than that.

Unfortunately, as moving as the young girl's entries

were, they left few clues as to what had happened the night of her death. Maybe Nina needed to read further ahead, but she wanted to get the whole story before arriving at a conclusion.

After showering fast and getting dressed even faster, Nina moved quietly through the still house. The sound of Will's footsteps on the stairs startled her — right as a flash of movement drew her attention away from the mirror and over to the window.

Nina was staring outside when Will entered the bedroom with a cup of coffee. But the mysterious figure who had appeared out of nowhere at the end of their driveway was already gone.

She turned around and Will offered her the mug with a tentative smile.

"I brought you coffee."

"Thank you," Nina said as she took it.

"But really, I just wanted to apologize for being a shit yesterday." He gave her a sheepish smile.

"Well then, thank you even more." She smiled back as the warmth seeped deeper into her fingers.

"What were you looking at?"

Her gaze returned to the window. "I thought I saw someone in the driveway. And I figured it had to be you, but I could also hear you on the stairs. And now you're here. So it was obviously just my imagination."

"You don't sound like you really believe it was your imagination." He joined her at the window and scanned the empty driveway. "Where did you see him?"

Maybe he was only humoring her after being such an asshole last night, but Nina appreciated his finally hearing what she had to say, regardless of the reason.

"Somewhere near the gate." She pointed vaguely

toward a spot outside. "I'm not exactly sure. It was a flash, gone by the time I was actually looking."

"Wait here. I'll go check it out. Give me a wave when I get to where you saw him."

Where you saw him. Instead of, *Where you think you saw him.*

Nina nodded.

Will grabbed the gun, then disappeared downstairs.

Nina stayed at the window, sipping her coffee while staring at the empty driveway, waiting to wave at Will. She pushed the window open. Cool morning air kissed her face as she leaned out.

A moment later, he emerged from the house, stepping down from the porch and moving briskly toward the driveway.

She watched intently, her heartbeat starting to gallop despite the lack of danger.

"STOP!" Nina shouted when Will reached what seemed like the appropriate spot in their driveway, her voice sending a slight echo into the morning stillness.

He scanned the area.

"I don't see anyone!" Will yelled back with a note of confusion.

His attention shifted to something on the ground.

He bent down and retrieved a small object that Nina couldn't see.

"What is it?" she called out.

But Will didn't reply. He just stood there, examining whatever it was in his hand.

Nina hurried downstairs, her coffee splashing onto the steps as she descended through the living room and out the front door.

She met Will in the driveway. He was holding up a small, familiar-looking packet.

"It's a box of Pop Rocks." He sounded bewildered.

The revelation made sense to Nina, and it chilled her blood to hear the words *Pop Rocks* out loud after reading them in Panda's journal. What if Sloth was the intruder?

That didn't make sense — if Panda was dead, why would Sloth want to hang around the house?

Unless he, too, was trying to find the killer.

Or… he could *be* the killer, trying to scare Nina and Will off for fear that they would discover his identity.

But she couldn't share her theories with Will, not without revealing the journals and the tunnel and the secret basement room.

"Pop Rocks?" She asked casually.

Will shrugged, staring at the packet in one hand while still gripping the pistol in his other one. "I guess whoever you saw dropped them."

Nina took a closer look at the packet. Vibrant colors and a cartoonish explosion on the package seemed oddly out of place in the morning serenity. "Seems like a strange thing to lose."

"Maybe it was just kids fooling around. They could have been daring each other to step foot on the 'haunted property.'"

"I don't think it was a kid." She shook her head.

"What did this person look like?"

"He was too far away to make out any real details." Nina shrugged, doing her best to remember. "Dark coat, jeans, boots. He had a hood up, so I couldn't see his face. And he was gone in a blink after I got to the window."

"Could it have been a woman?"

Why would he ask that? Was there another woman in the picture that she needed to worry about?

"I guess so, if she was tall and slender."

He looked relieved by that, and Nina couldn't help but wonder if he had a short, curvy mistress in Chicago.

She tore open the packet of Pop Rocks and watched the colorful candies as they tumbled into her palm. She had the odd feeling that they had been left just for her, even though that was ridiculous. Like so many other things that had been happening recently.

Except… What if Sloth had been sneaking in through the tunnel to spend time in the hidden room, to remember Panda? He would have searched the basement and found the diaries.

And when Nina took the diaries upstairs to hide them in her nightstand, he might have come back and found them missing.

If he'd read them, he'd know that Nina would eventually read the entry about how Sloth had introduced Panda to Pop Rocks. He could've left the candy as a message: *I'm still here and I haven't forgotten.*

Nina raised her hand toward her mouth.

Will's eyes widened in disbelief. "You're not seriously going to eat those, are you?"

"The package was sealed. And they haven't been out here for long. Why let them go to waste?" Popping the candies into her mouth, she felt the familiar crackle and fizz. She tried to imagine Panda tasting them for the first time, after a lifetime of Polar's bland cooking.

Will scanned the surroundings again, his gaze intense as he looked up and down the road. "Did you see a car?"

She shook her head again. "No car." A thought crossed her mind, and she blurted it out before she could stop herself. "Do you think it could have been Steve?"

"Why would it be Steve?"

She wished she could un-say it. Now Will was scowling at her so hard, she wouldn't be surprised if he accused her of cheating on him with Steve. But she couldn't explain that she'd been wondering if Steve could be Sloth.

"He's our closest neighbor, and a mile isn't too far to walk." Nina shrugged. "Maybe he was just out for a walk or something."

"Maybe he has a thing for you."

"Don't be ridiculous."

"I'm assuming your first interaction with our neighbor was the last interaction with our neighbor?"

Nina hesitated, then admitted, "He came over for dinner when Annie was here. She wanted to talk about the thing you don't want me to even be thinking about. He was there when it happened."

Will's expression darkened, a storm brewing in his eyes.

He didn't need to voice his displeasure because he said everything that he needed to say with his face. Nina definitely wasn't about to tell him that Steve had been the one to find Panda's body.

Pop Rocks were still exploding in her mouth.

Will stomped back toward the house, his steps heavy with unspoken anger.

Nina trailed after him, the candy fizz now fading.

Back inside, Will's movements were brisk and determined as he snatched the car keys from the wall hook.

"Where are you going?"

Will didn't respond as Nina followed him to the car, walking faster to keep up with his long strides.

He slid into the driver's seat, his movements sharply decisive.

"Get out." Will glanced at her as she dove into the passenger seat.

"I'm not going anywhere. We need to talk."

He revved the engine and gunned the Infinity in reverse down the driveway.

The sudden motion was jarring, and Nina's heart

leaped into her throat. It stayed there as Will kept going, swinging out onto the highway—

A semi-truck barreled right by them, its horn blaring in a deafening protest against his reckless driving.

Nina flinched, the sound reverberating through her body.

Will seemed unfazed by the near miss, his focus solely on the road ahead as he raced down the highway.

Nina buckled her safety belt, feeling anything but safe.

Chapter Twenty-Eight

THE CAR SURGED FORWARD AS WILL FLOORED the accelerator.

The highway was a blur of motion and speed. Nina's heart pounded against her ribcage, too much fear now fueling the frustration swirling inside her.

"Will, please, slow down. Be sensible," she begged, her voice barely rising above the roaring engine.

But Will was unresponsive, locked in one of his moods.

The kind where he retreated into a shell of silence and anger, leaving her feeling helpless and stranded on the outside.

"Where are you going?" Nina asked.

Will still wasn't answering her, but she had a decent idea where he was headed after turning onto the highway right in front of that braying semi.

She probably knew before he even got into the car.

After what felt like an eternity, he abruptly turned off the highway and proved her right, racing up to a farmhouse where Steve's truck was parked in the driveway.

As Will got out of the car and charged toward the front

door, Nina grabbed her phone and tapped out a hasty message to Steve: *I'm sorry. Will found out you were at the house.*

Her fingers trembled as she hit *send*, then she tucked the phone away and hurried after Will, wondering exactly how terrible the next two minutes might turn out to be.

Hopefully not so terrible that Officer Rivera would be adding another entry to Will's file. Unfortunately, right now Nina had no problem believing that Will could get angry enough to leave a dead bird at his ex's place as a threat.

He reached the front door just as Steve opened it.

Nina rushed up behind him, grabbing his arm in a desperate attempt to hold him back. "Stop, please!"

But Will shook himself out of her grip and spoke in a thunderous roar. "STAY THE HELL AWAY FROM OUR HOUSE!" he bellowed as his face contorted with anger. "AND LEAVE MY WIFE THE FUCK ALONE!"

Will's fists clenched and unclenched at his sides, blazing with an intensity that was both frightening and unfamiliar. Veins in his neck stood out like cords, pulsing with his words as he spat.

Nina's heart kept on pounding; she had no idea what to do.

Steve stood rooted, his face a mask of confusion and disbelief. He glanced at Nina as if looking for clues, but there was nothing in his expression that suggested he was the one who'd left the Pop Rocks or that he was trying to communicate some sort of secret message to her. Calmly, Steve said to Will, "I have no idea what you're talking about."

Nina burned with embarrassment and worry. Her cheeks felt hot as she turned to Steve, her voice apologetic. "I'm so sorry. This is all a big misunderstanding."

"I gathered," he replied with a nod. "Maybe it would

help if you told me what this misunderstanding was all about."

"YOU KNOW EXACTLY WHAT IT WAS ABOUT!" Will shouted.

"I'm so sorry," Nina repeated, her hands trembling as she navigated Will back to their car, exerting more physical effort than she had ever imagined using on him, her breathing short and rapid as she heaved him toward the passenger seat.

He shrugged her off again, but got into the passenger seat and slammed the door without another word.

Nina tossed one last apologetic glance over to Steve, still standing on his porch while observing the scene — even that fleeting look filled her with shame — then she slipped into the car behind the steering wheel and white-knuckled the thing as she executed a tight turn and drove them away from Steve's farmhouse.

The vehicle moved smoothly, but her heart was a flurry of beats.

The drive back home were swallowed by a suffocating silence. Will was a statue in the passenger seat, his posture stiff and unyielding, face turned away to stare blankly at the blurring landscape.

Her throat felt tight, mind reeling to find the right words, gaze flickering between the road ahead and the man beside her, hoping for any sign of softening, or indication that things were okay.

But Will remained distant, his profile etched against the window.

She pulled into the driveway and he was out of the car before she killed the engine, stalking inside without a single glance behind him.

Nina sat in the car, collecting her thoughts before daring to enter the waiting confrontation.

Her phone buzzed with a new message from Steve: *You ok?*

She texted back: *We spotted the intruder on our property again this morning. Will thinks it's you for some reason. I'm really sorry. I know that you had nothing to do with this.*

She waited a full minute for Steve's response. None came.

So Nina got out of the car with a heavy heart, and approached the house with a lead blanket of dread on her shoulders.

The front door shut behind her with a heavy thud that echoed through the empty living room. She went to the kitchen, needing to ground herself in routine.

So she started cooking, knowing what she would be making for lunch before grabbing the first ingredient.

An hour later the oven's warmth greeted Nina as she checked on the shepherd's pie. The rich aroma of cooked meat and herbs filled the air, making her stomach growl.

She set the table, then slipped down to the basement, leaving the door ajar just enough to hear any movement from Will upstairs, not wanting to get caught doing what she was so eager to do.

She went to the hidden room and settled on the bed, the dim glow of her laptop screen casting an eerie light in the darkened basement. Opening the forum, she clicked on the new message from Byrd91.

Byrd91: *I'm not Koala, just so you know.*

Nina: *I don't think you are. This morning's incident ... it was someone else.*

Byrd91: *Incident? What happened?*

Nina: *Someone was in our driveway. Dropped a box of Pop Rocks. Like in Panda's story.*

Byrd91: *Pop Rocks? No way. Panda wasn't allowed candy. Ever.*

Byrd91 had denied being Koala, but how else would they know that Panda wasn't allowed candy? Unless they were Kodiak, the uncle? Or was that the kind of thing that anyone in town would have known?

Her instincts said that few people had met Panda prior to her death, trapped downstairs like she was. Byrd91 had to be close family, someone who knew her intimately.

Byrd91: *What story?*

Nina: *The one I read in her journal. I think Sloth might have paid us a visit. Or maybe the uncle.*

She snapped a photo of the entry mentioning the candy, then attached the jpeg.

Byrd91: *The uncle moved to Europe, and took Koala with him. He paid the papers not to mention it. You're chasing ghosts.*

It hadn't occurred to Nina until that moment that Koala could've been their visitor. Maybe Koala wanted to finally come home, only to discover that someone else had bought the house. So she was trying to scare Nina and Will out.

Nina: *Koala would be in her late twenties or early thirties now. Either one of them could have come back.*

Byrd91 didn't respond.

Nina: *Panda mentioned a Kodiak in the journal. I think he's the uncle. But I don't know why he would have killed her.*

Byrd91: *The uncle loved them. And there was nothing left to inherit. The Byrds were totally broke.*

Nina's fingers paused as she processed this new information. Then she typed: *You said 'the uncle loved them.' How would you know that? Are you the uncle?*

The cursor mocked her with its blinking.

"Nina?"

Her heart skipped a beat at the sound of Will's voice.

She slapped the laptop shut, then hurried back

upstairs, meeting him as he was peering down the basement stairs. "I was just folding some laundry."

"With your laptop?"

"I was listening to a podcast."

"It smells like lunch is ready?"

Nina nodded, her hands tightening around the laptop. "I was just about to take it out of the oven."

His gaze lingered on Nina for a moment longer before he turned away, suspicion hanging in the air like an unspoken accusation.

Nina's phone buzzed and she reached out to grab it, grateful for the distraction.

The screen lit up with a message from the unknown number again. Another photo of Will in what looked like the same bar as before, his face hidden as he leaned close to a woman. Also same as the last time; she had an air of effortless beauty, cascading blonde waves framing her striking features, full lips and icy blue eyes.

Will definitely had a type.

Who is this? Nina typed.

The reply was immediate. *A friend.*

But a friend would never have sent pics without explanation.

She pressed *Call*, desperate for answers.

The phone on the other end rang and rang, but no one picked up.

So Nina decided it was time to get some answers from Will.

Chapter Twenty-Nine

WILL and Nina sat across from each other at the table. The rich scent of shepherd's pie did little to dispel the unease between them. Tension had continuously tightened ever since they'd moved out here to the middle of nowhere.

Now it was like the eerie calm between a bomb set to detonate and that final BOOM.

But Will did seem to be enjoying his casserole, making involuntary humming sounds as he repeatedly dipped the spoon into his mouth.

He finally met her eyes, looking at Nina from his side of the table as he cleared his throat. "I'm going to buy you a washer-dryer set that'll fit in the mudroom near the back porch. It's not a good idea for you to spend so much time in the basement." Then he cleared his throat again. "Or *any* time in the basement."

"I like it down there. It's quiet. A good place to think." Nina made sure her voice didn't sound argumentative, but strong enough to let him know that she wouldn't be backing down. This was her house too.

Will sighed, his fork tracing patterns in the shepherd's

pie. "I'm sorry for how I acted earlier. About Steve. I just … I don't want you hanging out with that guy."

Nina paused with the fork halfway to her mouth. This was the perfect opening.

She set her fork back down, tines clinking against the rose-patterned china that Panda and Koala had probably eaten off of. She looked directly at Will, her gaze unwavering.

"If we're going to set boundaries about who we can hang out with, then we need to talk about this." She pulled out her phone and slid it across the table.

Will looked down at the photo of him with the blonde at the bar.

The woman who looked eerily similar to Nina.

His expression darkened. "What the hell? Has Annie been following me around, trying to drive a wedge between us?" His lip curled in disgust. "Is she seriously so jealous of our relationship that she would stoop this low?"

"Don't you dare blame this on Annie!" Her hands clenched into fists as anger sparked in her chest. "You're the one who was so eager to go to Chicago without me. And after your embarrassing display of jealousy over Steve, without *any evidence whatsoever*, you have no right to criticize me for feeling suspicious after seeing this picture. Who is this woman, Will?"

The fight seemed to drain out of him, his shoulders slumping as he averted her gaze. "You're right. I should have told you about her from the start."

"Yes, you should have," Nina agreed, her tone frosty. "So start talking."

He drew a deep breath, as if steeling himself. "Her name is Sara. She's my ex-girlfriend."

Her stomach turned to lead. "You've been cheating on me with your ex?"

"No!" His head snapped up, his eyes pleading. "It's not like that at all. Sara is the one who left the dead bird. She must have found out about our engagement somehow and decided to start stalking me again. She wants to break us up."

Nina stared at Will in disbelief, her mind tumbling through a parade of uncomfortable thoughts.

Until a cold realization struck her. "Funny you should mention leaving dead birds for exes."

"Why do you say that?" Will asked her.

"Aren't you the one with a history of doing exactly that?"

The color drained from his face. He looked like he might be sick. "How … how do you know about that?"

"It doesn't matter how I know!" Nina snapped, though she was glad he didn't try to deny it. "What matters is that you owe me an explanation. *Now*."

He seemed to deflate before her eyes, all the fight gone out of him. His voice was full of defeat when he said, "I never did that." He shook his head. "Sara lied to the police."

Nina raised an eyebrow. "So there was no dead bird?"

"No, there was, but …" He ran a hand over his face, looking pained. "The bird was mine. A cockatiel I'd named Rosie. I got her before I even met Sara."

He paused, as if gauging Nina's reaction. When she remained silent, he continued. "Sara was always jealous of that bird. She accused me of loving it more than I loved her. Said I'd never gotten over my Rosie and was trying to turn her into Rosie's replacement. She claimed that the bird was proof, though I'm still not even sure how that argument even makes sense."

Nina stared back at him, unblinking.

"I wasn't, I swear. I know Rosie's gone." His voice took

on a pleading note. "Naming the bird after her … it was just a way to keep her memory close. To remind me how much she loved me before I lost her."

Nina maintained her blank expression.

Will swallowed hard, the words spilling out of him like water from a perforated dam. "I went out of town on a business trip. Asked Sara to watch Rosie for me. When I got back …" His voice cracked, eyes going distant. "I found that poor bird's corpse in the garbage can. Sara had let her out of the cage, and the cat killed her."

Tears shone in his eyes. "I confronted her, ended things right there on the spot. And when I refused to come back, she … she dug the bird out of the trash and went to the cops. Told them I'd left it on her porch as some kind of twisted message after she dumped me."

Nina chewed on her bottom lip, still unsure of how to respond. It sounded so over-the-top ridiculous, but Will seemed as sincere as she'd ever seen him. Was she going to believe him or the police report?

"She's crazy, Nina. Completely unhinged. I would never …"

Nina was already shaking her head, torn between disbelief and disgust. "If you're telling the truth, if she's really been stalking you — *terrorizing us* — then you've been lying to me this entire time, Will." Her voice rose with each word until she was suddenly shouting. "You knew who was breaking into our house and yet you said nothing! YOU LET ME GO TO BED OVERNIGHT SCARED OUT OF MY GODDAMNED MIND!"

"I was trying to protect you," Will insisted as desperation crept into his tone.

"*Bullshit.*" Nina's eyes flashed with hurt and anger. "You were trying to protect yourself."

He seemed to crumple under the weight of her accusations. "You're right. I should have told you the moment I suspected it was Sara. But I swear, I only hid it because I was trying to keep you safe. I went to Chicago to confront her, and finally put an end to all of this."

"Really?" Nina scoffed. "Because it looks to me like you went to Chicago so you could cozy up to your ex in a bar."

"These pictures don't tell the whole story," he argued. "Yes, I met with her. She tried to seduce me, but I shut her down hard. Told her in no uncertain terms that *you're* the one I'm marrying. And that if she didn't leave us alone, I would slap her with a restraining order hard enough to make her see the paperwork in her sleep."

Something in his tone made her pause.

"What did she say to that?" Nina asked.

"She denied everything, of course. Swore up and down that she had never even heard about the bird. Claimed she had no idea we'd left Chicago, and asked why I would ever think that she would drive all the way to North Dakota to drop a dead bird off in person when she could have just mailed it." He vented humorless laugh. "Like I'd ever believe a word that comes out of her poisonous mouth."

Nina fell silent, her mind churning. She wanted to believe him, but seeds of doubt had been planted in fertile soil and the germinating tendrils were already threading themselves through her heart.

Was she the idiot, letting him gaslight her into dismissing threatening behavior so clear that even Officer Rivera could see it?

Or was it possible that Will really was the victim of a crazy ex who'd decided to stalk him when she'd learned he'd gotten engaged to Nina?

Both possibilities were horrifying, but if their intruder was Will's ex, that meant the events since they'd moved into the house weren't fate somehow pushing Nina toward finding Panda's killer. They weren't a sign that she was getting closer to the truth. They were just some jealous woman's last-ditch attempts to break Will and Nina up.

Somehow, that just felt… disappointing.

But what did she really expect? Had she really been thinking that somehow fate had been leading her to the killer, one synchronicity at a time?Will pulled out his phone, navigated to an official-looking document, and handed the device to Nina. "I filed for a temporary restraining order. The court granted it this morning. Sara isn't allowed within a hundred yards of either of us."

Nina studied the screen, taking in the legal jargon, the bold letters spelling out Sara's name. It looked legitimate, but a nagging voice in the back of her mind still wondered if Will could have forged it. He could've noticed whoever had taken the picture, or had a feeling that he was being watched, and prepared the document just in case Nina found out that he was cheating.

But then, if he'd gone to such lengths to cover his tracks, surely he would have had a more plausible story prepared. Something better than a crazy ex-girlfriend he'd never mentioned who just happened to show up and start leaving dead animals on their doorstep. Wasn't it more likely that Will's file was correct, and that he was the one who'd left dead birds both for Sara and for Nina?

She found herself comparing her own features to Sara's. The resemblance was uncanny — they could have easily passed for sisters. Blonde, blue-eyed, delicate.

"She looks like me." Said with a flicker of unease, as Nina didn't know if she was asking a question or making an accusation. "Enough that we could be family."

Will at least had the grace to look guilty. He nodded, unable to meet her eyes. "I know. I … I guess I have a type." A helpless shrug. "Plenty of guys do, even if they won't admit it."

Her insides twisted again. The knot kept getting tighter.

Nina thought of the woman Will had loved before her, the one whose death had shattered him.

"When were you with Sara?"

Another uncomfortable shift in his seat, still avoiding her gaze. "We met right after I moved to Chicago."

"Funny, considering you've always said you moved there to find me." Nina couldn't keep the bitterness from her voice. "Did you feed her that line too?"

"No!" The denial was vehement, his pleading eyes finally meeting hers. "I ended things with Sara the day we met. You have to believe that."

But Nina wasn't sure what she believed anymore. The man in front of her felt like a walking question mark. Had everything between them been built on secrets and lies?

Will seemed to sense her turmoil. He reached across the table and took her hand, his touch gentle but imploring. "I know I'm not perfect. I've made so many mistakes, and I'm sorry. I should have told you about Sara from the beginning."

He squeezed her fingers, his voice low and fervent. "I just wanted this to be a fresh start for us. I wanted our home to be perfect. Untainted by anything ugly from my past. I figured that if you knew Sara had followed us, and that she was trying to ruin what we have, it would color everything for you. Especially with the history of murders in our house." He shuddered. "Please forgive me, Rosie."

Chapter Thirty

Nina yanked her hand away from Will's, her eyes flashing with fury.

Will tried to grab it again, desperate to maintain their connection, but it was too late. The damage had clearly been done.

Horror washed over him as he realized the gravity of his slip.

It wasn't exactly his fault — he couldn't help but see Rosie in Nina, especially when she looked at him with such vulnerability.

And now, with one careless word, he had hurt his new true love in the worst possible way.

He felt a tingling in his hands and feet as his chest constricted — the beginnings of a panic attack, just when he most needed to prove to Nina that he deserved her.

"Nina, I'm so sorry, please—"

"I want to know how she died, Will."

Hearing her say the words was like a knife digging into his ribs. The hand of panic squeezed tighter, making it hard to breathe in, caging his heart until it beat harder and harder in the crushing grip of fear.

Nina thought she wanted to know, but she had no idea. If Will told her the truth right now, she would never be able to see him the same way again. He would lose everything, and he would deserve to.

He should never have bought this house.

"I'm serious, Will. No more secrets. If we're going to get married, I have to know what happened."

"Don't ask me to do that," he pleaded with beseeching eyes.

Her expression hardened. "I think Sara is right. You're clearly not over your dead girlfriend." Then, to his surprise, her voice softened. "You need to talk to someone about it, Will. Please, tell me what happened."

"Okay." He nodded as something snapped inside him, then the next words burst out of his mouth before he could even hope to stop them. "After you tell me what happened to your parents."

Her eyes narrowed, nostrils flaring with indignation. "You know I can't remember anything before I woke up in the orphanage."

"So you claim. But I've heard you talk through your nightmares."

A lightning bolt of shock flashed across her features. "You never told me that."

"Out of respect for your desire to move forward with your life." He forced himself to meet her gaze without blinking. "The same respect I'm asking you to give me."

She shook her head with a bitter laugh. "I would give anything to remember. Even if the memory is horrific, at least I would finally know where I came from."

But he didn't believe that, because he knew what it was

like to remember. "*I would give anything to forget,*" he whispered.

The admission had been ripped from somewhere deep inside him. He wanted to tell her, to share the burden of everything he'd been carrying around since Rosie had died. But then she would know how he'd failed Rosie, and he doubted she could love him after that.

"Sometimes we have to look back before we can move forward." Her tone was almost gentle.

His jaw clenched at that pop psychology pablum. "Did your therapist tell you that?"

"At least I've talked to a therapist." Her gaze narrowed on him. "You clearly need help, Will."

The hand of panic squeezed so tight, he couldn't inhale. His heart was hammering so hard he could feel each beat reverberating through his entire body.

What did she know?

Had that bitch Rivera done a background check on him?

How else cold Nina have found out about the dead bird incident?

The thought chilled his blood. Had they conspired to dig even further back, into his lost years after Rosie's death? When he had been nearly unhinged with grief?

Was it possible he had already lost all chance of making Nina love him as completely as Rosie had?

Will knew he could never get Rosie back. But he could have the life they had promised one another, if only Nina would leave the past where it belonged.

The darkness seemed to close in around him, untill all he could see was her face. The accusation in her eyes, the disapproving downturn of her lips, the unmoving set of her clenched jaw as she stared expectantly at him.

Nina's attention was smothering him. He would suffocate if he

His breathing hitched, his chest tightening as panic clawed at his throat.

He thought of the pills in his office desk drawer, the ones that could calm the storm raging inside him. But going for them now would only trigger more questions that she would demand answers to.

So he clung to his composure with every ounce of his will, his fingers digging into his palms hard enough to leave little purple crescents.

"Nina, I love you more than anything—"

"How did she die, Will?"

Could she have guessed the truth?

The idea made his heart start seizing in his chest.

"Did you kill her, Will?"

The knife in his gut twisted at her accusation. That Nina could ever think him capable of such a thing—

"*Will.*" She leaned across the table. "Answer me."

"NO! Of course I didn't kill Rose! I loved her — I would have done anything to protect her. She was—"

His breathing turned ragged.

Darkness closed in around him like a shroud, suffocating as pain lanced through his skull. Spikes driven into his skull with the metronomic rhythm of his heartbeat.

Each throb brought a fresh wave of agony, same as it had on that terrible, blood-soaked night.

He lurched to his feet, his chair clattering to the floor behind him. He had to get to his pills. Had to make the pounding stop before it split his head wide open.

He staggered towards the stairs, Nina's voice echoing behind him.

She called his name, but it sounded distant and

muffled, as if she were shouting from the far end of a tunnel.

Will felt her fingers brush against his back as he stumbled upward, but he shrugged her off, single-minded in his pursuit of relief.

Nina tried again, grabbing for his arm this time. Her touch burned like a brand, searing through his haze of panic.

He wrenched himself free with a snarl, his momentum carrying him forward.

And in that moment, the world tilted on its axis.

Nina's scream pierced the air as she tumbled down the stairs, her body striking the steps with a series of sickening thuds.

Then, silence.

Deafening, all-consuming silence.

Will stood frozen at the top of the stairs, his heart seized in an icy grip of terror as he stared down at her crumpled form.

Nina lay sprawled on the basement floor, her limbs askew like a broken doll, blonde hair fanned out around her head like a halo. Her face was turned away from him, obscured by shadows.

She didn't move. Or make a sound.

In that interminable moment, suspended between one tattered breath and the next, a horrifying question crystalized in his mind.

Had he just killed his fiancée?

Chapter Thirty-One

Nina lay crumpled at the bottom of the stairs in a state of panic-tinged disbelief.

Her heart was still pounding from the fall, a rapid drumbeat that sounded so much louder in the otherwise silent basement.

Pain radiated through her body, sharp and sudden, throbbing fiercely in her head, her ribs, her right hip. Her breathing was shallow, and she was afraid to draw a deep breath in fear that more pain lurked just beyond her awareness and that it would come rushing in along with the air.

Will's footsteps thundered back down the stairs, his face a blur of concern and fear as he crouched down beside her. "Nina, are you okay?"

His voice was tense with worry and guilt.

Her breath came in ragged gasps. She couldn't find her voice, the shock rendering her mute. She nodded slightly, her eyes wide and fixed on his.

Will gently slid his arms under her body, lifting her carefully with an unfaltering grip. The world spun as he carried her up the stairs, each new step sending fresh waves of pain through her.

His pace didn't waver, all the way to their bedroom, where he laid Nina on the bed with an attentiveness that was nothing like the anger that had overtaken him moments ago.

He hovered over her, scanning her face, torso, and limbs in search of injury. "Did you hit your head?"

She nodded and the edges of the her vision went gray. "I think so."

His face crumpled with remorse. "I'm so sorry, Nina. I didn't mean to … I wasn't thinking."

She wanted to believe him, but did she?

Only yesterday, Officer Rivera had asked her if she was afraid Will might turn violent, and Nina had said no… but she'd hesitated first.

Should she have said yes?

Or was this just an accident?

It was hard not to blame herself for pushing him too hard. She should have recognized that he had been heading into a blind panic. And she shouldn't have tried to touch him when he was clearly not in control of himself.

Or maybe he would've pushed you no matter what.

Because he's a liar and a cheater and who knows what else?

Was that an unworthy thought, or was that the part of her that saw Will clearly and had been trying to get through to him this whole time?

The part that had been reluctant to rush into setting a date for the wedding and that remained determined to keep the tunnel and the journals a secret from him.

Maybe it was time to start listening to that voice inside her.

But Will was staring at her in horror, waiting, she realized for some sort of reassurance.

He pushed you down the stairs but it's your job to reassure him?

For now, she would treat this like an accident.

Until she figured out what she was going to do about everything.

"It's okay," Nina reassured him, though her body ached and her mind was still reeling. "I think I'll be okay."

"Can I get you something?" His eyes were earnest, pleading for any chance to make amends. "Is there anything you need?"

"Some tea, maybe?" Her voice was weak, but she managed a small smile.

"Peppermint?"

"Yes, please." She nodded. "And my laptop."

He tucked the blankets around her, his movements now gentle and cautious.

She watched him walk out of the bedroom, his shoulders hunched, wearing the weight of the incident like a winter coat.

He left the door ajar.

She lay in bed, cocooned by blankets, her mind a torrent of swirling thoughts and emotions as she replayed the events leading up to her fall, questioning whether it had truly been an accident or something more sinister.

The look on his face when she'd asked if he'd killed Rose. Rage and guilt for sure. But that didn't necessarily mean he had killed her. Still, Nina felt sure that Will blamed himself, regardless of whoever had actually done the deed.

Which didn't make him a murderer — he could have been an innocent bystander.

But why wouldn't he talk about it if that were the case?

Nina wriggled her cell phone out of her hip pocket and started to text Annie, then hesitated. If she told Annie that Will had pushed her down the stairs, Annie would never believe it was an accident — she'd move from Red Flag mode to It's My Mission to Rescue You From That Asshole mode.

There was no going back, once Annie knew. She would never forgive Will, and if Nina decided that the shove had been an accident, Annie and Will would never be able to be in the same room again.

Which meant that Nina would have to choose between her fiancé and her bestie.

She heard footsteps on the stairs, so hid her phone under the blanket until Will had deposited her laptop on the bed and the teacup on the nightstand, alongside a bottle of ibuprofen.

Then he kissed her forehead like she was a sick child staying home from school and said, "I'll be working in my office if you need anything."

She nodded and waited for him to leave, then opened her laptop and logged in to the Byrd Murder forum.

No message from Byrd91. And no new chatter worth reading.

She sighed and closed the laptop, then popped an ibuprofen with several swallows of tea. Almost immediately, the queasy feeling in her stomach began to settle.

The magic of peppermint.

Will would probably escape his guilt at having hurt her for by immersing himself in work for at least a couple of hours. Maybe he was chatting with Bruce right now, making sure he heard Will's side of the story before Nina could tell Annie hers.

But Nina knew Annie would believe her no matter what.

She opened the drawer of her nightstand and pulled out Panda's journal.

Chapter Thirty-Two

KOALA'S BEEN ACTING weird lately. Like a storm has been brewing inside her for a while and today it finally all exploded. Yesterday, she hit me. It was more shocking than painful, like a jolt of lightning in our usually quiet world.

Her hand left a sting on my cheek, but the genuine hurt was deeper, like a crack in the trust we're supposed to have. If we can't count on each other, who can we count on? We've always had each other.

Although, writing that now I see why Koala might have gotten so mad.

It's because we've always had each other. Before Sloth, that was ALL we had.

After the slap, everything just burst out. We yelled at each other. Our voices were loud, and we kept going at it until we were both hoarse.

We were suddenly tearing everything apart, all the silent rules we lived by. I was so scared Grizzly and Polar would hear, and so was Koala, but neither one of us could stop.

Of course, they eventually heard us.

Worse than the punishment was all the worrying about what was *going to happen to me. Or worse, to Koala. Grizzly has been getting so mad about everything lately, I've started to think he would actually kill us. That he WOULD actually kill us.*

Maybe the first murder would be an accident, but then he would have to do it again to shut the surviving one of us up.

Grizzly marched in and screamed at us both to shut up.

Then I got locked in our room. I lay there, my mind racing with all kinds of terrible scary thoughts. What if Koala told them something bad about me? I couldn't even sneak out to meet Sloth. I was so scared of what might happen if I came back to Koala having finked on me.

The walls felt like they were closing in, and I just felt so alone.

But I have a really enormous secret. It both scares and excites me.

Sloth gave me a phone. It's like a miracle in my hand. A little window to the outside world. And a secret that only me and Sloth know.

I haven't even told Koala about it. I'm worried she might want to use it or might slip up and tell Grizzly and Polar. Even on accident.

Having a phone might not seem like that big of a deal, but I think it might be enough to make Grizzly want to bury me alive, while Polar watches him do it.

Keeping this from Koala is hard, but I have no other choice. She has a big mouth, even if it's usually on accident.

Everything sounded so quiet and spooky. I kept jumping any time there was even a tiny little sound. Koala finally came down to our room in the middle of the night. She was all sorry and stuff, saying she didn't tell Grizzly and Polar anything.

An enormous weight lifted off me. We forgave each other right there, and it felt like everything was okay. Koala told them we were arguing about whether or not there was really predestination. That's better than almost all the lies she's ever told them put together. They didn't even bother to interrogate me.

Although Grizzly might tomorrow, either before or after Bible Time.

Koala and I talked for a long time, just lying there in the dark. I told her that no one, not even Sloth, could ever take her place. And Koala said that she would always only love me.

I kept trying to explain that she might find someone to love one day, just as I had with Sloth. But Koala's eyes were as set as her heart, insisting that I was the only one she could ever love. She said I was perfect, an angel on Earth.

Maybe she wasn't old enough to understand what I was saying yet, but hearing it felt like a warm hug, especially compared to how Grizzly and Polar see me. Broken and tainted.

I've never been any of those things to Koala. She sees me as whole and beautiful. We fell asleep that night. Not just in the same room but in the same bed.

Grizzly found us together before dawn, and his fury was like a storm breaking upon us.

I tried to protect Koala, to shield her from the wrath. But Grizzly was relentless.

They locked me away, and through the walls I heard Koala screaming.

I don't think it's possible for me to hate Grizzly or Polar any more than I do.

I HAVEN'T BEEN *able to leave the house for more than a week now. I could physically sneak out, but I can't bring myself to leave on account of Koala's bruises. They are a constant reminder of my guilt, and what could happen if I dare to leave her alone at the wrong time, when Grizzly is in the wrong kind of mood.*

Not that there are any right kinds with them.

We spent our days in a silent pact, whispering apologies in the dark.

When I finally saw Sloth again, the air between us was heavy as he begged me to run away with him, a plea full of longing and desperation.

My heart ached at the thought, and of course I was more than just tempted by the promise of freedom and a life with Sloth.

But how could I ever leave Koala behind like that?

Sloth couldn't understand. He saw it as an impossible choice — either Koala or our future together. But to me, Koala was my past, present, and future. How could I choose between them?

Sloth gave me a necklace — a rose charm surrounded by a compass. It was the most beautiful piece of jewelry I've ever seen. A symbol of his love for me. Roses are my favorite flower. Sloth said the compass represents how we would navigate life together.

But the necklace felt too heavy around my neck, especially knowing that I would have to hide it as soon as I got home.

PANDA HAD DRAWN a picture of the necklace. She was a skilled artist considering her total lack of professional instruction. The sketch revealed a stunning piece: the rose itself was delicate, with metal petals unfurling in intricate detail, encircled by a finely wrought compass, the needle pointing toward an unseen destination.

But most remarkable, or startling, perhaps even terrifying, was that Nina had seen that necklace before.

Worn by the man who had bought her this house.

Chapter Thirty-Three

Nina shivered in fear.

What were the odds that Will had the same pendant Sloth had given to Panda?

And that he would then buy the very house Panda had been murdered in?

It was an unlikely coincidence, but not an impossible one.

The necklace was probably mass-produced — teenage Sloth wouldn't be able to afford custom jewelry for his girlfriend. Maybe the compass-rose design had been popular at the time and Will had simply bought it because it reminded him of his Rose.

But buying this house?

Nina was the one who had found the place, though she couldn't remember exactly how. She just remembered clicking through tabs on her laptop and there it was in all its Gothic splendor. She had been instantly captivated, although she hadn't shown the house to Will for a couple of days, because it had been so far from his personal taste that she hadn't seen any point.

Until the night he caught her fantasizing about fixing the place up and they started talking about buying a house after the wedding.

Will's pendant was similar to Panda's. That didn't make it the same. Maybe if she looked at Will's pendant more closely, she'd find small differences in the design that would prove that it couldn't have been Panda's. But even if she didn't, there could've been thousands of necklaces with that same design, sold all over the country.

Her mind raced with questions, each more unsettling than the last.

She opened her laptop and started typing in a search for that charm, sifting through images and descriptions of countless pieces of jewelry. She found plenty of variations, including a site called Sterling and Stone that had a near match, but all of the necklaces bearing roses with compasses and compasses with roses were in some way different from the intricate design that Panda had drawn on the page all those years ago, and that Will had worn since before Nina had ever even met him.

With trembling fingers, she took a picture of Panda's drawing of the pendant in her journal. Then she opened the laptop again and messaged Byrd91: *I need to talk to you right away.*

She attached the picture to the message and hit send.

Her heart pounded as she gulped down the rest of her tea, waiting for a response. After what felt like an eternity but was likely only a couple of minutes, Byrd91 replied: *What is that?*

Nina typed back frantically: *The necklace that Sloth gave to Panda.*

Byrd91's response made her blood run cold: *She wasn't wearing it when the body was found.*

Nina shivered again. That suggested the killer had taken the necklace.

Are you still there?

Nina's fingers shook as she typed: *My fiancé wears a pendant exactly like it.*

Does it have 4Ever inscribed on the other side?

The question made her stomach lurch.

Nina swallowed hard. *I don't know.*

Byrd91's warning appeared on screen to give her yet another start. *You could be in grave danger.*

Nina tried to rationalize it away: *It could be a coincidence. There are probably a lot of people who bought this same necklace.*

But Byrd91 wasn't buying it: *How many of them are now living in the Byrd house?*

Her heart was beating much too hard against her ribs. *I'll try to look at the other side.*

Byrd91's final message was the most bone chilling of all.

Be careful, if he killed Panda, he won't hesitate to kill you too.

Nina slammed the laptop shut, terror gripping her insides.

She had to find a way to look at the pendant without Will realizing what she was doing. But how? He never took it off.

The implications of what she might find made her head spin.

What would she do if his pendant bore that inscription? Go to Rivera?

Did she have enough evidence for the police to arrest Will?

Even if they did, what if they allowed him bail, and he came after her?

Nina had listened to so many true crime podcasts, but

none of them had prepared her for the possibility that her own fiancé might be a killer.

Desperate for answers, Nina started rereading the journals, combing through the pages for any clues that might suggest Will was Sloth.

But with a sinking realization, she understood how little she actually knew about his past. He grew up in a small Midwestern town, but she didn't know which one, and he always deflected the conversation whenever she asked.

Will claimed to be an only child and that his parents had both passed, but Nina had no idea how or when. And she had no way of knowing if Will was even his real name, or if he'd changed it at some point.

She didn't know Sloth's real name either.

Opening her laptop again, Nina started a deep dive, typing *William Henry* into the search bar. But the results were frustratingly generic. A sea of faces and names, none of them her Will.

She refined her search, including his university, job history, and supposed upbringing in Florida. Again, her efforts led nowhere, frustration fermenting her blood.

The blog post about William Henry, a marine biologist in Florida awarded for his groundbreaking research on coral reefs, revealed a secret life under the sea, but he was twice her Will's age.

The William Henry involved in a high-profile embezzlement case in Miami was currently serving time in prison.

Another William Henry was a free-spirited traveler, his page filled with photos from exotic locations around the world. That man wrote a lot, and for a moment Nina even believed she might have a lead, but his age and locations didn't line up.

She chased it down anyway, finally finding a photo, only to confirm yet another dead end.

And Will himself had no social media accounts — she'd found that charming when she'd first met him — and no real online presence aside from his profile on the company website, beneath Bruce's. When she did lookup searches, she found their address here and the address of his Chicago apartment, no residences listed before that. His history was a carefully erased chalkboard, leaving Nina grappling with a growing void where his past should have been.

Wincing from the pain, she hauled herself out of bed and found Rivera's business card. With shaking hands, she dialed the officer's number.

"Rivera."

"It's Nina." A single beat to gather her courage before she blurted the rest. "I need a favor — can you do a background check on Will? I need to find out where he was born, and if he's ever changed his name."

After a brief pause, Rivera said, "If I have a reason to do a background check on Will, I can. Is everything alright, Nina?"

Nina hesitated. If she accused Will of murder without evidence and the pendant turned out to be a coincidence, she would be putting him through the hell of an investigation for nothing.

"Are you feeling unsafe?" Rivera pressed. "Do you need assistance?"

She drew a shaky breath. "I'm okay for now," Nina lied. "I just …"

Nina heard Will's office door opening and it was like someone squeezing her heart.

"I have to go," she whispered hurriedly into the phone.

She ended the call and scrambled back toward the

bedroom as his footsteps approached. But by the time she crossed the threshold, he was already there, standing beside the bed.

With Panda's journal open in his hands.

He looked up at her, his expression darkening.

Nina felt the blood drain from her face as icy tendrils of fear gripped her heart.

His expression terrified her. Rage, betrayal, and something even more chilling swirled in his eyes as he glared at her, the journal clutched in his white-knuckled grip.

Nina knew with gut-wrenching certainty that her world was about to shatter irreparably. And there was nothing she could do to stop it.

Chapter Thirty-Four

The air between Nina and Will was charged like the static before a storm.

He clutched the journal, glaring at her with an alarming mix of fury and betrayal. "Where did you find this?" His voice was low and dangerous.

Her whisper was fragile like ice. "*There's a hidden room in the basement.*"

Will made a strangled sound, as if the air had been squeezed out of him. "How long have you had it?"

When Nina didn't respond, his voice rose to a roar. "HOW LONG, NINA?"

She was rooted to the spot, her desire to flee battling the paralyzing fear squeezing her throat.

Will stepped forward, his iron grip iron on her upper arm. "How could you keep this from me?"

His eyes burned into hers, and as his fingers squeezed it felt as if he were transferring his rage right into her bones.

Somehow Nina managed not to shatter. She might never have another chance to know the truth, for Panda's sake. And for her own peace of mind. If there was ever a time to be brave and stand up to Will, this was it.

"I need to see the other side of your pendant. Please, Will." She held a flicker of defiance in her trembling voice.

He sneered, the muscles in his jaw clenching. "You don't deserve to touch it."

Despite his words, Will flipped the pendant over with a swift, jerky movement, exposing the inscription: *4Ever*.

Nina's breath caught in her throat as it all fell into place. Rosie was Panda. He'd bought the house because the woman he really loved had lived here.

And Nina? She had no doubt that Will's "type" was any girl who resembled the woman he'd lost — maybe killed. For him to choose her over Sara, who'd been drop-dead gorgeous, Nina must be a closer match to the dead woman Will was obsessed with.

And had possibly killed.

When Panda had refused to abandon Koala, had Will lost control and become violent?

Just like he had with Nina, mere hours ago?

And when he realized what he'd done, he took the pendant back. Wore it as a remembrance or a trophy, maybe both.

"You're Sloth," she blurted.

"Yes," Will admitted, his voice now eerily calm. "But you'd already figured that out, hadn't you?"

Nina attempted to wriggle free from his steely grasp as her panic bubbled up in her throat like rising bile.

Will whirled her back around and hurled her onto the couch, positioning himself between Nina and the only exit.

The room felt smaller. Suffocating. Walls closing in on her.

Will visibly calmed himself. His voice was steady,

almost normal as he said, "Ask me whatever you want to as me, Nina."

Nina sat up, trembling with her back pressed against the plush cushions.

"Did you kill Panda?" The name felt alien as she said it.

"I would never hurt my Rosie. I would have done anything to save her." His response was immediate and vehement.

But the denial was not a clear *no*, and Nina knew she had to tread carefully or incur his wrath. Even if he wasn't insane, he was clearly unstable, and who knew what might trigger his fury?

But she had to know the rest. Even if it meant he killed her, in the same house where his first love had been killed.

Even in her terror, she could appreciate the irony.

"Then tell me what happened that night," she prompted him.

His gaze drifted away from her, lost in the past. "The night before … Rosie met me like usual near Mrs. Fuller's rose garden. They were her favorite." His voice cracked with the weight of memory. "We were supposed to run away, but instead of bringing her things, Rosie brought bad news."

"That she changed her mind?"

"Rosie couldn't leave her sister, Lizzie. They got into a big fight when Lizzie found out about our plans."

Nina noted the shift from Koala to Lizzie, and the name held a sick resonance that made everything feel more real. Koala was a character in the story that Panda — no, *Rose* — wrote about in her journal, but Lizzie had been a real girl who had suffered terrible abuse and had probably been out of her mind with fear at the prospect of being abandoned by the only person in the world who cared for her.

She suddenly saw the hidden basement room as the loathsome place that the sisters must have felt it to be.

And Koala had thought she was going to be trapped down there alone for the rest of her life.

"Keep going," Nina encouraged Will, though every word was a blade sliding deeper into her gut.

"I was devastated." Will rubbed his temples, the grief evident in his expression. "Rosie went back home and told me not to follow. I sat in the rose garden for a long time, then decided that even if I wasn't sure how to take care of us both, I'd agree to take Lizzie too. I would do anything if it meant being with Rosie."

"So, you went to her house?"

"*Yes*," Will told her in a whisper before catching his breath. "I was tapping on the basement windows, hoping to get her attention. I just wanted to talk."

"She didn't tell you about the tunnel?"

"What tunnel?" Confusion crossed his face.

"You'd never visited her before?" Nina pressed, seeking clarity amid the swirling accusations in her mind.

"She begged me not to. Rosie was terrified that her parents would catch us. She was sure they'd kill us both if they did."

The fear in Rosie's journal entries made that easy enough to believe.

"How did you know about the basement windows?"

"Rosie told me that one of the workers was a peeping tom who used to watch her and Lizzie through them when they were supposed to be working."

"And after you tapped on the windows?" Nina's voice was a thread, pulling at the unraveling edges of Will's story.

"Her father must've seen me sneaking around. I was hit on the back of the head and knocked out." His hand unconsciously drifted up to the back of his skull, as if he could still feel the lump.

Nina frowned, skeptical. "Are you saying you never made it inside the house?"

"I woke up in total darkness in the basement, but I don't remember how I got there." Pain flashed across his features. "My head hurt so bad, I was seeing double, and I threw up. Then ... I heard a scream."

"Panda," Nina said softly.

Will gave her an annoyed look. "Rosie," he corrected her.

"Right." She nodded, the details gnawing at her. Why would Grizzly and Polar bring Will inside if they'd wanted to keep him away from their daughter? It was easier to believe he was lying. "What happened next?"

"I crawled up through the darkness, found a staircase leading up to the larder, and staggered out. I heard someone crying." He paused, his eyes moistening with tears.

He'd known about the larder's secret door this whole time. Nina reined the flash of fury in, knowing that if she interrupted him, she might never heard the rest.

His voice broke as he continued. "I managed to get to the living room, where I saw ..."

"What did you see, Will?" Her voice was gentle, coaxing the words from him.

"*So much blood,*" he whispered in a hollow voice. "She was so beautiful, my Rosie."

Her heart ached for his loss, the horror and subsequent torment at finding Rosie dead. If he Will wasn't lying. Because she could also imagine another version of events, one where Will crawled in through the tunnel, fought with

Rose about leaving, then followed her upstairs when she fled his wild anger. She imagined Will seizing Rose in the living room, Rose's struggles to free herself as he took his anger out on her, coming to his senses only after her feeble movements stilled completely.

He would have stabbed her, then painted the Satanic symbol on the wall in an attempt to mislead the police. Took back the necklace so that no one would look for who'd given it to her. Maybe he'd stabbed Grizzly and Polar because they'd discovered him or maybe to prevent them from telling the police about him.

And it had worked. When Steve found Rose's body later, he must've seen Lizzie, alone in this house of bloodshed and secrets, and assumed she was a ghost.

This version had fewer holes in it that Will's. But truth could be stranger than fiction.

"Are you saying you didn't kill Rosie?" Nina needed to hear him say it out loud.

He shook his head, adamant with his tormented eyes. "Of course I didn't."

"Do you know who did?" Nina was afraid of his answer.

And she had every reason to be.

"You did," he said.

Chapter Thirty-Five

NINA THOUGHT her heart might burst through her chest as she stared at Will in utter disbelief. "You're insane. And that's impossible. I never set foot in this house until you brought me here."

"How long did it take you to find the basement? And the secret door that led to it?" He laughed bitterly. "Less than a day, Nina. You don't remember this house, but your body does."

She shook her head in vehement denial, but he wouldn't stop attempting to incorporate her into his sick delusions.

"You were brought to an orphanage in Chicago by your uncle, before he disappeared." His eyes were wild, his voice sharp and accusatory. Nina could only stare at him in shock as he continued to babble accusations. "You killed your sister because she was going to abandon you. You started with your parents first, thinking Rosie would stay if they were gone, that your uncle would raise you both."

"That's crazy," Nina replied in a trembling voice. "That never happened."

But Will was relentless in his delusion. "You blocked out the memory of what you had done so you didn't have to live with the guilt."

Nina felt a chill crawl up her spine.

Will seemed completely unhinged, lost in this twisted narrative where he was the victim and she, somehow, the villain.

He had projected all his guilt and insanity onto her in this pathetic story where she was responsible for the entire tragedy. Even to the point that he'd been taunting her with the Byrds' rose-covered dishes. She was sure now that he'd hidden them among the boxes for her to find.

In that moment, Nina had never hated anyone more in her life than she hated Will.

How dare he blame her for Rose's death, when *she* was the one who'd spent the past few weeks trying to piece together what had happened to poor Panda, not realizing she was unraveling the mystery of his lost love?

He'd been trying to *stop* her from figuring out what had happened?

Because he didn't want her to know the truth — that he'd killed Rosie. She felt sure of it — and equally sure that he hadn't meant to. So he needed a scapegoat to alleviate the guilt.

And he'd chosen her as a stand-in for Lizzie in his disgusting fantasy world, simply because she also had pale blue eyes and curly blonde hair.

She pushed her terror back at the thought that she'd let herself fall in love with him. Slept with him. Agreed to marry him. If she hadn't found the journals, how much longer would he have been able to keep up the facade before his madness slipped out?

Worse, if he genuinely blamed Lizzie for Rosie's death, wouldn't he want to punish her? It followed a gruesome logic, the kind that serial killers often followed: sweep her off her feet, take her back to the scene of the murder, and avenge Rose by killer Nina the same way he believed that she'd killed Rose.

What had he been waiting for? The wedding, maybe? Or had he been hoping to wake her dormant memories first?

All of the serial killer podcasts she'd listened to focused on reconstructing the killer's logic, but they'd taught her nothing about reasoning with a live killer.

How could she break through his demented narrative without throwing him into another panicked rage?

"What you're saying is impossible, Will." Nina needed to inject a dose of reality into the conversation. "Think about what you're saying."

"It's all I ever think about." It looked like he was trying not to snarl. "You took Rosie away from me. She would have—" His voice cracked. "We could've gone together, all three of us. But you ruined everything."

"It's me, Nina. Not Lizzie." Though, something within her was insisting otherwise.

That something agreed with Will.

And it boiled like lava.

She told herself it was because she had connected so deeply with Panda through her journals. That her familiarity with the house came from months spent obsessing over the case in forums, and not because she had grown up here.

But this place did feel like hers. Spooky as it was, she'd wanted to make it her own the second she'd laid eyes on it.

"Lizzie fought back." Will's words kept on punching her. "How do you think you got your scar?"

Nina's hand flinched to the scar on her cheek.

How dare he use her scar to anchor his horrifying fantasy?

He had spiraled into madness, overwhelmed by guilt enough to construct narrative where the world had conspired to take Panda away from him, with Nina painted as the villain.

Her mind reeled as the pieces fell into place with chilling clarity.

Will had clearly been seeking women who looked like Panda, desperately trying to find someone he could mold into the role of the woman he couldn't save — or perhaps, the one he had harmed.

Their fateful meeting in Chicago had not been serendipity at all; Will had surely orchestrated every step, possibly even securing his position at Bruce's company with the sole purpose of being introduced to her by Annie.

This wasn't just a series of tragic events — it was a calculated manipulation. A sinister replay of his past orchestrated by a man haunted by his actions.

"You made sure I saw this house, so you could pretend it was my idea to buy it." Her voice gained strength with the accusation.

"It's always been your house. You just don't remember." He sounded far away.

And Nina could hardly breathe.

"You look so much like your sister, she could be standing right in front of me. But then you'll give me a look or say something Rosie would never say, and I remember how much you're not her. She dies all over again, every time, right in front of me."

Pity and horror were at war with her disbelief. And anger. Anger at herself for not seeing through his facade the second she'd met him. Intuition should've warned her that there was something not right with Will, something permanently off-kilter lurking just beneath the surface.

Red flags.

Annie had warned her repeatedly. And repeatedly, Nina had rationalized each red flag away, defending Will. Why?

Because he'd seemed to care for her. No, because he'd seemed completely focused on her, charming and protective. He'd told her just enough of his sad story to make her feel like he truly understood her in ways that she didn't even understand herself. She'd spent her whole life feeling abandoned, and he'd made that feeling disappear temporarily by anticipating her needs often enough that it was easy to trust him.

If she got out of this alive, she was never going to ignore another red flag again.

"Rosie would want me to take care of you." His voice broke again.

"I don't want you to take care of me." And she didn't, not anymore.

"You can learn to be my Rosie."

That was Will's most insane statement yet.

Nina wondered if there was a way she could reach through to the other side of his madness. "I'm not Rosie or Lizzie, Will. You're just obsessed with me because I happen to look like her."

But Will shook his head, tracing the line of her scar with a finger, causing Nina to freeze in place. "I saw you standing over her, with blood all over your white nightgown, and the cut running from here to here. You looked just like a ghost."

Nina flashed back to Steve's account of seeing Rosie's ghost when he found the body, and a horrible thought grabbed her by the throat and started squeezing tight.

Could Will be telling the truth?

She tried to back away from him, but he grabbed her wrist to keep her near as he continued spewing lies at her.

"Your uncle, Edward, hid you in an orphanage so you wouldn't have to stand trial for killing her," Will told her in the coldest of voices.

"No." Nina shook her head, now seconds from sobbing.

"Why else would he make you disappear?" His sneer was contemptuous. "Your uncle framed the drifter before fleeing to Europe."

"Even if that was true, how can you possibly know any of it?" Nina asked.

It helped to feel incredulous.

His eyes narrowed, the muscles in his jaw tightening as he seemed to grasp at the last straws of his concocted reality. "Because I tracked down Edward's new family. He was dead by the time I caught up, but I told his wife I was a journalist writing a book about the case. She believed me. Gave me access to all of his papers."

"I don't believe it," Nina stated flatly.

But part of her did. She couldn't deny the quiver in the pit of her stomach as she thought about the journal entry about Koala fighting with Panda. She could imagine the scene so perfectly — looking up into her sister's tear-filled eyes as Rose pressed her palm to the cheek she'd just slapped.

Any sane person would've found the hidden room in the basement creepy as hell — Annie definitely had — but to Nina, it had felt like a refuge from the world. Curling up on the bed down there and reading while listening with one ear for a sound that might signify Will's anger had been awoken again… that was what most of Lizzie's life would have been like, living under the tyranny of Grizzly and Polar.

This house, the life that Panda described in the journal, even Will's touchy, obsessive behavior, it all felt familiar to her.

It felt like coming home.

Was it possible that she *was* Lizzie Byrd?

Could the trauma of seeing her own sister murdered have caused the amnesia she'd never been able to break through? And was it possible Will was telling the truth, that the amnesia was a mercy, her brain's attempt to protect her from the guilt of killing her sister?

"No," she said. "I refuse to believe it."

Will's fury escalated as he stepped closer, imposing his presence upon her. "You killed your sister to keep her from the life she would have had with me, so now you owe me that life." His hands shot out, gripping her shoulders with bruising force. "YOU OWE ME."

Nina's survival instincts surged. With a swift motion, she kicked at his kneecap.

He bellowed in pain, his grip loosening as his knee buckled.

Nina fled, racing to the basement with a pounding heart and lamming the door behind her, then shoving a heavy cabinet against it.

The room felt like a sanctuary and a prison.

As she leaned back against the cool wood, her breath ragged, a flash of memory flickered to lfie, showing her the basement from a child's perspective.

She was in her bed, the room dark and still as a dark shape emerged from the tunnel. She remembered waking up to see Rosie's hand clamping over her mouth to stifle her screams as a shadowy figure loomed over their shared bed.

Then it evaporated and Nina slid to the floor back in the present, her own hands covering her mouth as she tried to throttle a scream.

Hoping and praying that the monster would not find her.

Chapter Thirty-Six

WILL WAS TEMPORARILY STUNNED as he crouched on the cold floor, nursing not only the physical pain from Nina's desperate blow but a deeper, more excruciating agony.

The journal — private musings and deepest thoughts of his beloved Rosie — had been kept from him. As he'd flipped through the pages earlier, every line seemed to slice right through him, reigniting the grief had never fully dimmed.

It was as profound and paralyzing as the grief he had felt while cradling Rosie's lifeless, blood-stained body years ago. Will had lingered with her as long as he dared until Edward's unexpected arrival — whom Rosie had affectionately called Kodiak — forced him to flee.

And now Nina denied her role in their horrifically-tangled past, refusing to admit she had taken the love of his life from him. Each day, he had lived with the tormenting reality that he had not been able to save Rosie — that he lay unconscious in that damned basement while Nina brutally ended her sister's life.

After slaughtering their parents.

It was such an unbearable thought. Yet he'd given her a chance for redemption. A chance to repay the debt she owed him. A chance to step into the life he'd meant to give her sister, and to be cherished the way he would have cherished her sister. She'd had the power to make them both whole. They could've turned the past that bound them together into something beautiful, something Rosie would've loved.

But instead, she'd ruined everything. Again.

He despised the necessity of allowing Nina to touch his pendant. *Rosie's pendant.* It was all he had left of her, aside from the journal. He might have felt a twinge of gratitude for the discovery of the journal if Nina hadn't kept it hidden.

Had he known about it sooner, he would have shared everything with her, laid bare his soul in hopes of healing together.

But hate was a pervasive shadow in his heart.

He hated Nina for not trusting him.

He hated her for pretending that she was blameless, accusing him of the crime that she'd committed against her own sister..

Most painfully, he hated her for not being Rosie.

Rosie deserved the life he had longed to give her. And he deserved that life, which he'd been willing to share with Nina, forgiving her if she would walk in her sister's footsteps.

Resolute despite the pain in his knee — she hadn't broken it, but the ache was sharper than he expected — Will made his way down to the basement.

The heart of his nightmares beckoned him with a morbid pull. Just the thought of being surrounded by that darkness again, of being shut up in a space that small, kicked up a dust storm of panic that threatened to engulf him.

When he'd awoken in the basement that tragic night in agony, head throbbing and stomach roiling, thanks to the concussion, he could barely stand. But still, he'd forced himself up after emptying his stomach and groped his way upstairs when he heard Rosie's scream, desperate to protect her. He'd thought he'd be protecting her from her father — he'd been shocked to see Lizzie standing over Rosie's dead body, a kitchen knife only a few feet away on the wood floor.

The same kind of knife she'd used to chop the damned basil she couldn't stop going on about.

But there was no other way — he had to make Nina see the truth. That was the only path to redemption now. She had to accept her guilt, just like he'd accepted that he'd failed Rosie. She had to admit what she'd done and make amends to him.

For she was either his salvation or his damnation.

Will was exhausted by the unrelenting curse of living without Rosie's love.

He staggered into the kitchen for the flashlight while thinking about how Rosie would feel about the way things were unfolding. His true love would be devastated to know Lizzie — Nina — had learned of her past in such a harsh manner.

But Rosie would be even more disappointed if Will failed to protect her. He had chosen not to involve the police back then, a decision that allowed Nina to lead the life she now enjoyed, under false pretenses.

There was no way he would let her back out of their promised future together now.

The truth would set them both free, if he could force her to accept it. Then she would heal him, by being the

Rosie he needed her to be. And he would have fulfilled his promise to Rosie that he would find a way to protect Lizzie — whether Lizzie deserved his protection or not.

It was the only way to make things right.

Will steeled himself and descended into the darkness of the basement, palm throbbing from his grip on the flashlight.

The air grew colder. An oppressive atmosphere from the underground room enveloping him like a thick fog as he approached the barricaded door.

His heart pounded with dread and determination. But he was going to face his fear and overcome it. For Rosie's sake.

He banged on the door, his voice echoing off the concrete walls. "Nina, come out! I just want to talk."

Her scream from the other side was filled with defiance and fear. "Go fuck yourself! I've called the police! They'll be here any minute — AND I'M GOING TO TELL THEM EVERYTHING!"

He paused, breath hitching in his throat.

Had she really called the police? Doubt gnawed at him, but Will couldn't take the chance. He quickly pulled out his phone and dialed her number, hoping to catch her in a lie. The phone rang upstairs, its familiar tone mocking his spiraling emotions.

A grim smile teased his lips. Despite everything, he couldn't help but admire her fiery spirit — so reminiscent of Rosie's, especially when not directed at him.

His gaze then fell on a sledgehammer leaning against the wall.

"Nina, I'm coming in!"

He raised the sledgehammer and swung it at the door, the impact sending a jarring vibration up his arms.

Wood splintered under the force, a small hole appearing in the door.

He swung again, each hit dismantling both the physical barrier and the last vestiges of the life he had tried to build with Nina.

With each crack and tear of wood, his resolve hardened. He needed to confront her and force her to admit the truth, no matter how dark or painful.

The door slowly gave way.

Chapter Thirty-Seven

Nina's breath hitched in her throat as the unmistakable sound of splintering wood echoed through the basement like gunshots tearing through silence.

Every fresh strike of the sledgehammer sent another spike of terror through the back of her skull, where it rippled until she felt the vibration in her heart.

Trapped in this house — Panda's house — Nina felt history folding in on itself, threatening to crush her like a hydraulic press. The brief memory she had uncovered might not have been a memory at all. It might have been her fertile imagination running away from her, primed by Will's lies to reimagine the events of the journal from Lizzie's point of view.

But even if it was a real memory, she could never have killed her sister — the very idea was monstrous. That was another fabrication of Will's fractured psyche. The journals, filled with scribbles of love and frustration, showed a complex but loving relationship between the sisters that she'd been drawn to because it was a beautiful, haunting story. Exactly the kind of story that Nina would savor as she listened to another episode of *Riddles in the Dark.*

Except now, she wasn't listening to the story. She was living it.

This was all so surreal. A nightmare that Nina could not wake from.

Another blow landed against the door, louder and more desperate. Each successive thud was another strike of that sledgehammer on the walls of her sanity, fraying the edges of her nerve and resolve.

She scrambled toward the tunnel, her hands clawing at the trash bags stuffed with drywall fragments that she had used to block it. The bags were surprisingly heavy, and her fingers trembled as she pulled with all her strength.

But the bags were stubborn and tightly-wedged; one ripped and spilled bits of plaster and dust over the damp earth. A cloud of white dust billowed around her, turning her into a ghostly specter in the dim light as she wrestled with the bags and sent showers of plaster across the muddy floor.

She kept going, the tunnel clearly her only escape.

Another violent crash from Will's sledgehammer echoed behind her.

Nina dove into the narrow, earthy passage. Cold mud clung to her skin, seeping through her clothes as she wriggled forward with frantic energy.

The tunnel roof grazed her back as panic clawed at her chest. The oppressive darkness swallowed her whole and pressed down on her, heavy as the earth itself.

Nina bumped her head against the low ceiling. Pain was sharp yet fleeting against the adrenaline rippingthrough her veins. She gritted her teeth against the ache, determined to make her perilous escape as the tunnel curved and she kept crawling toward that sliver of daylight promising freedom.

She pushed herself harder, the light growing brighter with each desperate motion. Her limbs moved with mechanical determination, drive by a primal instinct to survive.

She emerged into the afternoon sunlight to a terrible riot of sound behind her as the door finally gave way under Will's relentless assault. His distant shouts mingled with the rustle of leaves in the breeze.

His presence loomed like a dark shadow stretching long fingers toward her — a cold whisper against the back of her neck.

She felt painfully vulnerable without her car keys or phone, but Nina knew she had to put distance between herself and the insanity behind her.

She stumbled around the house, her legs weak but moving, driven by sheer survival instinct. A truck slowed beside her as she reached the driveway.

A stroke of providence — it was Steve, as if fate had steered him toward her rescue.

She yanked open the passenger door and threw herself inside, still gasping for breath.

"Drive!" Nina shouted into his shock. "Please, just go — NOW!"

His expression was mostly concern and confusion as he accelerated away from the house.

"What's going on?" Steve asked her as he swung onto the highway. "Are you okay?"

"Will has totally fucking lost it," she managed to say in her still-shaking voice. "He … he was chasing me with a sledgehammer."

Steve handed her his phone without hesitation.

Her fingers fumbled as she dialed 911, her voice

steadying as she spoke with the dispatcher. "My husband is out of control … he's at the Byrd house. I'm headed to my neighbor's right now. On Locust Run."

Nina disconnected the call without waiting for the dispatcher to answer, then turned to Steve, her eyes still widened by lingering terror. "Thank you. If you hadn't shown up …"

"It's nothing." His voice was steady and calming, his brow furrowed with concern. "But I gotta ask, does this have anything to do with me? Is that why he snapped?"

"No." She shook her head vigorously. "It's about Panda's murder." Nina paused, gauging his reaction before she delivered the punchline. "Will is Sloth."

She'd expected disbelief, but Steve managed to hide his skepticism, putting on a patient expression. Humoring her, maybe. Or reserving judgment. Either way, she was grateful not to be dismissed, like Will had done so many times when he didn't want to hear another one of her theories.

Yet another red flag she had ignored at her peril.

"You better tell me everything," Steve said calmly.

"Will was Panda's boyfriend. They were planning to run away together the night she was killed."

"He was there?" Steve sounded like maybe he believed her. "That night?"

"I think he killed her." Nina nodded slowly. "He insists that I did, but …"

She trailed off as she registered the shock on Steve's face.

He was silent as he maneuvered off the road and turned into his driveway. Nina glanced behind them, but didn't see Will's Infinity behind them. He was probably searching the property for her, assuming she'd hidden from him.

She sighed with relief and exhaustion.

"You're safe here." Steve turned to face her. "Stay as long as you need to."

"I don't want to impose." She bit her lip with reluctance. "I'm going back to Chicago once Will is in jail." She managed a weak smile. "I'm just so lucky you happened by when you did."

Steve smiled back. "I'm just glad I could help."

She touched the cut on her face and forced herself to remember.

Waking up in the basement to an intruder …

Could she really be Lizzie?

The thought sent a chill down her spine. The name felt so foreign and familiar.

She had spent countless hours poring over Panda's journals, immersing herself in the girl's life and struggles. She'd identified with both Panda and Koala, longing to find the ending to their story and put their souls to rest. When Will had tried to convince her that she *was* Koala, that jolt of recognition could've been a recognition of truth — but couldn't it also have been an artifact of how deeply she had empathized with the sisters?

Didn't it make more sense that Nina was just the unlucky woman Will had chosen to target with his twisted manipulations?

And that the memory was a trick of her suggestible imagination trying to make sense of it all?

As shadows of doubt fogged her mind, Nina felt her reality start to unravel, thread by thread, grasping at the chilling possibility of an identity that was not her own.

Chapter Thirty-Eight

WILL'S body trembled with exertion and adrenaline as he battered the basement door with his sledgehammer. Each strike echoed through the hollows of the old house like the roar of thunder, a storm of his own making.

Wood splintered and cracked, protesting under the fury of his blows until it finally gave way. He pushed aside the wreckage, his breath now coming in ragged gasps and his heart pounding hard enough to echo off the cold basement walls.

Stepping into the dimly-lit room — a crude sanctuary reeking of damp earth and mold — he paused to catch his breath. The air was alive with the echoes of expired despair that still seemed to seep from the very walls.

This place had haunted his dreams for most of his adult life. Dreams of terror and regret. Dreams where he fought to change what had happened, but always failed.

For a long time, he'd wished that the blow to the head had killed him, so he'd never had to know Rosie's fate.

He held his breath for a moment, then blew it out slowly, fighting to regain control of his emotions.

This place where Rosie had spent most of her abbreviated life was barely even a dungeon. The walls were too close, and Will felt like he might have to drop his sledgehammer to keep them from crushing him.

How could she have ever stood being down here?

Rosie had been desperate to escape.

But for some incomprehensible reason, Lizzie had wanted to stay.

Even now, she seemed to want to spend time down here. She had apparently been down to this cursed room a number of times since he bought her this house. Part of the new life she never appreciated.

Rosie would have been bowled over with the gift of a house, especially the chance to turn her childhood prison into the home she'd never had. Nina didn't deserve what Will had given her. After all these years, he'd thought the punishment she earned for killing her sister — the shame of her scars and the loss of identity — had taught her a lesson.

He only wanted for her to make amends for his loss. Then he would have given her everything.

The claustrophobic room was lined with peeling wallpaper and faded photographs. A small bed with a threadbare blanket lay in one corner. Religious icons watched over the room like idols, their eyes seeming to follow him as he moved.

Another surge of betrayal twisted in his gut at the sight of several trash bags full of broken drywall she had hidden from him, here in this wretched room, just in case he managed to overcome his panic and come down to the basement.

Although Will would have seen the door, so what was the point?

Or maybe he wouldn't have, given that the light was

burned out and it would require an awful lot of patience to look around with the flashlight. He'd done his best to hide his panic that day she'd insisted he come down to look at the water valve, but Nina was perceptive. She could probably sense his aversion, even if she had no idea why.

Although he wasn't completely convinced that she didn't. How could she spend weeks in this house and never recover a single memory from the time when she'd lived here?

He saw the hole in the wall and remembered Nina saying something about a tunnel entrance. That must be how Sara had sneaked into the house.

Hard to imagine Nina crawling through the dirt; she used to get annoyed whenever she chipped her nail polish. The day she'd claimed to have been gardening but acting strangely — she must have found the tunnel then.

Another secret Nina had been keeping from him.

Yet another reason she didn't deserve all that he had given her.

She hadn't deserved Rosie, either, as she'd proven so long ago.

No doubt she had crawled through the tunnel on her belly like the snake she had proven herself to be. But she wouldn't get far, barefoot and without any keys or a phone on her.

Will stormed out of the basement and up the stairs, knee throbbing with his steps, emotional torment dwarfing the physical pain.

Reaching the upper floors, he dashed over to the front windows just in time to see Nina at the end of the drive, climbing into Steve's truck.

Of course she would run to him.

She must have called Steve before Will found the journal — she'd already been planning to leave him. So he'd been right to be jealous. Nina had obviously found comfort in Steve's arms while Will had been in Chicago stopping Sara's harassment — for both of them.

The sight of Nina escaping — seeking refuge with another man — was a visceral blow confirming his worst fears. Her infidelity, her rejection, and her disdain for the life he had offered her. She had betrayed everything that Rosie stood for, everything that was good and pure in this world.

He was tempted to let her go, but he couldn't give up on her when Rosie had refused to. Panic and rage clouded his judgment as he dashed back to grab his gun and keys. Still there were where he had left them, on the small table by the door, the gun cold and heavy in his shaking hand.

This was it — the moment of reckoning. He couldn't let her go, couldn't allow her to unravel the threads of the future he had so meticulously woven for her.

But as he burst through the front door, Will's escape was cut short by the sudden arrival of a police cruiser, dust billowing behind it as it skidded to a stop.

Officer Rivera stepped out of the car, her expression stern and hand on her holster.

Nina had called the police too? Did she seriously think he wouldn't tell them the truth?

Now she would spend the rest of her life in prison for murder, and it was her own goddamned fault. He had been willing to forgive and move on, but she just couldn't let go of the past.

He hoped Rosie would forgive him for failing to protect her sister.

"Put the gun down, Will!" Rivera commanded.

He hesitated ... then slowly lowered his weapon while turning the possibilities of over in his mind.

"Where's Nina?" Rivera approached cautiously.

"She's gone," Will replied with despair and defiance. "She left with Steve."

Her eyes narrowed, stance defensive. "Drop your weapon and get on the ground!"

Compliance seemed his only option. He set the gun down carefully on the gravel and raised his hands in surrender.

Then he made one last appeal to Rivera. "Nina is a murderer and she's getting away right now. You can leave me here if you want, but go to Steve's and arrest her before they run off together. I have evidence of what she did in the house."

Rivera tossed her cuffs to Will's feet. "Put them on."

She wasn't going to listen to him. She'd probably already taken Nina's side, thanks to the police report that Sara had filed to spite him. Once again, Nina would get away with murder, and Will would be destroyed again.

He bent down to pick the handcuffs up, but then grabbed a handful of gravel and threw it in the officer's face.

He tackled Rivera and her gun went off as he wrestled with her, trying to take the weapon away. He slammed her into the cruiser face-first and knocked her out cold.

Rivera fell to the gravel.

Will checked her pulse. She was alive. Good. He cuffed her hands, then picked up his gun, jumped into his car, and peeled out for Steve's house.

He wasn't sure how he was going to fix this mess, but he owed it to Rosie to try.

Chapter Thirty-Nine

NINA SAT in a rocking chair with a blanket draped over her shoulders and a steaming mug of tea cradled in her hands. Steve's living room was a sanctuary compared to the nightmare she had just escaped. He sat on the couch, quietly sipping his own drink, a calming presence amid the chaos.

"I know I've only known Will for six months, but I can't believe I didn't see that he's crazy. Am I stupid, or did I see it and lie to myself about it?"

Steve shook his head with a sympathetic expression. "You can't blame yourself for what your fiancé hid from you."

"Ex-fiancé," Nina corrected him with a wry smile.

Steve returned the smile, a flicker of approval in his eyes. "Good."

Nina sighed, her shoulders slumping. "Annie saw the red flags. I should have listened to her."

"Your friend Annie gives good advice," he chuckled, "when she's not flirting up a storm."

"I'm sorry about that." Nina felt a flush of embarrassment. "She's … Annie."

"Nothing to apologize for." He waved off her apology. "A man needs a little flirting every now and then."

Their moment of levity was shattered by the sound of a car zooming up the driveway and skidding to a halt out front.

Nina's heart leapt into her throat, panic surging through her veins as she jumped up from her rocking chair and rushed over to the window, peering out with dread coiling in her stomach.

Will emerged from the Infinity, clutching a gun.

Nina stifled a whimper, her mind racing.

Rivera had been on her way to the house.

Had Will killed her? If the officer was dead, that would be all Nina's fault.

"NINA!" Will's raw scream pierced the air.

Nina turned to Steve, her eyes wide with fear.

"You don't have to go out there." His voice was steady and calm. She was equal parts grateful for his protection and guilty that he now stood between her and Will. Steve was a near-stranger, but he was willing to face down her crazy ex-fiance despite having no reason to be involved in any of this. He hadn't deserved Will's jealous fury, and he'd gone through enough trauma finding Rose's corpse all those years ago. It was only chance that he'd been driving by when Nina ran out to the road, but now Will might shoot him, after possibly having killed at least one police officer.

Steve strode to the mantel and retrieved the shotgun mounted there.

Then he positioned himself beside the window and cracked it open, his movements precise and deliberate.

"Go home," he called out to Will. "She doesn't want to talk to you."

"You send Nina out or I'm coming in," Will snarled. Then another bellow: "NINA!"

Steve tossed his phone to her. "Call dispatch again."

She dialed the number with shaking fingers, relaying their location and the situation to the operator.

"Is Rivera okay?" she asked, her voice tight with worry.

"Officer Rivera was dispatched to the Byrd house but is currently not responding. We're sending the sheriff and several deputies. Please stay inside and stay on the line."

Will's movements were jerky and erratic as he started up the porch steps.

Steve fired a warning shot, the sound cracking through the air.

Will scrambled back down, crouching below the porch for cover.

"The next one ain't gonna miss," Steve warned. "Sheriff's on the way. Set your gun down and get ready to turn yourself in, unless you're planning on suicide by deputy."

Will's voice rang out with a desperate plea. "I just need to talk to Nina."

She steeled herself while approaching the window. "Did you kill Rivera?"

"It would've been on you if I *had* killed her!" Will spat. "But I'm not the murderer here."

"You're insane," Nina said as relief washed over her. "I'm going to make sure you spend the rest of your life in prison for killing my sister."

"Like I said ..." His manic laughter was sharp enough to cut her. "If you remembered that night, you would know I didn't kill her. *I loved her.* But don't worry, I forgive you, Lizzie. You just have to find a way to forgive yourself."

Nina glanced at Steve.

He pointed a finger at his temple and made the *cuckoo* sign.

Another wave of relief swept through her. Standing next to someone sane, Nina realized just how long she had been living with Will's insanity.

And how normal that had started to feel.

"You say you can't remember, but I think you can." Will's voice rose again in pleading accusation. "The blood gushing from Rosie's neck and pooling around her. Her fierce expression — she must've fought you good. You saw me come in, right after you killed her."

An image flashed through Nina's mind, vivid and horrifying.

A younger version of herself standing over Rosie's body in a sea of blood. She wanted to scream, but her throat constricted, allowing only a strangled squeak to escape. Pain seared the side of her face and neck.

A figure loomed before her, the silhouette of a teenage boy, details lost in the shadows, his face obscured by the darkness and the haze of her fragmented memory.

In the deafening silence, Nina's old ghosts went from whispers to screams.

Chapter Forty

"Put your gun on the porch, then back away, and I'll come out," Nina called out to Will, her voice surprisingly steady despite the fear like a tornado spinning wildly in her gut.

Will blinked, caught off guard. He had expected her to cower behind Steve until the authorities arrived. But there she was, emerging from the front door, looking pale yet determined as she stood in the doorway.

She had never reminded him more of Rosie. The resemblance was so striking, Will could almost forgive her. *Almost.*

"Did you kill my sister?" Nina asked, meeting his gaze, her eyes searching his.

He held her stare. "She was already dead when I found you standing over her."

Color drained from Nina's face, a stricken expression crossing her features.

She was finally starting to see that he had been telling her the truth all along. Maybe his outburst had jarred some of those memories loose. He didn't love that it had happened that way, that she had fled from him as if he was some kind of monster, but if that was what it took for her to stop lying to herself, then it was worth it.

He would visit her in jail. Keep his promise to Rosie, to make sure she was as okay as she could be, given her situation.

But then she slipped back into denial again, shaking her head. "I wouldn't."

"But you did," Will said with sorrowed resignation. "You took her away from me."

He saw the indecision on her face as she wrestled with her desire for it not to be true. Truth won, he saw the moment that it did, and his heart lifted. A moment of justice for Rosie, her killer finally acknowledging the horrible crime that she had committed against her own sister.

He'd kept his promise to Rosie.

Then Steve shoved Nina aside and raised his gun at Will, firing without hesitation.

Nina's scream pierced the air as Will felt a fiery explosion of pain rip through his chest. He staggered backward, betrayed once more, and hit the dried-out grass with a thud.

Will gasped for breath, choking on the blood filling his punctured lung.

Nina rushed to his side, dropping to her knees beside him as if she actually cared, as if she wasn't the one responsible for his death, just as she had been for Rosie's.

Hate and love warred within him, a twisted tangle of emotions Will could no longer unravel.

At least he would be with Rosie soon, while Nina would have to spend the rest of her life tormented by the knowledge of what she had done.

The truth he had forced her to remember was a small comfort in his final moments.

Slow footsteps creaked on the wooden porch, and then Steve appeared in his field of vision, still clutching the gun.

"You shot him!" Nina cried out in disbelief.

Steve shrugged, his expression unreadable. "I thought he was going for the gun."

"We were just talking!" she protested, her voice raw with emotion.

"Better safe than sorry," Steve replied coolly.

Nina stared at Steve in shock before turning her attention back to Will, still gasping and choking on rivulets of blood leaking out of his open mouth.

"*I didn't mean for this to happen,*" she whispered, tears streaming down her face. Just like she didn't mean to kill Rosie. But she had.

Steve pressed the gun into her hand. "He killed your sister. If you want revenge, finish him off now and I'll swear it was self-defense."

"I'm not a killer," Nina said.

Unbelievable that she could deny it again, even as he was dying. "Not saying you are," Steve drawled back at her. "But after what he did to you? I wouldn't blame you a bit. No one would."

Nina didn't resist as Steve wrapped her fingers around the weapon.

He would welcome it if she killed him. To die at the same hand as his Rosie had felt fitting. A perfect end to the tragedy that his life had been.

She looked down at him, her body shaking. With grief? With rage? Or with the same she deserved to feel after what she'd done?.

"Confess," she demanded. "You were faking the intruder and blaming it on your ex. You bought the house and set this whole thing up to gaslight me, trying to turn me into my sister because you're fucking nuts. When I finally discovered the truth, you tried to make me believe that I killed her."

Will shook his head weakly, breath coming in agonized gasps. He would try one more time to redeem her before he died. Would she finally stop denying the truth?

"I loved you," he insisted in a rasp. "I still see Rosie in your eyes, and in your smile. I love that part of you so much. It doesn't matter if you kill me or not."

Her grip on the gun tightened, but then she shook her head. "I'm not going to shoot you. You're going to rot in jail for murder."

She handed the weapon back to Steve.

With his last ounce of strength, Will forced out the words. "You killed your sister and your parents. Think about it, Nina: if you didn't, who did? Who else was in the house?"

Steve gently took the gun from her and helped Nina to stand.

Then, with no hesitation, he aimed his barrel at Will and pulled the trigger.

The shot echoed through the air like a final verdict.

Chapter Forty-One

NINA SCREAMED in horror as blood erupted from the hole in Will's forehead, the light fading from his eyes as he stopped making that awful gurgling noise.

His throat stopped working, the rose pendant glinting in the sunlight with a final mocking reminder of the twisted path that had led them here.

"What did you do?" Nina's voice was raw with anguish.

Steve lowered the gun, his expression unreadable. "Now he can't hurt you anymore."

He offered her his arm, but Nina hesitated, a sinking realization settling in her gut. There had been no need to shoot Will when the sheriff and his deputies were already on their way — he hadn't been anywhere close to his gun. And there had been no need to kill him when he was already bleeding to death in Steve's driveway. What was he going to do to Nina, bleed on her while he died?

But Steve had killed him anyway, no hesitation, and no remorse now.

Going to Steve for help had been a mistake, but she

was afraid not to go back inside with him now. If he could so easily kill a defenseless man, what would stop him from turning the gun on her and spinning a tale to frame Will?

The sheriff would believe it, especially since Rivera was aware of Will's background and Nina's request for a deeper investigation into his past. For all she knew, Rivera might have been on her way to the house with damning information about Will's true identity when the dispatcher sent her chasing Nina's frantic call.

It would make a tidy narrative: Will, in a fit of rage, chasing Nina with a sledgehammer; Nina fleeing to Steve for protection; Will pursuing her, only to be shot by the heroic neighbor.

Nina would emerge as the innocent victim, Steve the savior who stepped in to rescue her from domestic violence.

But the cold, blank look in his eyes as he pulled the trigger and the raw sincerity etched on Will's face as he said he still loved her … none of it felt right.

And then there was the flash of bloody memory, a piece of the puzzle refusing to fit.

That horrific possibility kept gnawing at her.

Nina remembered standing over Rosie's lifeless body, her own nightgown soaked in crimson, and a figure looming over them both, the right shape and size for a teenage boy. It had to be Will.

But his face remained obscured, lost in the haze of her fractured recollection.

What if he hadn't been lying?

What if Rosie had already been dead when Will arrived on the scene?

The unthinkable question whispered in her mind, insidious and persistent. Could she really have been the one to attack her own sister like Will believed? She had worked so hard to stop being ashamed of that scar. Was it possible that she'd been right to be ashamed of it — because it was the mark left on her by the sister she'd murdered?

Nina wanted to reject the notion, but his sincerity, even in death, had triggered a vision that would forever haunt her.

Was his accusation coming from the conviction of a madman, born from a warped fantasy?

Or was it the truth, terrible and inescapable?

Had she murdered her own parents, abusive as they were, to prevent Rosie from running away?

And when that failed, had she turned her rage on Rosie, extinguishing the light she had sought to keep?

Unsure what else to do, she let Steve guided her back inside and over to the rocking chair, his touch gentle yet unsettling.

"It's not your fault," he assured her. "None of this was. Will was clearly demented, killing his teenage girlfriend and then stalking her sister more than a decade later. I'm not sure it can get much sicker than that."

She shook her head, tears blurring her vision. "I don't know what to believe anymore. And now there's no one left alive who knows the truth, unless ..."

She trailed off, feeling the weight of her missing memories like a lead cloak on her shoulders.

"You said you helped your father in the garden at the Byrd house. Did you ever see the sisters?"

"Old man Byrd kept them locked away most of the time, but occasionally I'd wave to them through the basement windows."

Nina suppressed a shudder, remembering Panda's mention of a peeping tom. And the look of reverence on

Steve's face when he'd said that Panda had been "a beautiful girl."

"How long have you known who I am?" she asked breathlessly.

"Recognized you that first day I knocked on your door. But you introduced yourself as Nina, so I thought you wanted to avoid the kind of hubbub people would make if they knew Lizzie Byrd was back in town, so I respected that."

Nina felt like she'd been gut punched. Another man hiding things about her past from her, out of "respect" for her feelings. He'd sat in her house, telling the story of how he'd found her sister's corpse, knowing the whole time who she was — maybe that's why he'd been so uncomfortable when Annie had insisted on peppering him with questions. Especially when he'd described the ghost.

Or maybe he'd been watching Nina for a sign that she remembered, that it was okay for him to tell the rest of the story.

It was completely understandable that he wouldn't bring it up without a sign from her that it was okay. But she hated him for keeping quiet anyway.

"The ghost you saw," she said hesitantly. "Was that me?"

Steve sighed. "The police made me change my story after your uncle carried you off. Guess he paid some them off to keep you out of the limelight. He was protecting you."

It seemed that her entire life was a series of lies told by men who wanted to "protect" her.

"You don't remember anything?" Steve probed, his gaze intense.

"*Shadows and blood*," she whispered. "I remember a

person there, but it's all fuzzy. I can't tell if it was Will or someone else."

Steve shrugged, a casual gesture that felt out of place. "Will had the pendant, didn't he?"

A bolt of surprise jolted through her body. "How do you know about the pendant?"

The realization struck her a second later. The only person who Nina had told about the pendant besides Annie was…

"You're Byrd91," she breathed, her voice tinged with disbelief.

Steve met her gaze, unflinching. "Guilty as charged."

"Why didn't you say anything?" Nina demanded, her mind reeling.

"Didn't want to cause a problem with that fiancé of yours, and I didn't know if he might be snooping on your computer," he explained without hesitation. "But I figured you could use someone to talk to."

His answer was reasonable, even kind — he'd been offering her a confidant without any pressure to confide, knowing that she'd returned after a terrible trauma. But it only served to heighten her unease.

He'd looked her in the eye and pretended not to know that she was Lizzie Byrd returned to the house where her sister was murdered, because he thought her new name was a sign she didn't want to talk about it. Out of "respect" for her desire to move forward.

She was sick and tired of being lied to, and it didn't matter the reason. Steve studied her, then tilted his head toward the kitchen.

"You look like you need something stronger than tea. Can I get you a drink?"

Nina nodded, desperate for a moment alone to process the whirlwind of revelations.

Steve disappeared into the kitchen, leaving her to stare blankly out the window in a tangled web of doubt and suspicion.

If he was so cold-blooded that he could hide his knowledge of her identity, what else could he be hiding?

What if he hadn't just stumbled on Rose's body? What if he'd also seen the killer?

If she asked, would he tell her that she had killed her sister, that the police had told him not to talk about that either?

And did she really want to know?

By shooting Will, Steve had given her a chance to wipe the slate clean. She could claim self-defense, repeat the story she'd already told the dispatcher, and the case would be closed. No one would look deeper.

No one would find out that someone else — maybe Nina — should be rotting in jail right now, instead of Galen Green. Sudden pain stabbed through Nina's skull, followed by another flash of memory, vivid and terrifying. Nina standing over Rosie's body, the blurred shape of the killer resolving into a teenage Steve, clutching a bloody gardening knife.

The truth hit her like a punch to the gut, stealing the breath from her lungs.

Will had been telling the truth.

Steve had killed Rose.

Then he'd killed Will. Because Will was a loose end who'd come back to unravel Steve's story.

Now Nina was the only loose end left.

Chapter Forty-Two

NINA'S HAND instinctively went to her scar as the horrifying realization sank in.

She needed to get the hell out of here. *Now.*

She stood slowly from the rocking chair, careful not to stay quiet and keep from alerting Steve in the kitchen.

Then she tried to run, but he lunged out and grabbed her, throwing Nina into a chair and pointing the gun at her head.

"*It was you,*" she whispered, wishing her voice hadn't trembled.

His expression was cold amusement frosting his twisted satisfaction. "You're going to tell the police the story I tell you to, or I'll blame you for shooting Will."

Her mind raced as puzzle pieces finally clicked into place. "You were in love with Rosie, too."

Steve nodded, a sick smile playing on his lips. "You were almost as beautiful as your sister. I used to watch you both through the basement windows. Then later on I would sneak into the tunnel to spy on you."

"Why did you kill her?" Nina asked, forcing herself not to whisper.

"Your sister wouldn't leave without you, and your late fiancé was going to give in and take you with him too, help her raise you. But she deserved better than him. I tried to show her that it would be better if she loved me."

The leer on Steve's face made his intention all too clear.

Another flash of memory assaulted Nina, this time of a terrible struggle. Rose on her back, nightgown pulled up, Steve on top of her, holding a knife to her throat.

"You didn't have to kill her," Nina choked out, tears streaming down her face.

Steve shrugged, his eyes even icier. "If I couldn't have her, nobody was going to have her."

"Will was telling the truth. You knocked him out."

"I thought he'd take the fall, but he must've woken up and gotten out of there before your uncle found her and whisked you away. That's why I had to frame the grifter."

The next question was burning her tongue. "Why did you kill my parents too?"

"I didn't." His laughter was harsh and grating. "You did."

"That's insane," Nina protested.

But her heart kept on pounding like it was for a reason.

"I watched you take the rat poison from the garden shed and never said anything. I even did you a little favor, stabbed 'em so no one would suspect what actually happened to them. *You're welcome.*"

Nina was speechless.

Steve was not.

"I saw how awful they were to you," he continued, his tone almost conversational. "Didn't blame you a bit for wanting to be free of them."

"You're the one who gave me these scars," Nina whispered, her fingers tracing the raised tissue on her cheek.

"Sorry about that. You attacked me after seeing your sister, and I was just trying to fend you off. Forgot I had the knife in my hand."

Nina vibrated with fear, trapped and seeing no way out.

"So now what?" Her voice was hollow. "We pretend it never happened?"

"Why not?" He nodded. "You can go back to that pretty house of yours. I won't bother you anymore. You should seal up that tunnel, though. I'm not the only one who knows about it."

Another realization crashed over her like a tidal wave. "You're the intruder. You left the dead bird. But why? Neither Will nor I had any idea that you were the killer."

"I recognized Will right away, too. Couldn't imagine why else he'd buy the Byrd house if he wasn't back to find the killer. Then you and your friend were posting clues all over the forum—"

"Which you were watching to make sure no one ever found the right ones," she finished with a churning gut.

"Keep your friends close and your enemies closer." A predatory smile. "And you told me everything."

Not everything, but Nina bet that a background check on both her and Will had told him the rest. And he'd been taunting them both — with the dishes, the dead bird, the Pop Rocks. Testing to see what they knew, and what they were going to do with that knowledge.

"So, now what? You're going to let me go and trust that I'll keep my mouth shut?" Nina asked, disbelief coloring her tone.

"That's up to you."

"Please." Desperation clawed at her throat, but still she

refused to whisper like her voice kept wanting her to. She would give anything to be back in Chicago right now. She understood now why Will had said he would give anything to forget. "I just want to go home."

"Eventually." Steve stood and aimed the gun at her again. "But for now, I'm afraid you'll have to get reacquainted with basement life again."

Steve gestured toward the kitchen with the barrel of his gun. "Go through that door."

"What are you going to tell the sheriff when he gets here?"

"Maybe I'll say you ran off after you shot Will."

She rose on shaky legs, her heart pounding a frantic tattoo as she walked toward the kitchen, feeling the weight of his gaze like a second gun on her back.

Her fate would be sealed once she stepped through that door.

One way or the other, eternal darkness was waiting to greet her on the other side.

Chapter Forty-Three

NINA ENTERED the kitchen with her heart beating frantically against her ribs.

Steve's voice was cold and commanding behind her. "Open the basement door and go downstairs. You turn around even once and I'll pull the trigger. Nod if you understand me."

She followed both orders, facing forward as she nodded and opened the door.

But she didn't step through.

Terror was a suffocating force as she wondered whether it would be better to let him shoot her, or descend into the basement full of nightmares and forgotten memories?

Panic kept clawing at her insides. And Nina understood Will's fear with a clarity that was both heartbreaking and terrifying.

She decided she would rather be shot. At least then Steve would have to explain to Rivera why he'd shot her when she'd come to him for protection.

"The fuck are you waiting for?" Steve growled at her. "You need me to count?"

"Sorry. I was just—"

She turned around and lunged for the hot pot simmering on the stove before Steve could react, and in one swift motion she grabbed the handle and hurled the contents at his face.

Scalding liquid splattered her skin, burning as it splashed everywhere, but Nina barely felt the pain as Steve staggered back, screaming as he clawed at his face.

His weapon clattered to the floor.

She swung the empty pot again. A dull clang reverberated through the kitchen as it connected with his head. A jolt ran up her arm from the impact.

Steve crumpled forward, but as Nina tried to run past him, his hand shot out and grabbed her ankle.

She fell hard, face down on the linoleum.

Twisting her body, she kicked at his face with all her might.

Steve let go with a grunt, and she scrambled forward on hands and knees, desperate to reach the living room.

Her lungs burned, each breath a ragged gasp as she clawed at the cheap carpet.

Then Steve's weight was suddenly on her, pinning Nina to the floor.

He slammed her head against the ground, pain exploding behind her eyes as the world swam in and out of focus.

They wrestled in a tangle of limbs and raw desperation.

The coffee table toppled over as they crashed into it — knick-knacks flying hither and yon as his hands found Nina's throat, squeezing, cutting off her air.

Her fingers scrabbled across the floor, searching for something — anything to use as a weapon.

They closed around a pen, and with a burst of adrenaline she plunged it into his eye.

Steve's scream was ear-splitting as he fell off her, clutching at his face.

Nina bolted for the door, throwing it open and stumbling onto the porch, past her former fiancé's lifeless body and into the driveway.

Footsteps pounded behind her.

She risked a glance over her shoulder.

Steve was close, the pen still protruding grotesquely from his eye socket.

Her foot caught on a loose stone, and she fell hard, landing on hands and knees. She twisted to look over her shoulder as she tried to scramble away.

Steve loomed over her, Will's gun in his hand, aimed directly at her head.

The roar of an engine cut through the air as Rivera's police car careened around the bend in the driveway and slammed into Steve with a sickening thud.

The officer stumbled out of the vehicle, hands cuffed in front of her. "Are you okay?" she called out. "Neighbors reported shots fired."

She nodded, chest heaving as she tried to catch her breath. Adrenaline kept pumping through her veins, mingling with overwhelming relief.

"I'm not sure I'll ever be okay again," Nina admitted. "But at least I'm still standing."

She had survived.

And that was enough for now.

Chapter Forty-Four

NINA STOOD in front of the Byrd house, a *For Sale* sign planted firmly in the overgrown lawn. Annie was by her side, a comfort amid Nina's still-churning emotions.

"Are you sure about this?" Annie's voice was soft with concern.

Nina nodded, staring at the house that had once held so much promise, now forever tainted by the secrets she had uncovered within it. "It's time to go back to Chicago and start over."

Galen Green's lawyer had been happy to receive Nina's recounting of Steve's confession — minus the mention of the rat poison that Steve had claimed she'd stolen. She had no way of knowing whether he'd been lying about that. He'd needed her to cooperate with him, and believing that she'd killed her parents was a way to manipulate her. Just like Will had manipulated her.

She was done with being manipulated by men. And she was done with the Byrd house.

Steve had murdered her sister, and he'd died for it. Galen would finally go free. It was over.

They entered the house together, into a suffocating silence as Nina made her way to the bedroom and began to pack her belongings.

Annie tackled Will's office, sorting his stuff into piles for donation.

As Nina carefully placed Panda's journals into a box, one of them fell open.

Her eyes fell on the entry and she started to read.

I found something terrifying under our bed today. Rat poison.

When I confronted Lizzie about it, she claimed she had seen a rat scurrying around and wanted to get rid of it before Grizzly and Polar found out.

I didn't believe her for a second.

We've never had rats down here before. Even if we did, Lizzie knows better than to mess with something as dangerous as poison.

She's just a kid. Lizzie doesn't understand how deadly it can be.

I sat her down and gave her a stern talking-to about the risks. I told her that even a small amount could make her really sick, maybe even kill her if she ate enough of it.

The thought of losing my little sister to something so preventable made my stomach twist into knots.

Lizzie insisted that she wasn't going to eat it, that she really did just want to kill the rat. I made her promise to never, ever touch the stuff again.

But it felt like she wasn't really listening to me.

Nina closed the journal, not wanting to read anymore. Her heart ached with the implication that Steve had been telling the truth. She, as Koala, had intended to poison their parents.

The realization hit Nina like a punch to her gut.

She was just as twisted as Will and Steve.

Maybe she deserved to spend the rest of her life in jail.

She showed the entry to Annie with still-shaking hands.

"I'm a murderer," she whispered in her voice cracking. "I should go to jail."

Annie read the passage, then shook her head. "You don't know that you actually gave your parents the rat poison. Maybe your sister took it away from you so you couldn't. Or maybe she ran with your idea and poisoned them herself."

"I don't think she would've done that," Nina argued.

"But you don't know for sure," Annie said. "And there's no way to prove who did it now."

Her stomach felt hollow and echoing, a cavern filled only with the chilling winds of her own inexcusable actions. "The journal proves I thought about it."

"Okay, worst case scenario, you did," Annie conceded with a shrug of obvious indifference. "But you were an abused little girl trying to get away from her abusers. It was self-defense."

Nina flinched: Steve had used the same justification for killing Will.

Annie seemed to sense her discomfort. "It's not an excuse, Nina. It's an explanation for something that's long past and no longer matters."

"You don't think it matters that I could have killed my parents?"

"I think what matters is that you're not that person anymore," Annie said. "Your uncle got you out of there so you could be raised by people who cared about you. Now you're the kind of person who couldn't hurt your fiancé, even after the terrible things he did to you. And you could've shot Steve with Will's gun after he tried to kill you, but you didn't. *You're not Koala anymore.*"

Tears welled in her eyes as she pulled Annie into a fierce hug.

"Thank you—"

Nina was interrupted by the doorbell.

She wiped her eyes and made her way downstairs, opening the door to find the postal worker with a delivery.

"Package for Nina Turner," he said, holding out a large manila envelope.

Nina signed for it, excitement mingling with apprehension as she carried it back inside. She carefully opened the envelope, her breath catching as she pulled out a pair of birth certificates.

The names jumped out at her: *Esther Rose Byrd* and *Elizabeth Violet Byrd*.

A wave of emotion washed over her: sadness and relief. The documents made her past feel real and finished. A chapter finally closed.

Nina tucked the birth certificates into one of the journals with a tidy smile.

She might not remember most of her past, but she knew her real name now.

More importantly, she knew who she wanted to be: Nina Turner.

And she would build a new life from the ashes of a past that no longer mattered.

Chapter Forty-Five

*T*ODAY WAS … *awful.*

Koala and I had one of those arguments that shakes me to my core. I should have seen it coming, I guess. Telling her about Sloth's plan was bound to stir up a storm. And oh did it.

I mean, it's not like we never argue, but today was different. It was like a hurricane hit us out of nowhere. I guess it's my fault, sorta. I mentioned to Koala about Sloth's idea of us running away together, and oh boy, did that set her off.

Koala totally exploded. She started hitting and punching me. It hurt more than I would have thought she could hurt me. But mostly it just shocked me. Koala's never been like that before.

In the middle of all the yelling and screaming, Polar came down. She asked what was going on, and I just said Koala was upset about the cat. I don't even know why I said that, it just came out. But Polar bought it and left us alone. Useless like always.

I was still pretty shaken, but I had to be the strong one. I told Koala she's coming with me and Sloth, but only if she can keep their temper in check. And her mouth shut. I meant it too. I can't have Koala losing it like that, especially not when we're trying to escape this place.

Koala broke down, getting on her knees and begging, promising to be good, saying she would do anything I asked. I told Koala it was my job to take care of her.

I also needed for Koala to meet Sloth before we could make any actual plans. And she had to swear on her life that she wouldn't breathe a word about any of this to either Grizzly or Polar. If either one of them got even a whiff of our plan, then we would be trapped here forever. If not dead.

Because I was getting surer and surer that neither Grizzly nor Polar much cared if we were breathing each morning or not.

Koala promised, and I believed her.

We had to trust each other; it was all we had.

So I took Koala out to Jackrabbit Ridge. We rode on the back of my old bike, and it felt like we were breaking free, even if just for the night. At least while we were out, we could pretend it was forever. All the stars were out, and the night air felt like a friend.

Freedom was close enough for me to dream that I could touch it.

Sloth was waiting for us in the shadows of the ridge. My heart was pounding in my chest by the time we arrived. I was so nervous about how Koala and Sloth would react when they finally met each other.

Sloth brought Pop Rocks and told us his plan, using his parents' car to get us across the country. We could sell it on the other side and start over, he said.

The plan sounded solid, and I felt a surge of hope.

We agreed to set it up for this weekend. It felt right, like everything was finally falling into place.

The ride back home changed everything. Koala had been quiet during the meeting, but once out of Sloth's earshot she had plenty to say. Starting with how little she liked and trusted him. She was sure that as soon as we got away, Sloth would leave her somewhere so that he could be alone with me.

Sloth knows how important Koala is to me. We were a package deal; Sloth said he understands that. Promised it even. But Koala didn't believe it.

Her words came fast and sharp, like arrows finding their mark.

"We don't need Sloth," she hissed, her eyes burning with the words.

"We're trapped here then. Forever!" I argued. "Is that what you want?"

Koala stared at me for a long time before she said the next part. And I could tell that she knew how dangerous the words were before they even left her mouth.

"We can just poison Grizzly and Polar. Then we'd be free forever. It would just be you and me on this farm for the rest of our lives."

The weight of those words made me recoil.

"Shut up, Koala!" I snapped back, heart racing.

It was time for bed.

But that night, as I lay in the darkness, my mind echoed with Koala's words. And the more I really thought about it, the more I wondered if Koala might be right about Sloth.

Because whenever Sloth talked about the future, Koala was always an afterthought, something I had to bring up.

"Why are you so fidgety?" Koala murmured.

I didn't answer.

But in my head I was wondering two things over and over.

If me and Koala could really poison Grizzly and Polar.

Then, even more important, whether we could really get away with it after we did.

I only fell asleep after my breath grew steady and I finally believed that the answer to both questions was yes.

The End

About The Authors

Nolon King writes fast-paced psychological thrillers set in the glitzy world of entertainment's power players with a bold, insightful voice. He's not afraid to explore the darker side of human nature through stories featuring families torn apart by secrets and lies.

Nolon loves to write about big questions and moral quandaries. How far would you go to cover up an honest mistake? Would you destroy your career to protect your family? How much of your soul would you sell to get the life of your dreams? Would you cheat on your husband to keep your children safe? Would you give in to a stalker's demands to save your marriage?

Lauren Street has always loved a mystery. As a kid growing up in bible belt country she devoured every whodunit book she could get her sticky little hands on and secretly investigated all of her (seemingly) normal boring neighbors. Sometimes their pets and farm animals too. All grown up now and living in the UK with her thoroughly unsuspicious (and often unsuspecting) husband, she writes domestic psychological thrillers about families torn apart by secrets and lies. And she sometimes still peers over garden walls to check up on the neighbors.

Also By Nolon King

Replaced

Replaced

In Her Place

Irreplaceable

Cold Vengeance

Cold Vengeance

Cold Reckoning

Cold Retribution

Hidden Justice

Hidden Justice

Hidden Honor

Hidden Shame

Hidden Virtue

No Justice

No Justice

No Escape

No Hope

No Return

No Stopping

No Fear

Once Upon A Crime

Once Upon A Crime

Twice Upon A Lie

Three Times a Murder

Dead For Good

Dead For Good

Left For Dead

Dead Of Night

Wake The Dead

Dead For Life

Stand Alone Novels

Pretty Killer

12

Blown

Miserable Lies

The Target

Secrets We Keep

Close To Home

Heat To Obsession

A Simple Kill

Tell Me No Lies

Red Carpet Black

Fade To Black

Victim

The Bishop Smoky Mountain Thrillers

Hide Me Away

Fuel To The Flame

Closer By The Hour

A Gamble Either Way

Calling My Children Home

Too Far Gone

Here You Come Again

Replaced with Nolon King

Replaced

In Her Place

Irreplaceable

The Salazar Redwood Forest Thrillers

The Girl Who Couldn't Stop Dying